One Last Hurrah

by
Patrick G McLean

Copyright © 2013 by Patrick G. McLean

ISBN: 0615677266
ISBN 13: 9780615677262
Library of Congress Control Number: 2013916086
LCCN Imprint Name: One Last Hurrah, Saint Louis, MO

For my wife, Dawn, and the big kids, David and Eryn Bassett,
Randy and Vanessa Bassett, and Kelly and Ryan Tate. Also for
the five energetic little ones, growing up and getting smarter than their
grandfather by the day: Rivers Bassett, Madison Bassett, Isabelle Bassett,
Hadley Tate, and Hudson Tate.

ONE LAST HURRAH

Baseball will never be the same

by
PATRICK G MCLEAN

CHAPTER ONE

"Hey Sam," whispered Paul to the bartender, "was there a man who looked like Joe Fisher sitting next to me at the bar here last night? I must have been talking to this guy for more than two hours."

"Paul, you know we love that you've been in Rochester for the past two summers. You have been the reason why a lot of great college players come here to learn how to hit with a wooden bat before they turn pro. But I'm starting to worry about you. You were, as best as I could tell, by yourself the entire evening."

Sam Mello was owner and operator of the All Pro Sports Pub & Grill in downtown Rochester, Minnesota, and he had befriended Paul on the first day he came to town in 2009. Paul had eaten so many meals there and had thrown back his share of drinks, too, that Sam had jokingly installed a nameplate on Paul's favorite barstool to "endow" his seat when he showed up at the pub.

And thanks to the type of patrons All Pro attracted, everyone understood that the barstool was Paul's, whether he was there or not. Sam had been a vice president and COO of a food-products company based in the Minneapolis area before retiring at the ripe old age of forty and opening his own pub and grill in his hometown of Rochester. He was once heard to remark, "Owning this business is a lot like operating a psychology, political science, sports talk show, and baby-sitting service all rolled into one. And I wouldn't trade it for anything in the world."

Sam knew just about everyone in Rochester, from the rich and famous to the downtrodden. In his role as chief bartender, glass washer, and philosopher, he heard just about everything in his business. But he had never heard someone seemingly sane like Paul Kolbe talk to himself

1

for several hours and then swear that he had carried on a conversation with a dead man, particularly a dead man who had been the last to perform the seemingly impossible task of earning a Triple Crown in the National League. And that was more than seventy-five years ago.

Just what made the Triple Crown so difficult? Well, for starters, you have to have power, as part of the formula requires that you lead the league in home runs. Simple enough for your average oversized power hitter. But alas, another part of the formula requires you to lead the league in batting average. Generally, power-type hitters strike out, walk, and homer a lot, but they don't get enough singles and doubles to compensate for the outs they make with their mighty swings. Lastly, you have to generate a sufficient number of RBIs to lead the league, a feat almost entirely dependent on how many of your teammates stack the bases during the season.

You also have to be relatively injury free and play almost all your games. You have to be fairly good at defense to avoid getting taken out of games in the late innings for defensive purposes. And perhaps most importantly, you can never take a day off mentally. Every at bat, every pitch, is an opportunity to succeed or fail. And being successful—not to mention helping your team—is what the game is all about; it's the appeal it has on men to play a kids' game, albeit usually for a king's ransom.

Paul Kolbe would be the least likely candidate Sam could think of when it came to a discussion of who could be the next Triple Crown winner in the National League. For starters, he had been out of the majors for several years, having landed in Rochester, Minnesota as a hitting coach and mentor to aspiring pros who were currently playing college ball and using aluminum bats. Some of these college players had never used a wood bat, having graduated from peewee to grade school, middle school to high school, and finally to college, all the while playing baseball with aluminum or composite bats.

"Wood is a different animal," Paul told each new group of players at the start of their season. "At the major league level, bats have to be made of one solid piece of wood, traditionally white ash, but some more recently maple, and be no more than forty-two inches in length. They are always heavier than aluminum or composite bats, which means that a batter has to make adjustments earlier to his swing than with what he is used to. The ball doesn't go as far when hit with a wood bat, so the batter has to supply more of the power to hit the ball out of the park or into gaps. Inside pitches are much harder to handle with wood bats, as the 'sweet spot' is much smaller. Lastly, wood bats are less durable than metal or composite ones. A cracked or broken wood bat usually results in an out, as there is less of an opportunity to get enough follow-through on the batted ball. In sum, hitting is more difficult with a wood bat, and very few players are consistent .300 hitters in Major League Baseball. A .300 batting average, by the way, means you fail as a batter to get a hit 70 percent of the time, a testimony as to how difficult hitting is at the major league level.

"So, make the most of your time here and learn how to hit with a wood bat. I'm here to help you along the way!"

The Rochester team participated in the Northwoods League, an amateur collegiate invitational league designed to prep players for their eventual entry into professional baseball. Players on the various teams were sponsored by local businesses and stayed with families who supplied room and board for the players while they were on their respective teams.

Paul wound up in Rochester for a very specific reason: he needed a liver, and the Meyer Clinic was the best place to secure a transplant. If only Paul could beat his addiction to alcohol; it was an open secret that he was not helping his cause by going on benders from time to time. Rochester was just too small of a community for that kind of behavior to be kept under wraps. It also didn't help that Paul had a rare blood type, so when a liver became available he was not, at least so far, a compatible candidate.

Paul spent so much time at All Pro that Sam made sure Paul's "endowed" seat was the best in the house to watch baseball on one of the many flat-screen TVs Sam had mounted on the walls. It was not unusual for a shot of Jack Daniel's and a bottle of Rheinhold to be sitting in front of Paul. He didn't drink a lot, just a few each night, but his doctor at the Meyer Clinic warned him not to drink at all.

Paul's usual response to Sam after retelling the comment: "I can't do that, but I can cut back. I'll just have to be more discrete about it," he would say, explaining his predicament.

"Try that in a small town like Rochester," mentioned Sam one day. "You can't be discrete about anything here, Paul."

"Then I'll just have to quit and ruin your image by drinking Diet Coke. That will probably start a trend and run your business into the ground."

"On second thought, enjoy your drinks. I'll just pretend they are mine if anyone wonders!"

The little addiction problem aside, everyone in Rochester loved Paul, and he felt fortunate to have latched onto a hitting coach job with the Honkers. This position was achieved in part thanks to a good word or two from a former coach and sometimes mentor, Dave McFarlin, who was now first-base coach with the Saint Louis Cardinals. Kate Williams, sole owner of the Honkers, which she inherited from her father, knew the McFarlin family from her days growing up in the San Francisco Bay area, where Dave was a coach with the Athletics. She also claimed that she remembered Paul Kolbe as a young player with the A's, and that he was just an "average" hitter when she saw him play.

"Average? I was a regular Joe Fisher," said Paul. "Interesting," thought Paul, "that I would use Joe Fisher as a point of comparison."

"Joe Fisher was way before my time, Paul," said Kate, "so your comparison is wasted on me. Let's just say—no kidding this time—that as a contemporary of yours, you were a pretty good hitter then, and I bet that you still have a little magic left in your bat."

"Thanks, Kate," said Paul, "I appreciate the support you continue to give me."

Even though Paul had a somewhat troubled past, he, according to Dave McFarlin, had an almost perfect swing and understood grip, weight transfer, and follow-through mechanics better than most hitters and could also articulate the finer points of hitting to others. He was also readily available, having a keen interest in hanging out in Rochester to be near the Meyer Clinic if, and hopefully when, a compatible liver became available.

Paul had to chuckle to himself when he heard that Dave portrayed him as a near-perfect role model, but he knew hitting, and he knew what it was like to be both very good and very bad in the major leagues. And, as it turned out, he was perfect for the job in Rochester.

So on that evening in late February, Paul was at his accustomed seat, watching college basketball, reading *Baseball America*, and wondering who some of the college player invitees to Rochester would be in 2011. And he also engaged in a protracted conversation with someone that he knew could not have been sitting next to him at the bar.

"Damn, I could have sworn that was Joe Fisher I was talking to about hitting. You know, Sam, he was the last guy in the National League to win a Triple Crown."

"Paul, we had this conversation before. Are you going to keep bringing this up until I get tired and say I believe you?"

"I'm not saying it makes a lot of sense, but I'm telling you it was Fisher." At this juncture, Paul felt it best to drop the subject and go outside to get some fresh air. It was also the moment when he remembered that he had what looked like a tin of smokeless tobacco given to him by Joe Fisher. He had almost thrown it away, but he elected to put it in his car's glove compartment instead. For his own personal sanity, he went out to his vehicle, which was fortunately parked right in front of All Pro, and retrieved the tin.

"Hey Sam, I don't expect you to believe me without some kind of proof. How about a look at what he left me when he was here? Pine tar."

Thinking back on their "conversation," Paul recalled Joe Fisher saying, "Forget about wearing those fancy batting gloves that today's ballplayers wear. Use a dab of this stuff and you'll grip the bat like never before. And with your talent, you'll smack the cover off the ball. And this isn't just any old pine tar. It's from the woods just north of here. Wet springs, dry summers, cool falls, and crispy winters all go into making *this* pine tar the best of the best. There's nothing like it. Almost magical, I tell you."

"How 'bout that," thought Paul as he tossed the pine tar-filled tobacco tin back into the glove compartment of his vehicle and headed back to his residence.

Another evening, another battle with the bottle for Paul Kolbe. Paul at one time was the up-and-coming whiz kid who had six tools, not just the five that every major-league scout covets. And just what were those so-called tools? The traditional five were hitting for average, hitting for power, fielding your position, throwing accurately from your position, and using speed and judgment to steal bases and run intelligently for extra bases while on the basepaths.

And the sixth tool? That would be the ability to think ahead and anticipate what could happen during the course of a game and adjust accordingly. Scouts sometimes referred to this trait as "baseball sense." You know it when you see it, a scout once said, but it is hard to explain in words just what this trait is all about. It means moving based on the sound of the bat and ball, on which way the wind is blowing, on how the batter is positioning his front and back feet, and on what kind of pitch is being thrown. The game seems to slow down when you have that sixth sense. Not many ballplayers had it; Paul did.

But Paul had that weakness: he had difficulty controlling his drinking, and inevitably it cost him opportunity after opportunity to utilize his baseball skills. Now, at thirty-nine, he found his lot in life in Rochester, home of the summer-league Honkers.

But what happened in the years leading up to his medical condition sounds like a feature article for *National Geographic* magazine. Kolbe was signed in 1994 as a twenty-two-year-old college player by the Oakland Athletics. He stayed on the major-league roster for ten years, was finally released from the team in 2004, and then picked up as a free agent by the Boston Red Sox in 2005, by the Baltimore Orioles in 2006, by the Atlanta Braves in 2007, by the Pittsburgh Pirates in 2008, and eventually by the Rochester Honkers as a hitting coach in 2009.

The early major-league years were quite productive, featuring a career batting average of .327, with an average of 75 RBIs and 24 home runs per season. He had a great knack for picking up the rotation of a baseball, which helped with the timing of fastballs, the type of breaking ball, or even when a change-up was going to be thrown. In short, he hardly ever got cheated when he was hitting.

His fielding was outstanding as a younger player, but he increasingly had to rely on his keen baseball sense as he got older to position himself for fly balls and line drives. And he hardly ever threw to the wrong base.

In his later years, he became a nomad as mentioned above, playing only one season each for four different teams. Each season, his batting average and power numbers went steadily down, and, along with it, so did his at bats and ultimately games in the field. His last season with Pittsburgh was notable in that he spent more time as a pinch hitter than ever before and ultimately had less than two hundred total plate appearances.

Could he have played a few more years if he would have taken care of himself? No doubt. But injuries, temptations, pain-killers, alcohol, and other assorted issues had been the bane of many good-to-great ballplayers. Paul was not alone in having his career cut short by alcoholism. He retired after the 2008 season and wound up in Rochester, knowing that he had sufficiently abused his liver and that the only solution was a transplant and a severe lifestyle adjustment.

Now, going into his third season with the Honkers, the prospects of getting a transplant seemed to have faded with each succeeding year. But hope maintained a very strong tug on Paul. "Maybe this is the year it happens," Paul thought. Besides, he liked the slower pace in Rochester. The winters could be a little harsh, but Paul learned to love the days when it snowed and tolerated the weather when it was just plain cold. It was the early darkness at the end of the day that bothered him the most. And then spring happens: everything bursting out at once, which meant that baseball was not too much further behind, even in a short-season league like the Northwoods.

"Enough with the reminiscing," thought Paul. "I need some air." He walked out to the small patio area in the front of the pub. Just as Paul was about to sit down, who pulled up to the curb but none other than Kate Williams, owner of the Rochester Honkers and employer of record for Paul Kolbe. Kate was a very youthful-looking forty-year-old woman. Having inherited the Honkers from her father, she engineered a major makeover, including an expansion of the stadium, continuous year-round promotions, and total community involvement. Rochester felt a special kinship with the Honkers, thanks in large part to Kate's unflagging efforts.

"You know, Paul, I could fire you right now for being a poor example for our college men to follow. How many beers and whiskey shots have you had this evening, and what good do you think this is doing to your already damaged liver? You know I gave the Meyer Clinic my assurances that your drinking was far in the past. What do I tell them now?"

"Well, Boss Lady, with all due respect, you can tell them to take a flying leap for all I care this evening. I just had a long conversation with an old pro, and I feel like I could get back in the batter's box and face the best of the best right now."

"You may get your chance. Do you remember Dave McFarlin?"

"Sure, he was a coach in the Oakland A's system when I was working my way up the organization. He was one of the biggest supporters I had, and his opinion was helpful in my moving up faster than most guys my age. He's now a coach for the Saint Louis Cardinals. I consider him both a friend and a mentor. What about him?"

"He is here in town and wants to meet with you. How 'bout coming by my office tomorrow around ten o'clock and you two can get reacquainted?"

"Sounds fine. Do I have to be sober, or would it be okay to have a few drinks first thing in the morning?"

"I hope…I know you're kidding me, Paul. But please stop this crap. You know you don't have a chance in hell if you keep drinking."

"I've got this devil under control, Boss Lady. And I'll be glad to see my old friend Dave tomorrow."

"Denial, denial, denial. I'm not giving up on you, Paul, but dammit, you sure seem to have done so for yourself. See you tomorrow, and take a cab home when you're done here this evening. And quit calling me Boss Lady. As you might recall when you sober up, my name is Kate."

"I've never seen her so demonstrative before," Paul reflected as he returned to his favorite barstool. "Maybe she has a point. Or two," thought Paul.

"Hey, Sam. Can you get ahold of my favorite cab driver? I think I'll call it an evening, and I'll pick up my car tomorrow."

But the evening was not through yet. Sam's niece stopped by to say hello, and Sam introduced her to Paul. "So you're the famous ballplayer hiding out as a coach for the Rochester Honkers?" inquired Heather Alexander.

To describe Heather as attractive was like saying that there are a lot of tall trees in the North Woods; the statement was just not an adequate description.

She was around five foot eight, with curves in the right places and an air of confidence in everything she did. Her hair was shoulder length, strawberry blond, with a hint of curl at the ends. You could use a lot of descriptions—classy, sexy, articulate, fun loving—but not capture her essence. She had a way about her that made you feel like a million dollars when she looked into your eyes, like you were the most important and infinitely most interesting person in the room. She had beauty and brains, a combination not exactly missing in many women, but in abundance when it came to this particular one.

What possibly could she have seen in Paul Kolbe?

"I'm not sure," she confided in Sam when asked about the attraction somewhere along the course of their budding relationship. "Maybe it was the fact that he was good looking, but very vulnerable, yet a man's man, and also an open book. You didn't have to guess where you stood with Paul. He liked you or he didn't, with no drama wasted on the in-between stage."

"That's a good answer, I think," replied Sam as they both laughed at the likelihood that it wasn't.

"So, Paulie, why are you hiding out here in Rochester? Shouldn't you be coaching or even still playing in the bigs?" asked Heather.

"I wouldn't exactly call what I'm doing here 'hiding out.' I prefer to think of my Rochester experience as a sabbatical from the major-league wars. And Paulie? I haven't been called that since I was a little leaguer!"

"Sorry, it just seemed to fit."

So what do you do, and how do you know Sam?" asked Paul.

"Sam and his dearly departed wife were my favorite uncle and aunt. When my parents were killed in a car accident many years ago, they took me in and treated me like their own daughter. I live in Minneapolis, but I stop by to see Sam whenever I'm in town. And, bless her, I also visit my aunt's grave, too. She died of cancer a year or so before you came to town, Paulie, so I can attest to the fact that Sam has not always been the happy-go-lucky bachelor you see behind the bar!"

"That accounts for Sam. And what do you do for a living, Heather?" asked Paul.

Besides being drop-dead gorgeous, Heather was smart, having ma-triculated with a master's degree in political science from Macalester College in nearby Saint Paul. The college had gained renown as one of the top twenty schools in terms of student intelligence, based on extensive testing of over sixty thousand students at over four hundred colleges.

Heather fit right into this academic culture, so much so that she was offered the opportunity to pursue a doctorate degree in political science, along with a full-ride Fulbright scholarship to conduct research in a for-eign country.

Instead, she chose a riskier path as a political analysis consultant, joining a small firm based in Saint Paul. Within three years, she had become a junior partner and was up for a senior partnership within the next twelve months.

She had an extensive network of national high-end clients, built through referrals and word of mouth. She was a vibrant conversationalist and an amateur psychologist who knew how best to put clients at ease.

"I offer political advice to individuals and organizations at the rate of $1,850 per day, plus expenses, with a two-day minimum charge. I have plenty of clients, plenty of well-respected men and women of all political and professional persuasions. As such, my firm is rather unique. We work both sides of the aisle, if you know what I mean!"

"That sounds extremely interesting and rather sexy at the same time. Kind of like having to face someone with a ninety-five-mile-an-hour fastball, followed by a knee-buckling curve ball.

"And speaking of extremely interesting, I'm afraid I'm a little out of practice on this boy-meets-girl stuff. I have a lot of time in the off-season, but invariably I only seem to meet women during the baseball season when I have very little free time."

"Don't fret, Paulie. I won't throw you any fastballs, or curve balls for that matter!"

For the next hour Heather and Paul discussed their likes and dislikes about everything they could think of, including chili cheese dogs at the ballpark (yes!) to cottage cheese as a restaurant side dish (no! too healthy).

Finally, Heather looked at Paul and asked, "What if I told you that I was interested in some good, old-fashioned stranger-on-stranger sex with you? No strings attached."

"I'm not about to say no to your offer. But I must admit to having to pinch myself to make sure I'm not dreaming. Here I am, sitting here in my endowed seat at Sam's place on a random, late winter evening, and you walk in, and before you know it, we both walk out together. Tell me I'm not dreaming, or worse case, that someone has adulterated the drinks at this establishment."

With a laugh, Heather responded, "No, you're not dreaming. I'm a very busy lady, Paulie. I don't have time for the dance that goes into dating. I like you and this is my way of getting to know you better. A whole lot better! Besides, Sam, your friend and mine, has been telling me about you for some time, and now I feel like I've known you forever. That explains my side of the story. What about you? Do you always throw yourself at the first damsel in distress when you see her?"

"Well, Ms. Damsel, I'm not sure how much distress you are currently in, but I'd feel very ungentlemanly if I didn't help out where I could. And no, believe it or not, I generally don't spend time with female strangers. And for some reason, they do seem to flock to ballplayers, even though some of them—me included, are no longer teeing it up on the playing field."

"Well, I'm flattered that we have arrived at a mutual conclusion to this discussion," said Heather.

"So it seems like the right thing to do now is to leave before one or both of us change our minds. Gotta ask that question: your place or mine?"

"I prefer mine. Follow me, soldier. My humble abode is not easy to find in the evening."

"I'm not really in good enough shape to drive; I was just about to get a cab when you came in."

"No problem. You can ride with me and I'll bring you back here in the morning."

Paul followed Heather to her red Mercedes SLK with black convertible top. He was not a car buff, but he did appreciate an outstanding vehicle like Heather's, which more than likely cost two to three times what his current salary was with the Honkers.

"This is one beautiful car for an equally attractive lady."

"Why, thank you for the compliment. I always wanted an SLK, and last year I bit the bullet and bought a new one—cash of course."

"Of course. I do the same thing with the daily newspaper. But a car? I would need to hustle a loan for that."

"That little red thing is my only obvious extravagance. I prefer to remain as under the radar as I can."

"Hard to do with that SLK parked there, but thanks for clearing up that issue. I've done okay over the years and have a nice little nest egg socked away, but *that* is something beyond my reach. That being said, it fits you to the T!"

"You're not making a lot of sense, Paulie. But I will accept your comment as a compliment—I think. Now, shall we go up to my place and fool around for a while?"

"I never thought you'd ask. But, up to your place? You have a residence here *and* in Minneapolis?"

"This is not really mine. It belongs to the firm. I spend enough time down here that I suggested we buy a condo, and my firm agreed. Besides, it's a good investment in this part of town."

"So you're a real estate guru too? I'm impressed!"

"No, I saw an opportunity and jumped on it. Sort of what we're doing this evening, Paulie."

"Wow. I have to pinch myself. This time for real!"

"I have a better idea," said Heather, as they walked into the condo. "Let's get to know each other better," as she put her arms around Paul and proceeded to give him a tender kiss.

The rest of the evening and early morning consisted of various and sundry wrestling-like positions. At least, it felt like that to Paul. "That woman knows a thing or two about making love," thought Paul. Even though it was late, then ridiculously late, both Heather and Paul felt in tune with one another and eager to continue their spontaneous activity.

After all, neither party had to get up too early the following morning, so why waste a few glorious hours on something so trivial as sleep? The morning arrived in just a few short hours. Paul sat up in bed, stark naked, covers and sheets askew, and saw a gorgeous lady in the hallway clad in a pink nightie coming toward him with two steaming cups of coffee.

"You are a sight for a pair of very tired eyes—mine. What a lovely vision so early in the morning! I hope I didn't come off as some sort of goofball, only interested in a roll in the hay, Heather," said Paul.

"Not at all, Paulie. As I recall, I pressed you into your joining me last evening. Aren't you glad you did?"

"I am, but I'm embarrassed to say that every part of my anatomy is very stressed out. Never had that happen to me before!"

"I didn't think you were ever going to stop playing last evening, Paulie. You had a lot of pent-up feelings, and I was the fortunate recipient of same."

"Glad you remembered. I know I started out very well with you. I think we mesh together. But I must admit that the rest of the evening and morning was a blur. I think I was maybe two or even three sheets to the wind—and I'm not a sailor!"

"You've never been with a real woman who knew what she was doing, I presume. I'll try to go easy next time. Will there be a next time, Paulie?"

"I'm on board if you are. I must admit that I'm getting way ahead of myself, but I can see you and me spending a lot of time together."

"I hope so, Paulie. Now I understand that you have an important meeting at the ballpark. You're welcome to shower here, and I have enough supplies on hand for a quick shave and other grooming essentials. I'll then take you back to your car."

"Thanks, I'll take you up on your offer."

"Wow," thought Paul to himself as he stood under the steaming shower. "Now that was an experience—one of the best nights I ever had!" He hurriedly dressed and gave Heather a quick hug, and then they were off to Paul's car. After he gave Heather another hug and a nice soft kiss, Paul drove to the stadium and was excited about seeing his old friend.

CHAPTER TWO

"Hello Paul. How in the hell are you doing? Damn you look good, but you also look like you had a sleepless night," said Dave McFarlin as he greeted Paul at the offices of the Honkers baseball club.

"I think I was anticipating this meeting too much. In any event, it's great to see you again, Dave. It's been awhile!"

Dave and Paul's relationship extended way back to the Oakland Athletics days, when Dave was a new coach of the A's and Paul was a first-year player. Dave pitched batting practice to Paul, helped position him in the outfield based on batters' strengths and pitchers' tendencies, and worked with him on throwing to second, third, and home.

As a result, they had a bond of mentor and student, and it paid off. Paul not only became a good hitter, he also ranked high in outfield assists, range factors, and overall fielding metrics. And they also maintained their contact and friendship over the years. It was only fitting that Dave thought of Paul when the need arose for an outfielder that could help the Cardinals in the short run.

"Well as I recall, Paul, you never were much of a sleeper, although I saw you catnapping in the clubhouse from time to time."

"And I think I sleep even less now, Dave. My doc thinks it's some sort of chemical imbalance. In any event, I get about three to five hours per night, just enough to keep me going."

"I'm sorry to hear that. I hope you get some additional medical insight into that issue. Maybe do a sleep study? Those folks at the Meyer Clinic surely have an expert or two in that field. Seems like they have an expert staff involved in everything!"

"I've been meaning to talk to them about that issue. I have a greater one, and it's the reason I keep hanging out here in Rochester. My liver is shot, and I'm in need of a transplant. I've been on a waiting list for several years, but my blood type, which is not common, makes good matches tough. You of all people know that I have had problems with alcohol over the years, but I think that's all behind me. Not totally, but I'm managing what little drinking I do nowadays, thanks to good support here in Rochester. I really think this is the year I finally get the transplant, and when that occurs, the guy you're looking at becomes a teetotaler."

"I hope for your sake, Paul, that this works out for you. But selfishly, I hope it's not too soon. We have a serious problem in Saint Louis, and we think you might be able to help us and resurrect your career. Does that sound interesting to you?"

"Dave, I like it here, but I always thought I had 'one last hurrah' in me. I certainly wasn't ready last year, but I've been taking batting practice as part of my off-season conditioning program, doing roadwork to improve my stamina, and spending a considerable amount of time in the weight room. The net result of all this effort has been that I've cost the Honkers a goodly portion of their supply of baseballs. I need to come back here, Dave, for medical reasons at some undetermined point, but I think I do have some hits left in my Louisville Slugger. What gives?"

"Well, you know we signed Lance Champlin right off the street as a free agent after he was traded last year by the Houston Astros to the New York Yankees. He was still hurt when the trade was made, didn't play much, and wound up being released at the end of the season. He contacted his old club, and they professed sincere gratitude for his many years of service but advised him that they were committed to their youth movement.

"Thanks to good scouting and our own medical staff, we invested three days in wooing Lance to Saint Louis. We're projecting him as our everyday right fielder, even though he hasn't played the position for a number of seasons. We think he can do some damage in the middle of the lineup, plus be a good influence in the clubhouse. There are also several budding prospects on the team. We see some mentoring opportunities for Lance as well.

"Long story short, we picked him up for a song, and he is in great shape, so much so that because of Al Robles being a fixture at first base, we had to think out of the box and project him playing his old right-field position.

"In center, we have Colby Rakers, our 'can't-miss' prospect. He couldn't miss, unless he was batting, playing the outfield, or running the bases. He still has great potential, but you know how Tony LoDuca feels about potential. He'd rather see a proven record.

"And that is where you come in. You know we signed Matt Bradley to a long-term, big-money contract that runs another five years. We're obviously committed to him for the long haul. Last week, however, he separated his shoulder chasing a ball off the wall in spring training. The official word is that he is out two to three weeks, so we don't appear desperate if we have to pull the trigger on a trade. In reality, he is probably out at least till the All-Star break, and it might even be longer, depending on his range of motion after rehab.

"Meanwhile, we have a season to play, and the skipper thinks we are a contending club for our division. That was before Matt got hurt. Tony remembered you when I brought up your name—who wouldn't? But I gotta be honest, Paul. I need to know if you have a handle on your drinking problem, plus now the transplant issue you brought up.

"We cannot afford a public relations misstep if we bring you on. And don't be surprised or take it personally if the media doesn't accuse us of being cheap by signing someone past his prime versus getting a player with more immediate name recognition and proven performance.

"We need a quick fix, but also a quality fix that doesn't compromise our future by a trade that weakens our farm system or by a pricey—sorry about that one, Paul—free-agent signing."

"Dave, my batting practice workouts have become appointment viewing at the ballpark. Folks show up because they know I take BP at the same time every weekday—eleven a.m. I would need a little conditioning time, but there are still four-plus weeks of spring training. I realize the organization exposes itself if it signs yet another older player, but if you can stand the publicity heat, I think I can fill in long enough until you get Matt back. I'm confident about my hitting. Base running? I'm not going to BS you. I've been doing roadwork, but not enough to be okay at a high level. I would need to get in better shape, plus I would need plenty of throwing to build up my arm strength. Fortunately, there aren't too many plays from left field that require more than two hundred feet of accuracy."

Dave looked at Paul and could see a sense of determination in his somewhat bloodshot eyes, which was a hallmark of Paul's previous success. Which Paul would the Saint Louis Cardinals be getting? Could Dave personally survive his own job with the Cardinals if Paul became a liability or an embarrassment to the organization? At this stage of his own career, Dave thought that a risk that just might turn into a reward was worth taking. "Besides, where else could the team find an impact player at the eleventh hour that didn't cost them a young player, a draft pick or two, and/or a wad of cash?" thought Dave.

"Well, old teammate, I think we can cut a deal with you if you're willing to take a 'Major-Minor' contract. Make the team, and you're in the bigs with a one-year big league salary. Look good but don't make the team, you're in the minors, making minor-league money, and serving as 'insurance' in case someone else goes down. Wash out, and I suppose you're no worse than where you're at now.

"Do we have a deal, Paul?"

"How can I say no to your offer, especially if I wipe out? My only caveat would be that I'd like to eliminate the "Major-Minor" option. I either make the team or you cut me. I'm not interested in being 'insurance' in case one or more of your rookies isn't maturing enough to fill Matt's shoes. I realize that this is not exactly what you had in mind, but I think I have one more season left in me, and I don't want it to be at triple-A. The only other stipulation I have to make is that I'm waiting for a donor match for a liver. It's the sole reason I've hung out here in Rochester. I can't control when or even if I'll get a chance at a new one, but I'm ultimately a goner without it. There is the slim possibility that I could be called by the clinic during the season, which would end mine. But I've been on the watch list now for two years. I think I could finish the season, or at least get you to Matt's return to the ball club."

"Let me check with John Nowicki, our GM, real quick," said Dave. After making the phone call, Dave reported back to Paul.

"We're willing, and even glad, to accept the conditions you outlined for your signing.

"It would be great if the Meyer Clinic could wait till Matt is available, but life doesn't revolve around a pennant race, does it? Since this matter is a rather delicate one, our senior management group and I believe it would be best to not advise Tony LoDuca of your condition for a while. Our concern is that he would not play you and urge us to find someone else to fill in for Matt. If you got off to a slow start he would be carrying a chip on his shoulder with senior management for forcing you on the team. A few good months of performance would give Tony the feeling that he could piece everything together. We'll at least be able to buy some time with him. Once you start hitting and generally find your place on the team, there will be time to introduce your medical condition to him.

"I'm putting myself out on a limb here, Paul, but I don't think there is a better candidate out there than you. It will be up to you to prove me to be right."

"I'll follow your lead on this matter, Dave. I'm sure the skipper will ultimately be upset when he finds out he was kept in the dark, but I'll try to make myself as indispensible as possible in the meantime," said Paul

Later that evening, back in the comfort of the All Pro, Paul mentioned to his friend Sam, "I might be on my way back to the big leagues. Can you believe it?"

"I suspected that you might be leaving us one day for bigger and better things. What about the Meyer Clinic? Aren't you concerned about being called by them while you're out of town?

"Sam, I've been waiting for two years for the darn transplant. What are the odds of getting one over the next few months?"

"You sure about that, Paul?"

"Sam, I'm only sure of two things—cold Rheinhold and room temperature Jack Daniel's."

"What about your friend—and my niece—eyeballing you. Are you sure of her?"

From the other side of the bar, Heather looked straight at Paul.

"Hi, Paulie. Care to buy a girl a drink?"

"I'd love to, but I'm going on strike to eradicate the use of 'Paulie' as it relates to addressing me," he said, smiling. "As you know, I haven't been called 'Paulie' since I was in the first grade. I'm guessing that if I make a big deal about it, I'll never hear the end of it."

Heather laughed as she moved to his side of the bar.

"Not so, I'm not vindictive. For example, I could be grilling you as to why you haven't called me all day since our initial love fest. You do remember we had a great time all night long at my place last night, don't you?"

"Of course I do. And I agree. It was a great time. I don't know why I haven't called. Call me stupid. On the other hand, it has been an extremely fast-paced day."

"Well news travels fast in this town and I have to ask this question: are you now finally going to get to chase your dream one more time? If so, please tell me it's with the Twins so I can see you once in a while, assuming of course, that you can overcome your prejudices against pushy women like me."

"The Twins? No. Back to the big leagues? Yes. But with the Cardinals in the other league. They do come to Minneapolis to play the Twins once this upcoming season for three interleague games. Otherwise, I'll be out of the state until the fall. And as far as seeing you again, you can count on it. I just don't know when."

"I can handle a little long distance. Who knows? I just might pop up in Saint Louis one of these days, or even some other city where you might have some road games. I usually wind up with a few new clients each year, and I never know where they will be headquartered.

"In the meantime, I'm meeting some ladies for dinner this evening. Would you like to come by later, say eleven o'clock or so, and keep me company until the cock crows tomorrow morning?"

Paul thought about it for just the slightest part of a second. "How can I resist your offer when it includes crows? Yes, I'll be there. Looking forward to seeing you again so soon, Heather."

Heather then left to get ready for her dinner party. Having some time to kill, Paul put it to good use downing a few Rheinhold Supremes and throwing back a shot or two of Jack. A little dinner followed, and then a few more drinks.

Paul found himself in one of those half awake, half asleep states and thought he had a conversation with someone about gripping bats, swinging through the pitch and completing a full swing in order to generate power and consistency. Then again, he thought he might just be making all of that up. "Maybe it was really time to start cutting back on my drinking," thought Paul.

CHAPTER THREE

"I can't pass out," Paul thought to himself. "I have 'obligations' later in the evening."

And so after Paul had apparently dozed off, Sam asked him if he was ready to close his tab. "Yeah, sure. What's this tin, Sam? I don't chew tobacco."

"Well it just so happens that your mystery friend was by to see you. You know the one that you said was Joe Fisher, the great ballplayer from the thirties? If it was him, he looked pretty damn good to me for someone about a hundred years old!"

"Damn, I could have sworn that I was talking to someone," thought Paul. Opening the can lid, Paul discovered a pungent and sticky goop. "This is the same stuff I got from Joe Fisher during our first meeting, and I tossed that stuff in my glove compartment before throwing it away!"

"Your centenarian friend said it was pine tar from the North Woods. He said he came here every off-season and collected enough of the stuff to make sure he held his bat tightly and in a perfect position to square it up on the ball. It sounded like he knew what he was talking about. And, he said, "don't use bullshit"—his word, my friend—"batting gloves with this stuff and to just grip the damn bat like a man." Lastly, he reiterated that North Woods pine tar wasn't just pine tar. It has almost magical properties when it is applied to a bat."

"That's what he told me, too. Nowadays everyone uses batting gloves. The players would laugh at me if I didn't. I'll keep this gooey mess, but I'm not sure what I'll do with it. As far as magical properties?

This is starting to sound like that cornfield-in-Iowa movie I saw awhile back."

"Maybe you should try the stuff, Paul. After all, you're not getting any younger, you know?" advised Sam kiddingly.

"Maybe you should stick to bartending, Sam. But maybe you're right, too! I might need a little magic to get through, however long this baseball season turns out to be for me!"

"Meanwhile," thought Paul, "I'd like to find out a little more about where this stuff comes from. I'd also like to really talk to 'Joe Fisher,' because he is driving me crazy. Is he real? Is he some sort of figment of my imagination? I seem to manifest his image only when I'm at some level of drunkenness. And I remember now. He said, "Don't blow this chance. It's the last one you'll get." Gee, thanks for the pep talk, you friendly ghost, you. But then, Sam did say he talked to Joe Fisher. Plus, he keeps leaving this gooey stuff for me to try. Doesn't he understand this in not the 1930s anymore?"

Getting back to Sam, he said out loud, "So I'm *not* crazy!"

"Doesn't seem so. Any idea who do you think your mystery man really is?" asked Sam.

"Maybe he is a relative of Joe Fisher's. For now, I hope we're done with Joe the helpful ghost, as this whole scenario has me a little creeped out."

Paul was tired, very tired, but he did not want to disappoint Heather.

Thanks to his favorite cabbie Mario, Paul reached Heather's comfortable residence near Silver Lake in the northeast section of Rochester right at the appointed hour of eleven o'clock. Mario wasn't his real name, but Paul called him that because he resembled a certain video-game character. So the name stuck, and "Mario" was okay with whatever he was called, as long as he was busy with good customers like Paul.

"Do you want me to pick you up at a certain time, Paul?" asked Mario.

"Let me call you in the morning. I'm not sure what my schedule will be like tomorrow. And thanks for showing up this evening. I know your firm has a lot of drivers. I'm just very comfortable with you. You're dependable, and you know your baseball. Works for me!"

As Paul walked up to Heather's address, she answered the door in a sheer black nightgown and black high heels, leaving little to Paul's imagination.

"Come in, Paulie my dear," she said as she handed him an old-fashioned martini with gin, vermouth, and several pimento olives.

"The drink I don't need, but I'll take it anyway, Heather. My, you look…what's a word beyond *gorgeous*? Whatever it is, you qualify. Wow!"

"So get comfortable and tell me: what's the next step with the Cardinals?" asked Heather.

Paul kicked off his shoes and sat down on a small love seat facing Heather. "I have some paperwork floating around between my long-lost agent, who probably had given up on me, and the Saint Louis Cardinals. I also have to pass their physical in Saint Louis in a few days. If that all goes well, I'll go down to Jupiter, Florida, and get in baseball shape before the start of the regular season. How long I stay with the Cardinals depends on the health of Matt Bradley, meaning how quickly can he get back in the lineup, plus how well I play in general. In my perfect world, I get the whole season in, but we'll just take it a day at a time. Regards the physical, I have an agreement that the Cards medical staff won't tell Tony LoDuca just yet about my liver issue, as he might not play me until management found someone else. I'm hoping that I do well enough to establish rapport with the manager so he can look past my health condition, which no doubt will deteriorate over time."

"I'm sorry to hear that you'll be leaving us so soon, but I'm also glad for you that you're getting this wonderful opportunity. And this pine tar goo that I heard you talking to Sam about, what makes it so special?"

"I don't know, but someone, possibly a relative of an old-time Cardinal, keeps giving me the stuff and encouraging me to use it. He has even told me the goo has almost magical properties regarding the ability to hold a bat tighter without the use of modern-day batting gloves."

"Do you believe in this magical goop?"

"I don't know what to believe. The guy says he's someone that has been dead for over twenty-five years. I did learn from him that pine tar quality can vary based on the age of pine trees, the type of soil present, and moisture conditions. Plus, if you want to get a little more technical, add the combination of aromatic hydrocarbons, tar acids, and tar bases. He seems to know what he is talking about.

I think I'll give the goop a try in spring training. I suppose I can handle a few chuckles from the other ballplayers."

"Enough of this baseball talk. Go into the master bedroom and slide under those satin sheets, Paulie. I'll be in to join you in just a minute."

Paul couldn't wait to cap off the evening. What better way than to be with his newfound favorite lady friend? He eagerly stepped into the bedroom, dropping clothes along the way. He made it all the way to the bed, laid his head on several oversized pillows, and closed his eyes.

As promised, Heather followed in her birthday suit, pulling up the sheets and snuggling next to Paul. He was physically and mentally cooked. He felt like a human pincushion for all that had happened in recent days and weeks.

So despite Paul's best intentions, he slept through the remainder of the evening. In the morning, there was fresh coffee brewed in the kitchen, a plate full of croissants, and a note: "Sorry we didn't (continue to) consummate our friendship last evening, as you slept like a newborn baby. You probably needed your rest more than a romp or two with me. I'll allow you a mulligan this time, but don't let it happen again. It's bad for my ego! I'm not sure when I'll see you again, but it better not be after the baseball season. Find a way back to me, slugger. Sooner, not later, Heather."

Paul drank several cups of coffee, stared out the window, ate a few pastries, stared out the window some more, and then gathered up his clothes, making a note of Heather's temporary address in town. He wasn't sure what, if anything, was appropriate, such as flowers, but he felt he had to do something before he left town to show that he was sorry and that he did want to see her again.

After contacting Mario for yet another cab ride, Paul picked up his car near the pub and then went shopping for something for Heather in downtown Rochester.

He settled on a fruit basket that he hoped would make it back intact to her and attached a simple note: "Heather, I'm sorry. I look forward to seeing you again. In the meantime, good luck and be careful out there! Your slugger, Paul."

CHAPTER FOUR

The next day found Paul in Kate Williams's office for a very different kind of meeting with one of his favorite women.

"So, Paul, we finally found someone to take your ridiculously low contract off our hands and our books. And it happens to be a major-league team to boot.

"C'mon, Boss Lady. You know I wouldn't be making this move if I didn't think this was my last chance to resurrect my playing career. The Cardinals came through with my request for a major league–only contract or bust. I really do enjoy coaching our kids and having them develop into competent wood batsmen, and I also like imparting some of life's lessons, such as 'Do as I say, not as I do.'"

"I know that, Paul. I just wanted to let you have it one more time. You know we love you here in Honker Nation. You can come back anytime, and we'll find a way to use your baseball expertise. Good luck, and we'll be watching your comeback from afar."

It was too early in the season for Honkers players to chip in with their good-byes, and the staffing for the team was at its traditional off-season low. Still, a few honest "we'll miss you, Paul" mentions went a long way in helping Paul realize that things were about to change in his life.

"Can I really do this?" thought Paul to himself. "Other than hang out and keep waiting for a liver, I never felt comfortable walking away from the big leagues the way I did. Then again, if I hadn't, I probably would have been kicked to the curb. That kind of ending does not lend itself to a nice job in the game, be it as a coach, a scout, or a front office manager."

Meanwhile, Paul had to make one more key stop in Rochester before he left town. He had to see his gastroenterology specialist, Dr. Richard Archer, at the Meyer Clinic.

"Hello, Paul. You're looking good. I'm glad to see you're staying fit," greeted Dr. Archer. "It will help your MELD hold steady. This means you're still a candidate, although there are many younger and/or more critically ill individuals in line. I'm still very confident we'll get a call for you. As a reminder, that means you will need to drop everything and get here to the clinic in less than twelve hours. And in the meantime, that means no alcohol, a low-fat diet, and moderate exercise."

"By the way," mentioned Paul. "Can you refresh me on what the acronym MELD stands for?"

"Sure, it's 'Model for End Stage Liver Disease.' It lets us know, in simplest terms, how healthy a liver is. In your case, Paul, yours isn't. But the good news is we're monitoring your score."

"And I'm thankful for that. The words *end stage* keep resonating in my mind," said Paul.

"And well they should," said Dr. Archer. "There is a point where your other organs will start to shut down rather than be poisoned by a nonfunctioning liver. We obviously don't want to reach that point, or your situation could turn fatal.

"Also, are we clear on what I reiterated as our terms on your transplant? I can almost assure you of a normal life, except for a few pills each day, when this is all said and done. You've been patient so far. Keep your chin up and keep plugging away, and we'll find a good match with your blood type and get this accomplished."

"That sounds great," remarked Paul, trying not to sound too disappointed (same old pep talk, doc!). "Doctor, I have some news I need to share with you. I've been offered an opportunity to go back to the big leagues with the Saint Louis Cardinals. I'm headed to Florida for spring training and then it's on to the real thing. So I'll be out of Rochester for the next six months, traveling half the time around the country when I'm not at my home base in Saint Louis."

"Paul, you know the routine here. If we contact you, you have twelve hours to be here. You'd be better off staying in Rochester and being ready when we contact you."

"Doc, with all due respect, I've heard that same scenario from you for several years now. I have a life to live, and I've been offered one last shot at playing my passion at the highest level. It's not about the money or the public exposure. At my age, it's about participating and contributing one last time."

"Paul let's be honest for one moment. You've been on the list for several years because of your age, your unusual blood type, and the fact that you haven't totally taken care of yourself. The clinic assigned a higher risk number to your case because they do not want to waste the precious organ on someone who will abuse a new one. You're still in line, and there is a good chance you will get one before your current one fails, but you have got to be ready to turn on a dime if you get the call from us. Are you prepared to address this matter if, not *when*, this happens? I need your assurance that we're not wasting each other's time, Paul."

"Wow, Doc. You don't mince words, do you? I understand. I haven't been hanging around Rochester these past two years for my personal financial gain working in the Northwoods Summer League. You call, doctor, and I'll make damn sure that I get here."

"Fair enough. And you know you have got to stop drinking. Your friend Sam rats you out whenever I see him. We frequent the same grocery store, by the way. Amazing what you can learn in the fresh produce aisle! Before you get too hacked off at him, he does have your best interests at heart, and he is a good friend. I think he does you a great service by slowing your consumption down as much as possible. And you probably thought it was because he was extremely busy! But the fact of the matter is that you shouldn't be drinking at all."

"Damn that Sam! He probably watered my whiskey down, too, come to think of it. Okay, guilty as charged. On the plus side, I've cut way back to a drink or two every other night. Plus, I won't have time with the Cardinals to do much drinking; I wouldn't be worth anything if I did anyway. I hear you, doctor. I'm not going to pretend that quitting the sauce will be easy for me, but there are multiple reasons, including a new lady friend I disappointed recently, to do so."

"I hope you follow through, Paul. I really do. Good luck on your way back to the big leagues. I hope it works out for you, and I hope you come back here to stay afterward."

With that rather tense discussion concluded, Paul had taken care of his loose ends in town and was ready to start his new adventure.

He started packing, very lightly, and noticed one of the tins given to him by Joe Fisher, or whoever he was. "Joe Fisher? Are you hallucinating?" Paul thought. Joe Fisher had been dead since 1975. He won the last Triple Crown in the National League way back in 1937, batting .374 while hitting 31 homers and driving in 154 runs. It was amazing that no one in over seventy-five seasons had approached this feat in the National League, given all the great hitters that followed Joe in the ensuing decades.

But the image of Joe Fisher remained firmly planted in Paul's mind. "What is this all about? Why is someone obviously messing with me?"

"Maybe," he thought, "I've been hitting the bottle way, way too much, and it's time to give it a rest." In any event, Paul concluded that he would take the pine tar with him as a souvenir of his meetings with the spirit, or whatever, of Joe Fisher.

CHAPTER FIVE

Getting from Rochester, Minnesota, to Jupiter, Florida, where the Cardinals trained, was not easy. There were several direct flight options from Chicago to Miami and from Minneapolis to Fort Lauderdale, but the flights were early in the morning (e.g., 6:30 a.m.) or late in the evening (e.g., 9:30 p.m.).

Paul opted for the early flight to Fort Lauderdale and then rented a vehicle for the short trip to Jupiter.

He checked into the team hotel and got situated with his new home for the next few weeks. "Not bad," thought Paul. A suite to myself, an ocean breeze, a sandy beach, room service. I could get used to this. Being in Rochester at the independent-league level for the past few years, Paul forgot how comfortable things could be in the big leagues. "Until you face a one-hundred-mile-an-hour fastball or knee-buckling curve ball," chuckled Paul to himself.

The next morning came very quickly. He made his way a few blocks in his rental vehicle and proceeded to the players-only parking lot. An attendant asked for ID and welcomed him to the team. "I'm good with names and faces, Mr. Kolbe," he said. "I won't have to check your ID again. Have a great spring here in Jupiter!"

The first person he met in the clubhouse was his buddy, coach, and mentor Dave McFarlin. "Welcome aboard, Paul," said Dave, shaking Paul's hand. "Are you ready to help us win some ball games?"

"You bet, Dave. I'm champing at the bit. Can't wait to start playing some competitive baseball!"

"That can wait a bit after some drills, more drills, and even more drills. You remember that routine! In the meantime, let me introduce you to the skipper, Tony LoDuca. I bet he's already obsessing over where he can put your bat in a variety of lineup situations!"

Dave and Paul walked over to Tony's office and stood in the open doorway. Tony looked up, rose immediately, and greeted them with a handshake and a motion to sit down on a couch facing Tony's desk.

"Paul, welcome. Glad we could work something out with you to bring you here. I just missed managing you in Oakland, but Dave was there for your entire career. He speaks highly of you, and I remember you as a very tough out."

"Thanks, Tony. I look forward to playing for you and the Cardinals. What a tradition. What a climate for a ballplayer. What a great opportunity you've given me!"

"I agree with you. It's great to be here, Paul. I can't believe Matt ever got hurt, as he was practicing taking balls off the left field wall and got too close to the darn thing. I'm more pessimistic about his shoulder than our medical staff, because I've seen these kinds of injuries linger for extended periods. That's where you come in. Our kids are not ready for an everyday assignment. Maybe by midseason, but not now. A trade would hurt our current team or our farm system. Signing a high-profile free agent would bust our budget, and who's left at this late date anyway? Oops, sorry about that, Paul. And then comes Dave's bright idea. Having you stashed away for just this occasion! Can you still get the job done at this level, Paul?"

"I wouldn't have agreed to this experiment if I wasn't confident that I could still hit major-league pitching. The fielding, throwing, and running will take some time, but I'll be ready come April first!"

"Sounds great, Paul. Do you have any questions while you have a captive audience?" asked Tony.

"Yes I do. An off-the-field one. I understand that the Cardinals have new ownership as of a year ago. That Anheuser-Busch sold the club to the Rheinhold brewery. I happen to like Rheinhold Supreme when I occasionally have a sip or two, but I wasn't aware that it was a Saint Louis product. My question is what kind of a deal did the new owners negotiate that allowed the stadium to keep its 'Busch' name?"

"A rather confusing deal if you asked me," said Tony. "The old man, Hank Rheinhold, loves baseball, and I think he would have thrown in his soul to the devil to acquire the Cardinals and the assorted pieces... the stadium, the land to the north, now referred to as BallYard Village, but not any of the minor-league affiliates. Anheuser-Busch has new ownership, and I think they just wanted to refocus their efforts on the beer business. And what a coup for A-B! They get to keep their stadium naming rights for ten years for a nominal annual fee to Rheinhold. Ten years!

"Hank is retiring from running his brewery and the Cardinals as of the end of this year. He will personally oversee operations for the club for this season. A new president and CEO will be named after our 2011 campaign, no doubt one of Hank's baseball jock protégées from the brewery. I wish it would be someone from our actual industry, but his baseball jocks came from the select baseball team sponsored by Rheinhold over the years in Saint Louis. Those select teams almost always finished first or second in regional tournaments. Whether or not amateur baseball and beer industry experience translates to running an MLB franchise remains to be seen."

With that conversation concluded, it was off to a physical and then a uniform fitting. Paul requested and received number forty-seven, reason being it was the only uniform that fit him in high school and he stuck with the number through college and all the professional teams he played on, including now with Saint Louis.

He was assigned a locker near the other outfielders and right next to newly signed Lance Champlin. Together, the two veterans had accumulated over thirty years of major-league experience. How many balls and strikes they looked at from the batter's box was anyone's guess. Suffice it to say, the Cardinals were adding some age with the acquisition of both these corner outfielders, and it would be evident soon enough if they were up to the task.

"Hey there, Paul," greeted Lance, as Paul sat down in front of his locker. "Pleasure to meet you. How long will it take before the club is accused of robbing the cradle to get both of us?" He asked this with a broad smile on his face.

"Hi, Lance. You're right about that. It's unusual for a contending team to have two youngsters like you and me on the same field!"

"Well I'm glad you're here, Paul. I consider myself a student of the game, and you put up some good numbers in your career. I think the club is in very good hands in left field until the big guy returns. Having gone through various degrees of shoulder, hip, and knee injuries myself, I think Matt is out for a considerable period of time. Maybe the rest of the season."

"That's my unprofessional take, too, Lance. And thanks for the compliment. I'd like to see some October baseball if possible. I'll settle for whatever works out. Midseason, end-of-season. Whatever. It's my 'one last hurrah.' I think there is a good fit here for me and I'm ready to get started."

The early days of spring training consisted of drills, which would hopefully lead to routine habits for the season. Paul rarely caught fly balls one-handed unless he had to sprint to a ball. It was unusual for him to see the number of young outfielders catch virtually all their balls that way. "They would get a stern lecture from me if we were in Rochester," thought Paul.

The first games in the spring were played with multiple players for every position so Tony and the coaching staff could get a look at everyone in camp. After the first week, players started being weeded out, as one by one they received a "personal invitation" to join Tony (and sometimes with John Nowicki) to hear the news of their demotion to the minor-league complex or outright release. It was never an easy process for Tony or the player, but a necessary one when there were over ninety players in camp at this juncture.

Paul's first encounter with Colby Rakers set the tone for the rest of their season together. He was batting in front of Colby during batting practice and fouling off a number of pitches. At Tony's directive, he was having an extended session at the plate and fiddled with foot location, nearer and farther from home plate until he felt comfortable.

"Hey geezer," said Colby, standing next to the batting cage. "You think you could give someone else, like me, for example, a chance sometime today, to take a few cuts, too? Maybe someone, like me, for example, to hit the ball in fair territory?"

Paul turned around, stopped concentrating on the pitcher, stared at Colby, and then returned his focus on the pitcher and the task at hand.

As he passed Colby, he looked at him and said, "I would appreciate your not calling me that."

"Okay. I'll just shorten it to 'Geez,'" said Colby with a smirk on his face.

"I'll deal with smartass later," thought Paul, "but not on my first day of spring training."

The first games of the spring were played with the remaining players still in abundance, at least two and sometime three deep per defensive position. Further review and evaluation continued the weeding-out process until there were just sixteen position players and fourteen pitchers, including six starters, two swingmen, and six relievers. As a result, the team was pretty well set, with just a few role players to be determined.

In between games there were fundamentals, fundamentals, and more fundamentals. Paul and Lance both paced themselves on throwing drills, using the cutoff man every time there was one. Colby, on the other hand, tried longer throws, including to home, with very little success.

"What an ass," thought Paul, "why do they put up with his crap?"

Week two started to get into the exhibition schedule, and the team began play against the Miami Marlins, their co-tenant at the Jupiter complex. Tony experimented with Paul batting anywhere from second to fifth, sixth, and seventh and settled into a flip-flop with Colby, based on whether or not the starting pitcher was left- or right-handed. For lefties, Paul batted second or sixth, with Colby batting seventh. For righties, Paul batted sixth or seventh, with Colby batting second.

Week three was a repeat of the second week of exhibition games plus more drills, and still more drills. Most players hit a wall by this time, but not Paul. He felt he needed every at bat, every catch, every throw, to get ready for the season.

The final days of spring training were different than the rest of baseball's preseason. By now, the roster was trimmed down to the core group of players, and very few jobs remained open—a fifth starter spot, a bullpen spot, and an extra infielder. Paul was assured of a starting spot in left field as long as he could generate some RBIs and field his position.

In Paul's case, he was always in fairly good shape, but nothing like the chiseled physical specimens playing the game today. But he had a swing, something you couldn't duplicate without natural talent. His plate demeanor seemed effortless, yet packed with enough power to lift the ball out of the park when centered correctly. The power was derived from torque utilizing his whole body in his swing, allowing for the ball to literally jump off the bat after Paul's follow-through. Somehow he had developed a consistency of swing to preclude prolonged slumps. He hardly ever got shut out in a three- or four-game series of at bats and usually would bounce back with a hit or two the next day if he went 0-4. Consistency, with some power, was his game.

Manager Tony LoDuca had finally settled on a starting lineup for the upcoming season. Paul glanced at the lineup card taped to the back of the dugout wall for the final preseason games in Florida against the New York Mets and was gratified to see his name as follows:

Rafael Martinez, SS
Scott Russell, 2B
Al Robles, 1B
Lance Champlin, RF
David Page, 3B
Colby Rakers, CF
Paul Kolbe, LF
Yadier Marcello, C
Kyle Flynn, P

ONE LAST HURRAH

Everyone else was projected as the starter at his respective position, so this was a good omen for Paul. What he found a bit uncomfortable was hitting seventh in the lineup. Not that he would have said anything to his new boss about it, but hitters are a funny breed; they get used to preparing for a game based on their spot in the batting order. Paul was always in the three, four, or five spots in his entire major-league career. Granted, he was an unknown entity, having been out of the game for two years, but seventh?

For the other regulars, assured of their place on the team and in the everyday lineup, the last few games of the exhibition season were reserved for staying healthy—no pulled muscles or broken bones at this crucial junction of training. Almost any error or mistake would be much less meaningful now versus the start of the official season.

And, of course, put a new guy in the lineup and the ball will find you. It was a blustery early spring day, and the wind was whipping around the park, showing great determination to knock someone over before it petered out. Paul would be tested before the day was done.

Paul thought that since this was still spring training, he would try to use the Joe Fisher goop and forgo batting gloves. "Why not?" thought Paul. "If ever there was going to be a time to use this stuff, it's now."

The first inning was uneventful for Paul. No at bat and no plays in the field. Things started to heat up in the second inning. He applied his pine tar to the curious looks of his teammates and manager, and he strolled out to the on-deck circle. "Hey, Paul," yelled third-base coach Jose Nieves. "Aren't you going to use batting gloves?"

Paul just shook his head no and refocused on the task at hand. His at bat was a classic one. With two strikes, Paul fouled off five successive pitches before flying out to the center fielder. Although he made an out, he sent a message to the league that he would be a handful when he came up to the plate.

In the bottom of the inning, though, he had the first of a series of run-ins with Colby Rakers, the fair-haired wunderkind of the minor-league system who was expected to make a huge contribution in his first full season with the club. Everyone expected big things from Colby, and he seemed to carry an air of importance about himself as a result.

The Mets cleanup hitter led off the inning and promptly drove the ball between Colby and Paul. Colby, being the speedster, got to the ball first and completely flubbed it. He let the ball go under his glove, and it headed toward the wall. Paul got to it as the runner was rounding second and lumbering into third. "Hey geezer, you think you could back me up a little? You made me look bad on that one. He should have only had a double and not a triple. Look, if you can't play your position, maybe you ought to DH in the other league."

"Look Colby, I didn't miss the ball—you did. And if you call me that again, you and I will have a discussion away from the stadium, and it won't be a pretty one for your face. Play your game and don't blame me when you screw up, pretty boy."

"Fuck you, old man," replied Colby.

"Hey, cut the bullshit," added Lance Champlin from right field. "Let's get back to baseball."

When Paul went into the dugout following the last out, Tony walked over to where he was fiddling with his bats and asked him what the "discussion" was all about. "Nothing, Skipper. Just getting our communication down on fly balls between us." Satisfied with the answer, and knowing that it was an attempt to diffuse the conversation, Tony went back to his station at the far-right top step of the dugout where the players would come and go. Meanwhile, Colby went back to the clubhouse, and moments later everyone in the dugout could hear what sounded like chairs being thrown about. No one went in to check on him, and he soon emerged much calmer than he had previously appeared.

The third inning was routine in the field for Paul, who had to catch a ball near the warning track. And since he had enough time, he had used both hands to ensure the ball wasn't dropped, something Colby Rakers wouldn't be caught dead doing.

"Nice two-handed catch, geezer; very retro," yelled Colby.

Paul just glared at Colby and eventually gave him a quick tip of his cap in acknowledgment, rather than engage in another confrontation with Colby.

With his team trailing the Mets 1–0, Colby led off the inning with a solid base hit to right field. Trying to get something going, Tony put on the sacrifice bunt sign for Paul, who laid a perfect one down the third-base line on the first pitch. Colby, not paying attention, stumbled from a modest three-step lead at first and was easily thrown out at second base. As he came back to the dugout, he glared at Paul, giving everyone the impression that he had been set up for an out at second base. Even the announcers noted that there appeared to be a rift forming between the two outfielders and wondered if this would affect team unity as the season progressed.

Paul didn't want to confront Colby in the dugout and make a public spectacle on the first day with the club, so he promised himself he would deal with the situation privately.

The seventh inning proved to be a lucky one for the Cardinals, as they punched home three runs to take a 3–1 lead. Paul walked in his third at bat and eventually scored a run. In the ninth inning, he got his first hit of the day in his fourth at bat with a seeing-eye double between the right and center fielders. He didn't score, but thanks to a two-run homer off the bat of Al Robles, the Cardinals came away with a 5–1 victory.

The curious looks continued as he headed to the hitter's circle during the seventh and ninth innings. "Better get used to it, guys," said Paul to himself. "I'm going to try to use this stuff for the rest of the season."

After the game, Tony, as usual, handled all the media inquiries. "Tony, it seemed today that your new left fielder and Colby were not on the best of terms. Are we gonna see fireworks between these two guys?"

"That answer is an unequivocal no. You know I don't tolerate discord on the team. They will have to work on their communication on how to handle fly balls and also how to deal with bunts and other calls. This is spring training, a perfect time to address these kinds of issues.

"Plus, Paul is brand-new to our club. He hasn't had the benefit of working with our center fielders, and he hasn't even played in two years. He knows he is a fill-in for Matt this season and that the kids will be ready next year or sooner to assume a bigger role on the club. We picked him up for his pure talent as a hitter. He will be okay in the outfield, too, even if that means our center fielder will have to cover more of left center and right center with Paul and Lance out there at the same time."

Meanwhile, smelling a potential story, Bernie Madlock of the *Post-Gazette* and STL.com found Tony Rakers, Colby's dad, and asked for his comments regarding the game. Bernie originally came to the Saint Louis market from working on the *Planet* staff in Baltimore. His job with the *Post-Gazette* was to write three weekly print and on-line columns and occasionally fill in on reporting assignments if the story was a big one.

So it was a bit unusual to see him hanging around the clubhouse. Bernie's angle was that he was following up on the persistent involvement of Tony Rakers in his son's professional baseball career. There also seemed to be, at least in Bernie's mind, a conflict between an organization professing to work through its farm system and promote from within. But that was precisely what the organization had elected not to do so this season, at least if one looked at the signing of Lance Champlin and now possibly an even older ballplayer in Paul Kolbe.

"Is there a story here?" asked Bernie to himself. "Maybe, and if there is, I'll run with it!"

The next day was a home game with the Florida Marlins at Roger Dean Stadium. Tony took the occasion beforehand to ask both Colby and Paul to step into his office for a brief meeting. "Look, gentlemen, I've been in this game for a long, long time, and I can smell a conflict in personalities a mile away. I'm on a mission here, and you should be, too. I want to win the World Series one more time, and I need your complete cooperation. It's tough enough to beat the other team, or sometimes to beat an inconsistent umpire or two as well. And let's not forget the occasional weather issue. But let's act like professionals out there on the field and at bat. I want to see the 'Cardinal Way' from you both. Am I clear here?"

As both players nodded in agreement, they started out of the manager's office. Rakers made the door first and promptly scooted out and headed over to his locker. As Paul was leaving, Tony stopped him for a brief moment and said, "Look, I don't expect you to give a Gold Glove performance out there in left field. And I haven't seen anything yet that would lead me to the conclusion that you can't play the position, either. The problem on that ball hit in the gap was plain and simple—a flub by Colby. You can't have your center fielder doing that, as neither you nor Lance can motor to dead center on those kinds of balls. And realistically, Colby is a bit immature at times.

"Plus, I'm not too happy that his dad likes to mouth off to the media whenever he thinks his son is getting some kind of raw deal. That has got to stop. By the way, I just wanted to say once again that I'm glad you agreed to come here. We need a good bat to replace Matt's. We still haven't confirmed the severity of his injury yet because we want to keep our options open in case we have to make a trade. If you come through for us in the meantime, we will be much better off than sacrificing some farm club or even parent club talent.

"And you don't have to win the Triple Crown or whatever for us, but we do need some run production in addition to adequate defense. Give us that, and I think we have a real shot at our division, and it's always a crapshoot after that. Let me know if the Colby thing escalates. I can't afford for you to kick his ass—which is probably what he needs—and I'll have to figure out with management what we can do to muzzle his father."

This was one of the rare occasions where Tony felt it necessary to have a disciplinary discussion with several his players. His style, though, was to do so behind closed doors. He appreciated this approach when he was a player and decided early on in his thirty-plus years of managing that it's too easy to lose players when they are dragged through the coals with teammates, the media, fans, and the general public.

At the very least, you diminish the value of your unhappy player if you feel compelled to make a trade. There is also a great risk of losing the entire team. When that happens, the manager is among the "walking dead" until ownership resolves the situation by terminating his contract.

Tony had weathered the storm for over three decades, having won World Series titles in both leagues and amassing the third-highest win total in MLB history. Unknown to the team, including management, his own coaching staff, and players, Tony was seriously considering retiring at the end of the season. He didn't want to distract from the progress of the team, so he kept his plans to himself. His ultimate timing would be based on how far the team went in the playoffs, if they indeed did so.

Tony didn't expect to have another conversation with Paul, but Colby was another story. He needed his bat and his speed on the basepaths, but his fielding was erratic at best. And the attitude—he'd love to punch the guy silly if he could. But instead, he continued to try to maintain a professional attitude to avoid confrontations and hopefully maintain the steady heartbeat rhythm of the long season.

CHAPTER SIX

"Funny that Tony should bring up the Triple Crown, which, of course, was last owned by Joe Fisher," Paul thought.

"Gotcha, Skipper. I don't anticipate any problems with Colby. He does have a lot of talent, and from what little I've seen, he's used to getting his way in life. Happens a lot to kids with a ton of talent and an overbearing parent. I won't let you down on either front, the ass kicking—or lack thereof—that Colby deserves or the run production that you need. You put me in whatever slot you think best for the team, and I'll respond. I appreciate the opportunity to be back in the big leagues with a class organization. This will, no doubt, be my last season, so I want it to be a memorable one," said Paul.

With that matter somewhat resolved for the time being, Paul headed back to his hotel suite in West Palm Beach, where the team stayed. He ordered an ice tea from the restaurant, chuckled at the thought of drinking it versus a tall, frosty draught beer, added an appetizer, and repaired to the patio to sit, relax, and reflect on the day's events.

The appetizer and drink arrived within ten minutes, along with a message from the front desk: "Call me if interested in having dinner. Welcome to the big leagues, Paul," signed Dave McFarlin.

Paul sat down for a moment, leafed through his mail, including some from Rochester wishing him good luck, and then picked up the phone.

"Sure, you buying big spender, or do I have to pop for one of your meals again?" asked Paul, kidding.

"You pop? I'd like to know what century that happened, buddy!" replied McFarlin.

Paul didn't bother to change clothes, as he had just done so at the clubhouse. He met Dave in the hotel lobby and they decided to walk a few blocks to a nearby Italian restaurant.

"So how does it feel to be back in the bigs, Paul?" asked Dave after they ordered steaks and assorted sides.

"It feels great except for the chatter between Colby and me. I suppose you saw the jawing back and forth."

"How could I not? I thought you handled our golden boy very well. And I assume that Tony advised you not to take matters into your own hands."

"Yes, he did. And wouldn't that be a nice way to introduce yourself to the team! I'm here to do what you and I talked about. Provide some offense, a respectable level of defense, and help the Cardinals win their division. And who knows what happens when Matt comes back. I'm assuming that the big salary comes into play, and you would try to get as many at bats for Matt as possible. I get it."

"That kind of perspective will play well with Tony. Don't be surprised if he moves you up to the two spot if you get off to a nice start. He loves to have someone with 'dangerous power' in that slot, and that fits you like a glove!"

The rest of the dinner provided both Dave and Paul the opportunity to reflect on many of their good and bad times in baseball and life in general, and they both concluded that it had been a good ride, both on and off the field.

Monday and Tuesday were the final exhibition games against the Florida Marlins, and the Cardinals dropped both of them, 4–1 and 4–2 respectively. Paul went 3-3 with a sharp double in the first game before being replaced, and then he went 2-2 in the last game of the Florida-based preseason, both in which Paul used the pine tar versus batting gloves.

And then it was on to Springfield, Missouri, to play two games against their double-A minor-league franchise. This kind of exhibition schedule accomplished several things: it got the folks in that part of the Cardinals' home state excited about the major-league club, and it also allowed management an opportunity to see how the double-A players handled themselves against major-league competition.

The park—John Q. Hammonds Field—was an approximation of Busch Stadium by design. This helped management determine how players might fare in the same park dimensions as the major-league club so that any double-A players who made it to the Cardinals were instantly familiar with their home venue.

Paul needed at bats to get ready for the season, so—just as Dave had predicted—Tony inserted Paul into the second slot for both games. And he did not disappoint. His first at bat was a classic one against last season's number one draft pick. Strike one. Strike two. Ball one. Foul off. Ball two. Foul off. Foul off. Ball three. Foul off. Foul off. Home run to deep center field. His second at bat, he drew a walk, as he did in his third. His fourth and final bat for the day finished like the first one—home run to deep center field. "Yes," thought Paul. "Tony wants 'dangerous power' at the number two slot in the lineup, and I'll have to see what I can do about that!"

The last remaining game in the exhibition season against Springfield was a similar experience for Paul. Facing the Cardinals' number two overall pick in the previous year's draft, Paul bounced a double off the right-field wall in his first at bat, reached first on an error in his second at bat, hit a home run on his third at bat, and finished the day replaced for a pinch runner after a walk.

"Nice work, Paul," said Tony.

"Thanks, Skipper. I don't mind batting in the lower part of the line-up, but I had a lot of fun today in the number two hole!"

"You've shown me you can handle that spot in the lineup. What I foresee doing is flip-flopping you and Colby, depending mostly on whether their starter is a lefty or a righty. But if someone is hot, then he stays in the slot in the lineup where he can do the most damage. I hope to see you in that number two spot a lot this season."

Meanwhile, Paul found a new hangout called D.D.'s Corner Pub, located around the corner from what he would later learn was the Sunset

Place cemetery, where Joe Fisher was buried. It was not the same as his favorite haunt in Rochester, although admittedly D.D., a lady in her early forties, was better looking than Sam! It was a place where Paul could vegetate away from the baseball crowd and just be Paul Kolbe. D.D. befriended him to the extent that she did not broadcast his status as a Cardinal to fellow guests, so Paul knew he could have a sandwich, watch other baseball games, and generally chill out when time permitted.

CHAPTER SEVEN

Paul would soon learn the rather complicated dynamic that represented Cardinals' ownership and was glad that his contact with the higher-ups generally stopped at the GM level, meaning John Nowicki.

Regarding the venue where he would be playing, this was the third stadium in Saint Louis baseball history called Busch Stadium and named after Anheuser-Busch Inc., the primary sponsor and former owner of the club. This particular stadium hosted a World Series winner in 2006, its inaugural season. This was shortly after a heartrending loss to the Boston Red Sox in the second Busch Stadium in 2004.

The current Busch Stadium continued the retro look started with Oriole Park at Camden Yards in Baltimore in 1992 and continued with the newest major-league facility in Minneapolis, Target Field in 2010. It had a brick facade on three-quarters of its outside footprint; the remaining side, the one pointing toward the Gateway Arch, was kept open for fans viewing the downtown Saint Louis skyline around the Arch.

And the irony of it all was that Anheuser-Busch sold the team, the stadium, and four square blocks of downtown land—destined to become a retail complex called BallYard Village—to a competing brewer located in their same city, H. Rheinhold & Sons, during the 2010 off-season.

Rheinhold was a throwback organization of sorts, in that they were an independent brewer that had not been swallowed up by a larger one. Its product line was simple: Supreme, Supreme Light, and Supreme Dark. Its focus was middle America, mostly male, ages twenty-four to forty-four. Baseball, especially in the company's hometown, seemed to be the ideal marketing vehicle to increase awareness, interest, and trial for its products at the ballpark.

PATRICK G MCLEAN

This decision to sell the team followed on the heels of the Anheuser-Busch acquisition by a foreign brewer and the new firm's interest in shedding nonbeer assets. The sale received a significant amount of positive media for A-B for the unique marketing agreement brokered with the other brewer, as well as their selling the team to a local organization.

The Rheinhold management team for the Cardinals was headed up by none other than Henry (Hank) Rheinhold Jr. himself, a Cardinal fanatic since virtually the day he could walk and talk. Hank even was willing to suffer the ultimate indignity—Anheuser-Busch was allowed to retain naming rights for the stadium for a nominal sum for a period of ten years before they reverted back to Rheinhold. Also, while he fiddled at the ballpark, he had a core group of managers running the brewery, some with an amateur baseball background who previously played for the Rheinhold select youth team. Contemplating retirement, he was debating with himself about who would be the ideal candidate to replace him with the Cardinals and the brewery. Maybe he would give himself the balance of 2011 and look toward 2012 for making such seismic shifts.

Meanwhile, his son, Henry Rheinhold III, and his daughter, Christina Reinhold, both employed by the brewery, asked Hank to meet with them when they found out he had brokered the purchase of the baseball team. It was widely assumed that Henry would take over the brewery's reins when Hank eventually retired, but Christina was the sibling with guts, greater brainpower, higher motivation, all coupled with an abrasive personality. It remained to be seen what her ultimate role would be at the brewery.

Christina, taking the lead in the discussion, started the conversation, mincing very few words.

"Dad, Henry and I wanted to have a sit-down with you about this acquisition that you made on behalf of the brewery. It's bad enough that you have peppered the brewery with a number of baseball jocks—and admittedly some of them are turning into good managers. Now you buy a baseball team, a stadium, and a retail development parcel?"

"Now Christina, you know marketing opportunities like involvement with this historic franchise don't come along every day. I jumped on this and the board of directors readily agreed that a business our size would be highly unlikely to be able to pull something off like this if it wasn't for A-B and their new ownership's desire to focus on its core business."

"And was it your idea or theirs to keep the Busch name on the stadium for a fucking decade, Dad?"

"Young lady, watch your language. They proposed and I accepted based on their position that it was a deal-killer if they didn't get to keep naming rights for a reasonable period of time."

"And you agreed that a decade, a fucking decade, was reasonable, Dad? Naming rights would have helped offset the huge debt we're taking on, not to mention the brand impressions from hearing and seeing Rheinhold Stadium. Ten years? Rheinhold may not survive that long with the debt service we'll have."

"There you go again with the foul language. It's very unbecoming of you! I appreciate your concern, but the deal is done. We are moving on. And I suggest both of you do so, too. I have a luncheon with the mayor to discuss BallYard Village."

"BallYard Village? A-B couldn't get that off the ground for the last five years because of the overall economy. And we can? Please do Henry and me a favor, Dad. Let us ruin our inheritance—not you. Please don't commit to some grand scheme for retail development that straps us even further."

"I'll keep your concerns top of mind. Now, if you'll excuse me."

And with that exchange, the stage was set to start the 2011 baseball season, hopefully with baseball taking front and center stage and front-office drama taking a backseat.

Then again, the ever-attentive Bernie Madlock had the following to say about Cardinals ownership:

PATRICK G MCLEAN

Are the Cardinals in Good Hands?

One of the most successful franchises in major professional sports resides right here in Saint Louis. Of course I'm referring to the Cardinals. The team has achieved consistently good results on the field, as well as incredible attendance, grossing more than three million patrons per season for the past decade. What could be better? The new stadium continues to be tweaked annually for improvements, the BallYard Village projects seems to be finally getting some traction. In sum, things are rosy. Not so fast there, readers. H. Rheinhold & Sons swallowed a lot of expenses when they acquired the Cardinals, the stadium, as well as BallYard Village. So do these folks have what it takes for the long haul? Anheuser-Busch set an incredibly high standard for ownership. Everything about the Cardinals had to be first class because this organization was a reflection of A-B. I don't know that much about Rheinhold to tell you that the high standards will continue. So maybe it's up to us to remain vigilant. Thanks for reading.

CHAPTER EIGHT

There's nothing like Opening Day in Saint Louis for a baseball fan. You can feel it in the air. People at work wear red whether they are going to the game or not. Almost as many people come down to the area around the ballpark to listen to the bands and visit the food, beverage, and merchandise tents at the currently vacant BallYard Village as they do to attend the game.

The pageantry is unparalleled in perhaps any sport, but especially in baseball. The village is transformed into a carnival-like atmosphere, complete with music, food, giveaways, and commercial entities, all interested in getting their name associated with Cardinal Nation.

And every radio and TV outlet in the metro area is represented by a satellite or otherwise functioning broadcast vehicle strategically parked someplace around the stadium. A number of bars, particularly on the south side of the stadium where there was once no activity, spring to life as if on cue, featuring loud music, open-air grilled meats, chilled drinks, and numerous customers in various states of soberness, all starting around 10:00 a.m. for a 3:10 game on March 31.

The gates open inside the sold-out stadium two hours in advance of the game, allowing enough time for most of the attendees to be seated when the festivities began.

Bernie Madlock had this to say in his "Bernie's Bytes" online column:

There's Nothing Like It, Fans

Opening Day in Saint Louis ought to be declared a local holiday. There will be at least the same number of people outside the stadium as there are inside. And the folks that aren't downtown will be wearing

*red in their offices and will be streaming or reading on their comput-
ers rather than working. So bosses everywhere take heed: let your
staff go home early because they aren't working anyway! Thanks for
reading.*

On this particular Opening Day, as late afternoon turned into early
evening, the Arch was lit up, and the view was spectacular. A new park,
a sold-out stadium: what could be better? How about forty-five red convertibles parading players, coaches, and staff along the edge of the playing field to the delight of a sold-out stadium?

The procession started with the right-field gates opening, and the first
convertible came out with Fredbird, the Cardinal mascot, and several attractive and energetic female assistants, who immediately started shooting
Cardinals T-shirts into the crowd. Fredbird was as animated as any Major
League Baseball mascot, and he was especially on his game for Opening Day.

The second convertible featured Tony LoDuca, entering his six-
teenth season as manager of the Cardinals. Tony had a way about him
that made you either intensely like or dislike him. Over time, the number of fans who liked him continued to rise, although even the more
strident supporter occasionally would second-guess some of his unorth-
odox moves. No one, however, could question his desire to win. He was
all business once he put on his uniform.

The next convertible featured several coaches, including longtime
pitching coach Dave Darren, who had been with Tony for his entire
Cardinals managerial career, and Mark O'Bannon, hitting coach and
former slugger for the Cardinals.

Next came popular third-base coach Jose Nieves, along with his
first-base counterpart, Dave McFarlin, another longtime associate of
Tony's. Dave, of course, was instrumental in securing Paul Kolbe for
the 2011 season.

Next came the reserves and pitching staff, including ace starters
Chris Mitchell and Adam Cartwright.

Last came the starting lineup in individual vehicles.

Catcher Yadier Marcello was the first starter, and he received thunderous applause. Next came first baseman Al Robles, who somehow received even louder applause. Second baseman Skip Russell was next, followed by shortstop Rafael Martinez. Third baseman David Page was in the next vehicle, followed by the three starting outfielders: left fielder Paul Kolbe, center fielder Colby Rakers, and right fielder Lance Champlin.

The lineup was solid but aging in a few places, with a bench filled with young, but promising, talent. The starting pitching was also solid, provided the injury bug didn't bite too deeply. The Cardinals had already lost left fielder Matt Bradley for an undetermined period with a shoulder injury. Another injury to an everyday player—or key starter or reliever—would most likely doom the team to watching the postseason on television.

"Who is the new guy?" seemed to be the prevailing question, as the convertibles deposited their riders at home plate. "Why do we need another aging veteran?" and "Don't we already have one of those guys in right field?" seemed to be the other common questions murmured in the stands. And lastly, "Are they gonna put roller skates on Colby to cover the two-thirds of the outfield that the old guys can't?" Bottom line, Paul had his work cut out for him if he was going to win the hearts and minds of the fans.

Announcer Mike Shaughnessy strode up to the microphone set up at home plate and began to address the crowd.

"Hello Cardinal Nation! Are you ready for some baseball? Some Cardinal baseball?" he said to thunderous applause.

"We have a special guest today who needs no introduction. Folks around here call him 'The Man,' and he still leads in key offensive categories in the National League despite retiring in 1963. That's fifty years ago, folks! Here he is, Stan Munson!"

The crowd stood up as one as ninety-three-year-old Stan Munson was escorted out in a wheelchair by his grandson. He was too weak to talk, but not too weak to smile broadly and wave at the crowd. The Cardinal players, managers, and staff all converged on him to say hello.

Just as they were all reassembling in a line on the first-base side of the diamond, Stan motioned to Paul Kolbe. He looked around and quickly went to Stan's side.

"You must be Paul Kolbe," Stan said in a whisper tone.

"That's correct, sir," replied Paul.

"My old friend Ducky—you know him, too, as Joe Fisher—told me that you are going to win the Triple Crown this year," and he let out a slight chuckle. "I was pretty good at your age, too, but not that good. The only advice I can give you is to keep using his pine tar and don't get caught up using the fancy batting gloves all these modern ballers use!"

"Thanks for the kind words and advice, Mr. Munson," said Paul.

He then hustled back to his position in line, wondering what the heck was going on with Joe "Ducky" Fisher that even the great Stan "The Man" Munson knew all about his secret pine tar.

Lastly, owner Hank Rheinhold strode to the microphone. "Welcome, Cardinal fans. Your 2011 team is ready to take the field, and I know a big part of their success this year, as in past seasons, will be the 'tenth man' they will have at Busch Stadium each time they play a home game. You have supported our team in the past, and you continue to today, with three million or more fans coming to the ballpark each season. This would be equivalent of five or six million attendance in some larger markets. Truly an outstanding attendance number year after year.

"Your support helps the cause immeasurably and represents an extra voice here at home. I can't promise you a playoff-caliber team every year, but I can promise that we strive for this result and, with your continued support, we think we can get there in 2011. Thank you, and the only thing left to say is 'Play Ball!'"

And then it was show time. The San Diego Padres were in town to help the Cardinals launch the new season, including games on Thursday, March 31, Saturday, April 2, and Sunday, April 3. Paul's initial game was nothing to write home about. He went 1-4 with a sharp single, but otherwise flied out three times to the warning track in a 5–3 loss to the visitors. As he dressed after showering, he noticed Bernie Madlock, the sportswriter, waiting at his locker.

"Hello, Bernie. Do you always hang out by a guy's lockers when he only had a so-so day and the team lost? Well, you got me, then."

"You know who I am already."

"I've seen you around the locker room in Florida and knew somewhere along the season our paths would cross. What can I do for you, Bernie?"

"Well, I really just wanted some background information in advance of any future stories. I'm also curious as to what your intentions are when Matt Bradley comes back from rehab."

"I haven't given that day a lot of thought. I was quite content in Minnesota, working with college players who hadn't had a lot of experience with wood bats. But I have a fire burning inside to play this game, maybe for the last time. More than anything, I think I can help this team while I'm here. It's going to be a fun ride for me, whatever the timing turns out to be.

"I think I can still contribute offensively and not embarrass myself and the club defensively. There's nothing like the postseason, and I don't want to get ahead of myself, but I'd like to think that I can help somehow when Matt comes back. I'm just keeping the spot warm for him."

"Paul, you've been schooled well. That sounds like a platitude coming from Tony. I'll accept that, though, as no one seems to know when Matt is coming back.

"By the way, I noticed that you have a tobacco tin on your locker shelf. I didn't see you using any of that stuff during the game. Are you a 'dipper,' and are you aware that Major League Baseball is campaigning to eliminate smokeless tobacco?"

"Well, I'm glad to report that I don't use chew. That is a tin full of black goop, or good old-fashioned pine tar."

"Pine tar—well I'll be. What is so special about the stuff to warrant keeping it in a tin?"

"You know, I'm not sure. A fellow in Minnesota gave it to me. Says he goes into the woods and collects a batch of the stuff every year and wanted me to try it."

"Have you?"

"I experimented with it in spring training and had good results gripping my bat. I felt my hands slipping a bit today, so I might go back to using it for Saturday's game. For now, it's a reminder of my home of several years and the nice people in Rochester."

"On the other hand," thought Paul to himself, "I might have had three homers today if I would have had a better grip on the bat. It kept slipping a little bit as I rotated through my swing."

And in an effort to give *Post-Gazette* readers a glimpse into what the club was up to, Bernie wrote the following in his "Bernie's Hits & Misses" column, which appeared every Friday in the *P-G*:

What Happened to the Youth Movement?

A funny thing must have happened to Cards' GM John Nowicki on his way to Memphis to collect the latest round of triple-A prospects. The first detour was in right field, where Lance Champlin now resides. Lance would have qualified as part of this movement by the club to get younger some 15 or so years ago. He's also set up to play a position he has not filled in more than a decade.

The other corner outfield position is manned by Paul Kolbe, most recently a first-base coach in an independent league. He'll be 39 years old this season, with his best years behind him. Granted, this is a temporary fix due to Matt Bradley's spring-training injury, but isn't this a great time to see what the kids can do? Otherwise, what is the point in investing in an elaborate player development system? Thanks for reading.

CHAPTER NINE

Friday, April 1, was a rare day off, designed to be a backup home opener in case of inclement weather the previous day. The extra time was especially helpful to someone like Paul, who had very little knowledge of the city.

While driving around to several locations in town, he noticed that he was near the cemetery where Joe Fisher was buried, according to his previous research on the subject. Why that might interest him when he had a ton of other things to do was something he couldn't answer. On a whim, he pulled into the church rectory on the property and walked into the administrative offices.

"Good morning," Paul greeted several middle-aged ladies near the front desk. "Can you show me on a map where Joe Fisher is buried? I bet you don't get asked that very often, do you?"

"Actually," said the one lady nearest him, "we get someone in here at least once a month or so asking the same question. Here is a map that shows you exactly where Mr. Fisher is located."

"I'm surprised. I didn't know there was that much interest in this gentleman."

"Oh yes. Did you know he was the last player in the National League to win the Triple Crown?" asked both ladies in unison. "And that was way back in 1937. We think the next guy to be able to accomplish this might be Saint Louis's own Al Robles, but even he has not been able to pull this feat off," advised the lady closest to Paul.

"There's that Triple Crown talk again," Paul thought. Out loud he said, "I appreciate your help and will say hello to him for you ladies!"

"That would be very nice," they both chided in unison as they handed Paul a map.

Finding Joe's grave was a snap. The gravestone was nothing spectacular, just a well-kept marble slab in the ground next to his wife's. The information on the slab, though, was anything but routine:

Joseph Michael Fisher

Born November 24, 1911

Died March 21, 1975

Outfielder for the Saint Louis Cardinals (1932–1940), Brooklyn Dodgers (1940–1943), New York Giants (1943–1945), Boston Braves (1945), Brooklyn Dodgers (1946), and Saint Louis Cardinals (1947–1948). Fisher was most famous for his days as a member of the Saint Louis "Gashouse Gang" that dominated the National League in the 1930s, including pennants in 1930, 1931, and 1934, along with runner-up finishes in 1935, 1936, and 1939. He was also instrumental in capturing two World Series titles in 1931 and 1934. His hard-charging style of play forced Commissioner Kennesaw Landing to pull him out of the seventh game of the 1934 World Series when Detroit Tigers fans started pelting him with garbage after he slid hard into third base on a triple.

Fisher was a ten-time All-Star selection and had a lifetime batting average of .324. Not particularly known as a home run hitter, Fisher won the Triple Crown in 1937 with 31 homers, 154 RBIs, and a .374 batting average.

Fisher met Pope Paul XII on a USO tour in 1944, and when asked of his vocation, he responded, "Your Holiness, I'm Joe Fisher. I, too, used to be a Cardinal."

Fisher was elected to the Hall of Fame in 1968.

After leaving the cemetery, Paul noticed how close he was to D.D.'s and decided to stop in and have a bite to eat. He pulled into the parking lot and walked briskly to the front door. He nodded to D.D. and selected a table on the outdoor patio, where he seemed to be the only patron willing to take on the heat of an unusually warm spring day in Saint Louis.

"Hello, Paul. I'm very glad to see you. I saw your opening day game, and you looked pretty good. Three balls to the warning track. Just a little more juice and those might have been taters. I also noticed that you, like all the other modern-day sissies, wore your batting gloves instead of using my pine tar and even had a glove on underneath your baseball glove in the field. What gives with that? Am I wasting my time trying to anoint you as the next Triple Crown winner?"

Paul turned around but didn't see anyone. "This is weird. If anyone is hiding out around here, quit playing games with me. And where did you come up with the information about the pine tar?"

No answer. "Figures. Is someone messing with me, and if so, what is their end game?" thought Paul.

"Okay, Joe," said Paul out loud. "I'll play your game. You're gonna see me gloveless next game, and my hands will be full of pine tar, straight from the North Woods, compliments of Joe Fisher. I'm sure the media is going to have a field day with my 'throwback' look, but if it works, I might have everyone else trying to copy what I'm doing—with your help—in short order. I sure would like to meet you sometime when I'm sober. I hope you realize you're messing with me something fierce."

Paul waited awhile and then decided that the conversation with Joe Fisher was over. He finished a quick sandwich and ice tea and spent the rest of the day working out and generally getting his mind ready for something he hadn't done in several years, until yesterday: play baseball at the highest competitive level. He knew he could hit—always could do that. But could he field his position? Could he make the throws? Could he run the bases? In short, was he kidding himself about this last hurrah? He was about to find out quickly enough.

Meanwhile it was back to the hunt for housing, and he ultimately found a place at a Marriott extended-stay facility in suburban Virginia

Heights and booked a suite through October. The location was just off an expressway about twenty minutes from the stadium.

The Padres were in town for two more games. On Saturday, April 2, Paul found his name in the seventh slot, behind Colby Rakers, as it started to look like that was going to be his lineup position for the foreseeable future. His performance was a virtual carbon copy of opening day: one sharp single, this one to right field, and three long fly outs. And all with the use of his traditional batting gloves. He was still reluctant to go the pine tar route for fear of ridicule by others, but hopefully not his teammates.

The team didn't do so well either, getting blasted 11–3. As can be imagined, the outfielders were busy. Paul fielded several routine base hits and took two doubles off the left-field wall, making adequate throws to the cutoff man in the infield. Colby, meanwhile, had a tough weekend. On Saturday, he lost one ball in the sun, looking helplessly at both Lance and Paul, both too far away to bail him out. He also ran in the wrong direction to try to take a ball off the wall, which caromed toward right field and was ultimately handled by Lance Champlin.

Lastly, Colby hesitated slightly on a ball hit straight at him just long enough for it to fall in for a hit, scoring two runs on what could have been an inning-ending out. And to further add to his frustration, John Keyes was brought in as a late-inning substitute, no doubt just to get some work in, but it nevertheless served as an embarrassment to Colby that he *had* to be taken out of the game.

Of course, Tony Rakers had something to say about Saturday's game to Bernie Madlock when he saw him on the runway going to the players' locker room. "My concern that Colby might become overextended appears to be happening already. Both the right and left fielders have good gloves and apparently respectable arms, but anything hit to the power alleys will go for doubles instead of singles unless Colby can somehow get over there, too. And as far as his hitting, I sure would like to see his videotape to see what he is doing wrong. He's 'oh fer' the season so far, and that is not like him; he's always been a fast starter."

And not one to miss a good story when he sniffed one, Bernie tracked Tony LoDuca down and advised him of Tony Rakers's comments. "I'm not going to get into a running dialogue with Colby's dad every time he has a complaint about his son. For some reason, he forgot that Colby is no longer playing American Legion ball and is a bona fide big leaguer with lots of upside for his career.

"I will say that the club has a full-time hitting coach and a full-time assistant hitting coach and access to plenty of advanced information on bats and other equipment, pitchers' tendencies, weather conditions, park peculiarities, and so on," said Tony. "Professional help is available on a regular basis for Colby and all members of the club."

"So much for not responding," thought Bernie.

For some reason, the Cardinals always seemed to play well at home on Sundays, and the third day in April was no exception. Even Colby had a good day, albeit batting from the seventh spot due to a lefty being on the mound. Colby had two hits, including a ringing double off the right-field wall that scored Paul all the way from first. "Maybe that'll calm some of the geezer talk in the stands," thought Paul.

And Paul, batting sixth, accounted for the other run with his first homer and solo RBI, a shot to the left-field bleachers above the Padres bullpen. And coincidence or not, Paul tried using the pine tar versus batting gloves and found that he did indeed have a better grip on the bat.

The problem he encountered, though, was getting the stuff off fast enough when he had to go to the field; the last thing a player wants when throwing the ball is to have it stuck in his hand. Working with the equipment manager, he came up with a liquid cleaner that he could soak on a towel and quickly rub the excess pine tar off his hands before he went onto the field.

And wouldn't you know it, Bernie Madlock smelled out another story, or at least a curiosity. "Hello, Paul," Bernie said as he sauntered up to Paul's locker after the game. "You told me you might try using pine tar. Do you attribute your homer to that good old-fashioned goop? You know you might be the only player in the pros not using batting gloves! So what's this stuff you're using? Just pine tar, or is there some kryptonite imbedded in that stuff?"

"Bernie, just good, old-school pine tar. I could lend you some so you get a better grip on your pen if you'd like," smiled Paul, hoping to deflect the subject.

"No thanks, just curious. You might want to pass your new approach on to Colby, as he seems to be struggling in the early part of the season," replied Bernie.

"I'm not taking the bait," Paul thought to himself. Aloud he said, "Have a nice day, Bernie. I've got to get a shower before I stink up the clubhouse."

CHAPTER TEN

The week of April 4 through April 10 was a mixed bag of three games at home against the Pirates and three games on the road against the Giants in San Francisco. The Cardinals continued to stumble at the start of the season by dropping two out of three to Pittsburgh. The entire club wasn't hitting, including Al Robles, the kind of player who could carry the club on his back for a month when he was hitting.

The trials and tribulations of Colby Rakers continued, with a dropped ball in the outfield on a rather routine play, several errant or weak throws back to the infield with men advancing extra bases, and his inexplicably giving up on a ball that should have been caught. The fans responded by booing Colby, something very rare for Cardinals fans at home games.

Paul continued his steady play against the Pirates and had a homer in the first game of the series followed by a two-run homer and a 3-4 day in the second game, the only one of the three they won. As Tony liked to keep his bench fresh, Paul did not play on the Wednesday afternoon getaway game, giving Alan Cooper his first start of the season in left.

"Bernie Madlock, you're back," said Tony.

"Yes, I am, Tony. I have a sidebar question for you, Tony. Your new left fielder—Paul Kolbe. He is sporting 'old-school' pine tar and no batting gloves. Isn't that a little too retro for 2011?"

"That's funny Bernie," Tony said as he chuckled. "If he keeps hitting like he has off the mark this season, then I'm going to encourage all our guys to throw away their batting gloves and start using pine tar. In fact, I think I'm going to ask the stadium operations personnel to stock some in the press box for you and your fellow writers, Bernie."

"Okay, Tony, you got me there. I know you're kidding me now, but seriously, isn't this a little strange for the era we live in to see this kind of hitting style?"

"Maybe, but Mark O'Bannon took one look at his swing down at Jupiter and declared he 'couldn't help him.' What he meant by that was that Kolbe had almost flawless mechanics. Just like Al Robles, there are some players that you just watch and try not to screw them up with additional advice. In Paul's case, if he found something was working for him that was a bit out of the ordinary, so be it. Sometimes in managing, less is more."

That comment seemed to satisfy Bernie, at least for the moment.

Thank goodness for charter flights. The team members quickly showered, dressed, and were on their way to an awaiting flight to the West Coast. They wouldn't get to their rooms until early in the morning, but they could sleep in the rest of the day for an evening game.

As this was the big leagues, hotels, transfers, and other amenities were first class. The Cardinals were no exception but preferred to stay as close to the ballpark as possible to avoid potential traffic delays on game day. For that reason, the traveling secretary chose the Pickwick, which was within walking distance to AT&T Park.

Upon arriving at his hotel room and given the time differential, Paul's immediate thoughts were on dinner. Little did he know what was in store for him that evening.

"Mr. Kolbe?" inquired the front desk supervisor as Paul picked up the phone.

"Yes, that's me," replied Paul.

"You have a note in your mailbox down here. Would you like us to deliver it to you, or would you prefer to pick it up at your leisure?"

"No, please have it delivered here, as I have no immediate plans for leaving the hotel room this evening."

The note arrived, and after an appropriate tip to the concierge staffer, Paul opened the contents and couldn't believe what he was reading.

For starters, the envelope and letter were scented with something very familiar, a perfume with which he had recently come into contact.

The note was a simple one:

"PK, meet me at my condo on Nob Hill at 8:00 p.m. Sharp. Don't make any excuses."

An address was listed, but with no name, Paul had no indication as to what excuses he could or should be mustering to not show up for the mystery meeting. Since it was a pretty swank part of San Francisco, Paul decided to let his curiosity overcome any fears of what this cryptic note might be all about.

So off he went in a cab to Nob Hill. He was aware that the skipper did not have a curfew per se, but woe to the ballplayer who couldn't answer the call the next day.

"So here we go," thought Paul, ringing the bell in the lobby of a rather imposing, yet inviting, condo complex.

"Take the elevator to the top floor, turn right to the end of the hallway. The door is unlocked," said a voice over the intercom. It was familiar, yet so succinct and businesslike that he wasn't quite sure whose voice it was.

But he proceeded as directed and went up to the twenty-fourth floor, turned right, and followed the hallway to the end. Looking at the numbers, there were only four condo units on this floor, quite a luxury with regard to space in the heart of San Francisco.

He opened the door and walked into one of the most awe-inspiring vistas of downtown San Francisco. An entire wall was nothing but glass, and seated outside on the balcony near a bucket filled with a bottle of Piper-Heidsieck Extra Dry (Paul's favorite champagne) was none other than Heather Alexander, looking stunning in a little black cocktail dress and black high heels.

"Hi, Paulie, I don't know how you can drink this stuff. It makes me pucker—it's so dry."

"Does it make you pucker up enough to kiss me?"

"You bet."

"Okay, let me guess," he said as he put his arms around her and gently kissed her. "You come out here often enough to justify buying some more of San Francisco's prime real estate!"

"Not quite this time. This belongs to a good client of ours who happens to be in the Far East. Pretty nice digs, don't you think? Well, don't get used to such treatment. I can't follow you around the country all the time. I was beaten into submission to present at a seminar here and didn't even realize you would be playing the Giants until I scanned the local paper. So let's enjoy the evening and see where it takes us."

"I'll be Paulie the Tiger tonight, but I do have to be back at the hotel in time for the team bus to leave for the park."

"And what time is that, my baseball hero?"

"Well, since it's a 3:10 p.m. start time, it will be about ten in the morning."

"I think that'll work just fine, Paulie, as I have my gig in the China Basin area and then I have to scoot back to Minneapolis for another seminar I'm conducting at the University of Minnesota late tomorrow afternoon. How about dinner in rather than out? You probably don't want to be seen out on the town anyway, do you? I've taken the liberty of ordering Chinese for delivery, which should arrive just after we've had time for a quick romp in the bedroom. Are you game?"

"Wow. You've thought of everything, Heather. That's why I'm madly attracted to you!"

The rest of the evening and early morning hours were a blur of bodies, food, wine, and a little sleep. After saying good-bye, Paul hustled back to the Pickwick and the real world.

CHAPTER ELEVEN

Paul wasn't hung over, but he was definitely exhausted from the previous twelve hours of activity. The good news was that he was back in the lineup. The bad news was that Colby Rakers was not, as he was struggling against left-handed pitching, and one of the best lefties in the National League was starting off the series for the Giants.

So, as Colby sulked on the bench as far away from the skipper as he could get, Tony Rakers fumed at home in Augusta, Georgia, when he saw the lineup card for the game online. He texted a message to Bernie Madlock, his new "friend," that said the following: "Check today's line-up out, Bernie. I guess if you're twenty-five years old or less and have been an organization man for five or so years, you can't play the outfield for the Cardinals. I don't understand."

"Damn," thought Bernie as he read the text copy. "This is too juicy to sit on. The Cardinals will have to comment on this after we publish it in tomorrow's paper. I love it when shit hits the fan. It's been way too quiet in Cardinal Nation the past few years. Time for some controversy, or at least dialogue to stir up the juices, get people fired up about this baseball season."

And that it did. The next day's publication of the *Post-Gazette* had a column by Bernie, featuring the headline "Time to Part Ways? Tony Rakers Thinks So." The story restated Colby's father's frustrations with how his son's major-league professional career was not progressing under Tony LoDuca.

Meanwhile, back in San Francisco, the team opened the Giants series with a one-run loss on Friday, April 8, followed by another one-run loss on Saturday, April 9, both as a result of the following formula:

double plays (hit into), not advancing runners in scoring position, and blown saves by the bullpen. At this rate, the team would be buried alive and out of the pennant race by July 1. Paul did not fare much better. He went 0-4 on Friday and 1-4 on Saturday after he had decided that the pine tar was "too much hassle" to deal with. Sunday, April 10, was another matter. Back to using the pine tar, he had a double and a home run in a 6–1 win over the Giants to salvage the last game of the series. Colby was back in the lineup Sunday at San Francisco, although he continued his season-long slump by not getting any hits and not catching several balls that appeared to be reachable if he would have had a good jump on them.

So the drama continued with Colby and the team.

The team now moved on to Phoenix for a three-game series with the Arizona Diamondbacks starting on Monday, April 11, and ending on Wednesday, April 13. This segment of the road trip went better for the Redbirds, who won two of three from the D-Backs. Then it was on to Los Angeles to take on the Dodgers for four games starting on Thursday, April 14. The Redbirds won three of four against the Dodgers. Paul piled up several more home runs, one each in Phoenix and Los Angeles, for a total of six on the young season, along with a decent batting average and RBI total.

He was not alone, as Al Robles, Paul's teammate; Joey Costa, first baseman for the Cincinnati Reds; and Carlos Vasquez, Colorado outfielder, were also bashing the ball at a similar clip.

CHAPTER TWELVE

Another off day loomed for the Cardinals on Monday, April 18, before a seven-game home stand began against the Nationals and the Reds.

Paul was hoping to duplicate his wonderful San Francisco experience with Heather in Saint Louis, but there were no return messages from her after he left a few advising her of the upcoming off day.

Ah, temporary home sweet home, at least for a few short months. After paying the cab fare from the airport, he walked toward his apartment and noticed several things out of place: there were no newspapers or mail lying around plus there were several lights on that he knew, or thought he knew, he did not leave on.

He approached the door gingerly, and it swung open. Now he was freaked out a bit, as he knew that he had locked the door. As he quietly dropped his bags in the foyer, he could hear soft, dinner-type music coming from the living room area. "Could that be my stereo system playing? Don't tell me that the spirit of Joe Fisher is bugging me again!" thought Paul.

Much to Paul's relief, he didn't have to face the apparition, spirit, or whatever of Joe Fisher, but rather a fetching Heather Alexander in high heels and a French maid's outfit cut low in all the right places. She walked toward him carrying a champagne glass and a feather duster, which at some point in the evening would be used for very stimulating purposes.

"We've got to stop meeting like this," said Paul, incredulous about the whole situation.

"I'm so glad to see you, but how did you get in here? Are you a B and E expert, too?"

"Hello, Paulie. I have many skills we haven't even tapped yet. Let's just say I figured out where you lived, and then I figured out a way to get into your place. Maybe someday I'll tell you my secret."

"Please do, because you are freaking me out. I may have to start calling you Wonder Woman. You continue to amaze and excite me!"

"The feeling's mutual, Paulie. That's why I keep chasing you around the country. Now you have an off day tomorrow and seven more home games. I can't stay for your whole home stand, but I can hang with you for a few days. I hope I have you all to myself tomorrow, and then I'd like to take in a game or two before I have to go back to Minneapolis."

The evening and early morning were glorious for Paul, and presumably for Heather, too. The next day, they shared a light breakfast at Paul's place, followed by a trip to the Saint Louis Art Museum to see an exhibit that Heather was particularly interested in. "French Postimpressionism?" Paul had said. "Okay, if you say so."

Paul and Heather then wandered over to the Deck House Restaurant near the art museum and had a bite to eat and a glass of wine. They then wandered the streets of Central West End, window shopping and spending a considerable amount of time at CWE Books, an old-fashioned bookseller that had embraced the information age, though it also specialized in preserving the lost art of marketing first-edition hardbacks.

The rest of the day and evening was a blur of arms and legs, as Paul and Heather renewed their interest in physical exercise, sans clothing. It was a great day, the start of a great week.

CHAPTER THIRTEEN

April 19 was the start of new home stand, with the Nationals coming to town for three games. Unfortunately, April in Saint Louis can bring showers or downright downpours, as it did this particular day. The game was rained out before the teams even showed up to the ballpark. The Cardinals and the Nationals, in conference with National League officials, adjusted the schedule to have a day-night doubleheader the following day on Wednesday, April 20.

The afternoon game was a sloppy affair, with multiple errors on both sides, which Washington won 8–6. Paul even had his first error of the season, dropping a ball after coming in a long way to catch it. It was ruled an error because he got his glove on it. He probably would have been better off letting it bounce first for a hit.

Paul virtually won the evening game on his own. He sat out the start of the game, but came into the contest as a pinch hitter with the bases loaded in the eighth inning. He hit the first pitch to the third level in left field, known as Big Mac Land, much to the delight of the home fans. The Cardinals, except for a sulking Colby Rakers, came to the top of the dugout to greet him. The fans were especially happy because everyone in the stadium could redeem their ticket stub for a free Big Mac at metro-area McDonald's restaurants the next day. It promised to be a busy day for the franchisees.

As Paul entered the dugout, the fans were standing on their feet, demanding that their new hero come out for a curtain call. He didn't disappoint, although he had to be pushed up and out of the dugout to honor their request. This would not be the last curtain call he would receive this season.

The Thursday, April 21, game with the Nationals was a day game, known as a "getaway game." Managers routinely substitute some of their key players, and although no umpire would ever admit to it, it seemed that getaway games had a tendency to be crisper and quicker due to an expanded strike zone.

This was no exception. The Cardinals won 5–0 on the strength of solid pitching by ace starter Chris Mitchell and good hitting up and down the lineup. Paul started the game and contributed a double that drove in two runs, and then he coaxed a bases-loaded walk in his second at bat. Tony LoDuca decided to improvise a bit the rest of the game and brought Paul in to play first base, while giving Al Robles the rest of the game off. Paul handled a half dozen chances without incident, including one ball that he dug out of the dirt to salvage an errant throw by third baseman David Page.

As he came into the dugout, Tony took a moment to congratulate Paul on his defensive efforts at the unfamiliar position. "Nice work!" he exclaimed to Paul.

"Let's not do this for any other positions, Skipper. I don't think you want to see me at shortstop!"

"I don't think you'll see that, Paul. I like my job, and I think I'd be run out of town if I did that," chuckled Tony.

Meanwhile, there had to be some drama over a long season, and Colby Rakers was ejected from the game in the sixth inning for arguing a called third strike and throwing his bat and batting helmet, the latter nearly decapitating the Cardinals' bat boy.

As he came into the dugout, Tony told him to see him in his office after the game. This sort of thing was difficult for Tony. He preferred seasoned ballplayers to rookies because they generally acted professionally while on the field and had their tantrums away from the cameras, microphones, media, and upper management, if they had tantrums at all. "Rookies," thought Tony. "They just keep reminding me why I lose patience managing them."

"You wanted to see me, Skip?" Colby said as he walked into Tony's office and sat down on a couch against the wall.

"Yes, I did. Do you mind getting up and closing my door? Thanks. Now, this won't take long. You may as well remain standing.

"Look, Colby, you and I both know that you have been established in the eyes of senior management as the best thing since sliced bread. You have a lot of talent, maybe five-tool talent. But you also still have a lot to learn, including taking direction from anyone, it seems, in our organization, including me.

"What you did out on the field today confirms my belief that you need to grow up. Jesus, Colby, you almost took the head off of our bat boy. Did you even say anything to him afterward? How do you think that looked to our fans? To the media? How did that make you feel? To help you think a little harder next time, and in this game there is always ample opportunity for a next time, I'm fining you five thousand dollars, which will be taken out of your next check and donated to Cardinals Care. I'm also 'resting' you for a few days. Maybe the break will help your attitude and also allow you to reset your game, 'cause you are not clicking on offense or defense right now.

"If you have a problem with this decision, talk to your agent and see if he wants to take this any further. I doubt it."

"Okay, Skip," Colby began. "I don't think you understand the kind of pressure I'm under to do well and live up to everyone's expectations, including yours."

"The only expectations I have for you are to remember that the name on the front of your jersey is more important than the one on the back," Tony replied.

With that comment, Colby left Tony's office and sulked back to his locker.

The defending division champion Reds came to town for a weekend series, and it was anticipated that both of these clubs would be in the hunt for the division flag this season, along with the surprising Brewers.

There was still an element of bad blood between these two teams based on a near riot on the Cincinnati field a year ago.

The opener for the series on Friday, April 22, was tied at 2–2 until the ninth when Al Robles did his thing by cranking a two-run walk-off home run. It was his seventh homerun of season, which tied him for the lead with three other players in the league: Costa, Cincinnati; Vasquez, Colorado; and Saint Louis teammate Paul Kolbe, the old guy in left field (although Paul preferred to think of himself as the seasoned veteran).

Paul had a good day, too, including two hits, a walk, and a sacrifice fly for an RBI. He was becoming that dangerous hitter in the number two spot in the lineup that he split with Colby, depending on whether and right- or left-handed pitcher was starting for the opposition. Tony LoDuca loved someone who could move the lead-off hitter over a base, but who could also crank an extra-base hit, even a homer, to disrupt the other team early in the game, and he hoped both Paul and Colby could fill that role.

The Saturday, April 23, game swung in the other direction, as the Reds won 5–3. Paul was getting hits in the series, but he did not display any power. Teams were starting to form a book on him and were starting to pitch him low and away. He either got impatient and started chasing some of these pitches, occasionally punching them to right field, or he walked or struck out. Clearly, he had to adjust to their adjustments.

And that didn't mean giving up on the "no batting gloves" approach to hitting, as the local radio talk shows and press speculated. On a local sports talk radio show (which Paul was generally averse to dealing with), Frank Luciano, a respected TV sports reporter moonlighting on radio, asked the question: "We're joined this morning by the newest Cardinal, Paul Kolbe, who is off to a terrific start. Paul, you have a real throwback approach to hitting. Would you care to elaborate on this matter for our listeners?"

"Good morning to you, Frank, and to your listening audience. Hopefully most of them are Cardinals fans! Frank, I'm not so sure my approach is much different than anyone else's. It ultimately comes down to situational decision making, including the count, the number of outs, and who is batting behind me."

"I was waiting for the classic statement, 'see the ball, hit the ball,' Paul," chuckled Frank.

"It ultimately comes down to that, Frank, but I was not going to go there!"

"What about your use of pine tar—not just any, but from the North Woods? And no batting gloves? You might be the only hitter in the major leagues that doesn't use them."

"Have you ever tried to use pine tar on batting gloves? It doesn't work very well! No, I'm not trying to be a throwback hitter or abstain from using something that obviously works for everyone else. I'm just trying to give myself the best opportunity to get a good grip on the bat. I've found through trial and error over the years, Frank, that a little bit of pine tar and the natural feel of wood works for me."

"Is there anything special about the pine tar you use? Apparently it comes from where you've been coaching the past few years, up in the North Woods of Minnesota."

"That's correct, Frank. I don't attribute any special powers to this stuff. It's just pine tar. I do think there is a certain consistency in the stuff that comes from that region that makes it superior to what you can get from somewhere else, but that's as far as I'll go with the 'magic powers' theory that I hear and read about from folks like you, Frank!"

"Okay, I'm guilty as charged. I do, however, find it intriguing that the last Triple Crown winner in the National League, our own Joe Fisher, used a similar product in the late 1930s. Do you see any resemblance to the season you're having with that of Joe Fisher's Triple Crown season?"

"Frank, I couldn't imagine competing for something like a Triple Crown. I consider myself a short-term solution until Matt Bradley comes back. I've been out of the game as an active player for a couple years, working as a hitting coach in Rochester, Minnesota. My goal there was to acclimate college-level players to the art of hitting a baseball with a wood bat. They, as you know, have used aluminum or composites, or anything but wood since their peewee days, and there is a difference when you start using something like wood."

"Why is that, Paul?"

"Frank, I appreciate that you're allowing me to address that question, because I know someone as savvy as you knows that answer already! For brevity purposes, let's focus on aluminum and perhaps save a discussion on composites for another day. First of all, wood bats are heavier than aluminum ones. This means that a batter has to commit to swinging earlier in order to catch up to, say, a high-nineties fastball. Also, the sweet spot on a wood bat, that area where a batter can do the most damage, is much smaller than on an aluminum bat. This means that the batter has to be more precise in hitting a baseball. Otherwise, you wind up fouling balls off, or popping up, or grounding out. Perhaps the most important outcome is that a pitcher can throw inside against a wood batsman, a useful tool if the batter has a tendency to crowd the plate. If the batter swings at an inside pitch with a wood bat, he probably will hit the ball closer to the bat handle and hit a weak pop-up or a weak groundout, and perhaps break his bat, too. With an aluminum bat, the weight is distributed equally and he can still hit an inside pitch as well as something across the plate. There are other differences too, such as product life, but I think your listeners get the point; the first time a college kid tries to hit against a good pitcher with a wood bat can be a rude awakening. Net-net: pitchers lose a big advantage in a nonwood bat league, but get it back where wood bats are used."

"Great answer, Paul. And I am impressed by what I hear from you about the art of hitting. Did you know the absolute master, Charlie Klaus?"

"Thanks, Frank. And yes, I ran across Charley in the course of my playing days, and I was constantly bugging him about the art and science of hitting. He was the best teacher I knew, and I tried to incorporate his theories into my own work in Rochester. Of course, I wouldn't be much of a teacher if I didn't try to deploy his teachings myself. And before you ask, probably the most important thing is to consider the situation while trying to extend the pitcher. The more pitches you see, the better your chance of getting one you can handle. One exception to this rule: if the pitcher is on the ropes, do him a favor and knock the ball out of the park. He'll get a quicker shower, and you will get some runs for your team. Now that's a win-win, Frank!"

"That's funny, Paul. I know you're off to the ballpark, but thanks for spending a few minutes with us, and we'd love to have you back on our show again to talk about the art of hitting."

"Thanks for the offer, Frank. Let's let your listeners weigh in on that one."

With that, Paul said his good-byes, hung up, and was satisfied that he didn't make a fool out of himself.

The last game of the series, on Sunday, April 24, went back to Saint Louis for a well-pitched game by Jake Hudson, as the Cardinals shut out the Reds 3–0. Paul walked his first two times at the plate and followed up with a ringing double off the left-field wall on a curve ball that didn't break. He was starting to show the league that if pitchers made the mistake of placing the ball in his power zone, they would pay. He finished the day with yet another double, driving in two of the three total runs for the Cardinals.

It was time for another comment by Bernie Madlock in his "Bernie's Bytes" online column:

So Far So Good

I've been critical of Cardinals management for bringing in several players well past their prime in Kolbe and Champlin, but so far the move has paid off. Both of them are off to a good start, and the rookie who 'can't miss' in center field? It's a rough start for Colby Rakers, but I hope management is patient and they let Rakers work through his slow start. Meanwhile, how long will Kolbe and Champlin be able to tee it up as the season edges into the long grind of 162 games? Thanks for reading.

Recognizing that Paul had was doing a bang up job in the second slot, Tony LoDuca started using him there more of the time, while deploying Colby Rakers further down in the lineup.

"Meanwhile, Tony LoDuca asked for a meeting with John Nowicki regarding his frustrations in dealing with Colby Rakers.

"Tony, don't bring up any thoughts about trading Colby," advised Nowicki. "You know he is the top prospect in our system and is tied up for six years at an attractive salary, notwithstanding arbitration. You also know that he has tremendous upside if you and the coaching staff can harness his talents. And he has accomplished everything we required of him at Memphis, so there's no point in bringing up the minor-league option issue."

"I understand all that, Wick, but the guy is disruptive, moody, and unwilling to listen to advice unless his dad says it's okay. And bottom line, he is a cancer in the clubhouse. And you know Bernie Madlock is generally a fair writer for the paper, but he seems to perceive Tony Rakers as someone the fans want to hear from. Needless to say, our two hitting coaches are not happy, and the day they see his dad in the video room is the day we are going to have some head knockin' going on in the clubhouse."

"Tony, I get all that. Please help me contain the situation by trying to get along with the guy. We're just coming off a season where we traded a budding all-star closer to Cleveland to get Jake Hudson, and, as well as Jake has performed for us, the talent we gave up was disproportionate.

"Trading Colby would not get us fair value back, especially in light of his well-known issues with you and the club in general. So bottom line, trading Colby Rakers would make us look like failures, and Hank Rheinhold, our owner, does not want the PR hit. Find a way to work with this kid, and I'll try to keep his dad off your back."

CHAPTER FOURTEEN

Monday, April 25, was another off day, but Heather had already told Paul that she couldn't come back to town due to previous commitments, so Paul was on his own until the team charter took off later in the day. He took the opportunity to get lazy and head for the pool with a sack of mail that had been collecting for some time. Aside from the usual fan mail, there was an envelope postmarked from Augusta, Georgia, with no return address. A one-page typewritten letter was enclosed.

Hey Dickhead (aka Paul Kolbe):

Just what are you trying to prove, other than you are making a fool out of yourself? You're costing younger players like Colby Rakers valuable development time. Why don't you take your geezer ass back to Minnesota and watch the games on satellite at the rest home you came from? You can take that other dickhead Tony LoDuca with you, too!

A concerned fan

"I must be making progress," thought Paul. "I'm good enough to get hate mail. I should just blow this off, but it also mentions the skipper, so it would probably be a good idea to share this letter—and now I see three others—with Tony."

And Paul did just that, having the opportunity to spend a moment in the charter aircraft terminal as they waited through the final preparations for their flight to Houston.

"Shit," said Tony. It was rather uncharacteristic of him, as he didn't use colorful language in front of the players, although rumor had it that he did save some choice words for umpires. "I need to show these to John Nowicki so he can inform our security department. They may see these as a threat or as simply the work of a pissed-off father, if you know what I mean."

"Hey Skipper, I didn't want to make a mountain out of a molehill, but they did reference you as well as me, so I thought you'd like to know."

"Absolutely, glad you did. Now let us take care of this matter. Your job is to get on base and drive in some runs."

The team was back on the road for the Astros series, a three-game set starting on April 26. The Cardinals dropped the first game 6–5, but they came back to win the last two of the series.

In the second game of the series played on Wednesday, April 27, Paul added one homer, moving his total to eight for the month of April. "Not bad for someone who hasn't been in the big leagues for several years," thought Paul.

Although it was only April, Paul could see that the season was going to be quite a marathon: six months of constant activity, half of which involved travel and sleepless nights, and of course games performed in front of thousands of "experts"—the fans, media, and team management. To an outsider, the job looked glamorous; to an insider, there was just pressure to perform. And that pressure never left. It just hung there over a player, day after day. "I'd take that," would be the most often heard comment by the average fan. And that fan no doubt would, perhaps until a ninety-eight-mile-per-hour fastball buzzed his ear.

CHAPTER FIFTEEN

Next, the team was off to Atlanta for a three-game series that began April 29. The first game of the series on Friday resulted in a win for the Cardinals. Paul did not have a hit, but he was still instrumental for the team, as he took a ball off his left arm during an at bat and eventually scored the game-winning run. Fortunately, it wasn't his throwing arm that was hit, but it still hurt, and a lump and bruise were already forming at the point of impact.

After the Braves game, Paul was getting a bit restless. He knew he shouldn't drink alcohol, but he was determined to see if he had "cured" himself by staying sober for the month of April. He didn't want to be seen around the team hotel, so he took a cab to Buckhead and was dropped off at a hole-in-the-wall establishment on Peachtree Street, a place that he knew from past experience would be open until three in the morning.

The place was also known for attracting beautiful people, and this particular Friday evening was no exception. Paul sauntered up to the bar and immediately noticed a mixture of twenty- and thirty-something men and women, mostly dressed for a hot date, with the ladies in slinky dresses and high heels, and the gentlemen in blazers or suits and open-collared shirts. Paul felt a little conspicuous with his tattered white oxford shirt and jeans—appropriately underdressed, but still kind of a standout with this crowd. He spied a stool in the corner of the bar and claimed it so he could get out of the traffic.

It didn't take long for a very attractive blonde, maybe ten years younger than Paul, to angle her way near him and ultimately sit down when someone else left the stool next to Paul's.

"Care to buy a lonely girl a drink, Sailor?" she asked Paul.

"First of all, I doubt if you're lonely, and second of all, how did you know I was a sailor?" kidded Paul.

Her name was Nikki Cole, and she was an upscale escort based in Atlanta. Nikki had a bit of a hard edge to her appearance, demeanor, and personality. She was not well educated, nor did she pretend to be. But she had a street sense that most men would find alluring. She also had a Georgia accent, full of honey and drawl, with an uncanny ability to occasionally make two-syllable words out of one-syllable ones. "And what can I get you, Ms. Cole?" asked the bartender.

"I'll have my usual R-O-C and Black Jack when you get the chance."

"Ms. Cole, I presume?" asked Paul. "You must come here often to be recognized in such a busy place. And by the way, I get the Black Jack stuff, but just what is R-O-C?

Royal Crown Cola, Sailor. I'm still loyal to my South Georgia roots. R-O-C was the drink of choice where I grew up. Add a banana moon pie and you have the makings of a great breakfast!"

"I'm surprised you survived your childhood with all that sugar and caffeine!" said Paul. "But truthfully, I've always been a fan of moon cakes, too and I actually like Diet Rite Cola, which was, as you surely know, a Royal Crown product."

Beyond the idle chitchat, Paul learned that what Nikki liked most of all was money and sex, and so she found a profession to combine the two, maybe not for a long-term career, but for as long as she continued to be unattached.

"Nikki, you are a very attractive lady, and I could see myself investing my hard-earned dollars in an hour or two of your company, but I don't operate that way. You're probably better off spending time with someone else this evening," advised Paul.

"Relax, Sailor," she said. The name "Sailor" was now ingrained in her mind as Paul's handle. "I'm not working this evening, and I only do so by appointment anyway. I actually have an administrative associate who handles those details for me."

"Okay," said Paul, "then I will gladly buy you a drink…when you're ready for another one and maybe even a late dinner if you're interested. I've got the late-night munchies this evening."

"I'm up for a little bite to eat, but not here. Let's go near my place in Buckhead, and I'll show you a great little eatery that caters to late-nighters."

"Fair enough," he said. And they were off. Getting a cab on Friday night was no problem. Getting into the little place that Nikki wanted to go—Bistro Blanco—was. Even at this relatively late hour, there was a small line waiting outside the front door to get seated. The place was tiny but striking in that all the furniture lived up to its name—antique white. With the kind of crowds they had there, the hand-rubbed finish was probably updated on a regular basis to keep the place looking fresh. Best of all, the people watching was spectacular. For the guys, there was one good-looking lady after another—for the ladies, one good-looking hunk after another. Paul, in his relative ruggedness and maturity, and Nikki, in her sensuality, fit right in.

An attractive cocktail server offered them a complimentary glass of wine while they waited, and before long they were seated at a great patio table that overlooked Peachtree Street.

Paul couldn't help himself. He observed the exceptional features that Nikki possessed, starting with the proper amount of understated cleavage, and moving on to the lovely display of thighs exposed under her appropriately cut skirt. She was a looker.

"Are you staring at me, Sailor?" asked Nikki after an extended period of silence. Both Paul and Nikki started laughing.

"You caught me, Ms. Cole. Yes, I was staring at you. Point in fact, I am still staring at you. I'm trying to figure out what your best feature is, and I've decided that it's a tie for first place—hair, smile, physique, eyes, the whole package."

"Are you trying to hustle me now, Sailor? I'll tell you what. I live just around the corner from this place. We can walk. I'll put you up for the night, and we'll see how it goes. If we click, then I expect to see you again."

Whether it was the forbidden fruit, the booze that he had for the first time in a month, or the fact that Nikki was just knockout gorgeous, he wasn't about to let the opportunity pass by. Thoughts of Heather—and what she might think of this situation—crossed his mind but were quickly pushed to the back of his consciousness. "I'll deal with those feelings later," thought Paul.

"And lest you think this is business, I told you I'm playing tonight, and I've picked you, Sailor, to be my boy toy," laughed Nikki.

"It's okay. I'm used to being a sex object. Hope you enjoy it!"

After a quick bite to eat, another drink or two, Nikki and Paul walked two blocks to Nikki's condo and hardly got past the front door before clothes started flying off in all directions. They barely made it to Nikki's bedroom.

The sex was different with Nikki. It was more physical than emotional, maybe even mechanical, and somewhat "needy" as Paul tried to rationalize in his mind what he was experiencing. "Now don't overanalyze the situation," Paul thought. "Here you are, with a drop-dead gorgeous woman ten years younger than you who is interested enough to bang your brains out. Under the circumstances, going with the flow is apropos," chuckled Paul to himself.

Morning came very quickly, and Paul knew he would be in trouble if he showed up late for the team bus to the ballpark. "I've got to go, Nikki. I never got the chance to tell you what I do for a living. I'm a baseball player for the Cardinals. We're in town to play your Braves. If I don't show up on time, ready to rock and roll in the hotel lobby, then I'm in deep doo-doo."

"Wow, now that's way too cool. I'll watch the game today when I can. I have some family commitments that won't allow me to see the whole thing, though. Did you intend to ask me out to dinner tonight?"

"As a matter of fact, I think that is a great idea. You just got ahead of me a bit. Thanks for speeding up the process. Can you book a reservation somewhere, and I'll call you later to confirm our evening?"

ONE LAST HURRAH

Paul cabbed it back to the team hotel, ordered some room service (including a large pot of coffee), showered, and was ready to board the team bus at the appointed time with his teammates.

Saturday's game with the Braves closed out the month of April for Paul and the team. Of note was that Al Robles was starting to heat up. He finished the month with seven homers, just one behind the club (and league) leader, none other than Paul Kolbe. The so-called Triple Crown race, of which there had not been one for years, seemed to be forming with as many as four players involved: Robles and Kolbe from the Cardinals, Costa from the Reds, and Vasquez from the Rockies. There had been many a batting title race through the years, but all three offensive categories, with four players? The 2011 season promised to be a historic one, although it was extremely early to contemplate such a feat as a Triple Crown.

The Cardinals won the Saturday, April 30, game 3–2, thanks to solo home runs by Al Robles, Lance Champlin, and Paul Kolbe.

Before Paul could even get out of the clubhouse, his newfound friend Nikki called and left a message that she had made dinner plans at La Grotta for eight o'clock. "That should give us enough time to enjoy a nice meal and for you to get some rest after I abuse you for a while. I also wanted to let you know that I took the liberty of pulling numbers off your American Express credit card last night. It's a protection device that I learned a long time ago. I didn't think you'd mind too terribly if I picked up a dress for this evening. I found one, a Parker kimono sleeve sequin minidress off the rack at Nordstrom. It was only $385."

"Only $385? What in Sam Hill have I unleashed on myself? A lady who is very street smart, that's what," said Paul to no one in particular. "Is this a good place for me to be? Especially since this new friendship is outside the scope of my budding relationship with Heather?"

Paul didn't know what to think. He had "invested" in Nikki so she could look great for the evening. He called her back from his cell phone while waiting to board the team bus over to the hotel. "Hello, Nikki?

87

How are you? I got your message, and that sounds great, Nikki. But could you do me a favor?"

"Sure, Sailor. What is it?"

"Please check with me on the credit card usage in the future. I'm not comfortable having that kind of information in another person's hands. I trust you will not make any more purchases without consulting with me."

"Sure, Sailor. Of course. I just wanted to look good for you!"

With that issue settled, Paul shook his head on the bus ride back to the hotel and none other than Tony LoDuca noticed what appeared to be a bewildered Paul Kolbe. "Hey Kolbe," said Tony, directing his line of sight at Paul. "I hope you're not upset because you only had one homer today."

"Now that would be a trip, wouldn't it, Skipper? No, nothing like that. Just some personal stuff twirling around in my brain. Fortunately nothing too major. Just the everyday stuff we all have to deal with."

"Okay. Just checking your mood, Paul. You know better than most players on the club that an even keel in the best way to handle the long season. Too many highs or too many lows and you're exhausted by September."

"I hear you, Skipper. I preached the same thing to the college kids in Rochester."

With that exchange, the conversation ended.

Paul dropped his personal bag off at his room and quickly hailed a cab to Nikki's place in Buckhead. Nikki opened the front door to greet him and all Paul could say was "Wow!"

"That's it?" said Nikki.

"You took my breath way for a moment. You look fantastic in that dress!"

"Worth three hundred and eighty-five dollars to you, Paul?"

"I'll tell you later. Just kidding. Absolutely."

Dinner and the rest of the evening was a blur. As with the previous evening, sex with Nikki was different. It was very physical, again maybe even mechanical, and somewhat "needy." But nevertheless, it was a wonderful time with a great lady.

In the morning Paul said his good-byes and promised to stay in touch. He truly meant it, but he was not sure it was a good idea.

He made the team bus with all of a minute to spare and then it was time to get back to the business of baseball.

The Sunday, May 1, game was close, but the Cardinals ultimately lost when closer Ryan Jefferson blew the save, his seventh in the month. Needless to say, the team was going nowhere if its closer continued to let games get away at such a great pace. When asked about the situation in his postgame press conference, Tony became irritated with the subject matter. "I'd like to remind you folks that Ryan had a significant number of saves last season, and sometimes it takes a veteran like Jefferson awhile to get into regular season form."

"But," interjected the beat writer for the *Post-Gazette*, "most closers don't blow seven saves all season, Tony. Ryan has done so in just one month. How long can you continue to go with Ryan as your closer?"

"This isn't worthy of any additional discussion. Ryan is our closer. Case closed. Let's move on to the next subject, if there is one."

"I understand that you're trying to protect your players," continued the beat writer, "including Ryan Jefferson. But at some point, I'll ask my question again, and we'll see if you have a different response."

"I think you adequately covered your concerns. Now are there any other questions from any other media members?"

With that, the press conference came to a close, and Tony retreated to his office.

Bernie Madlock waited five minutes to let the manager collect his thoughts, and then he knocked on Tony's open door. "Got a minute, Tony?"

"Only a minute. And by the way, tell your beat writer that I'm going to throw his butt out of the next postgame interview if he so much as mentions Ryan Jefferson. I'm aware that Ryan has looked horrible. I'm trying to make it work because the alternative is to shuffle the entire bullpen, something that might take all season for the staff to get accustomed to with their new roles. I know it's crazy. A reliever can be very effective in the seventh or eighth inning, but gets caught up in the hoopla of the BS if he gets moved into a different role."

Meanwhile, Paul had been using the pine tar rather religiously and had become concerned that he might run out sooner than later. Perhaps he could make a run to Rochester the next day off.

The next series, starting on Monday, May 2, pitted Miami against the Cardinals for four games. The Cards lost the first and third tilts, thanks to bullpen breakdowns, but they won games two and four with strong efforts from younger members of the pen. The days of closing for Jefferson appeared to be nearing a conclusion. Paul continued his hot hitting, with seven hits in thirteen at bats, including a home run.

Next came a three-game series with the Brewers beginning on Friday, May 6, which was a teaser for the season-long pennant race in the National League Central Division. The Cardinals shut out the Brewers 6–0 in the first game, but the Brewers came back and won the second game 4–0. The rubber game of the series went to the Cardinals 3–1, as Al Robles hit a two-run walk-off homer against the Brewers' closer. Paul sat out the first game to get a break and give some at bats to one of the Cards' youngsters. He came back strong the next two games with two hits in each contest.

CHAPTER SIXTEEN

So what to do with a whole day off on May 9? Paul called his old friend Sam Mello and told him that he was going to visit Rochester and see if Mr. Fisher would show up and deliver more pine tar.

"That sounds like a long shot, Paul, but you're welcome to crash on my couch," Sam advised.

"I'll take you up on your offer. I don't know how else to contact the guy."

"And," Paul thought, "how do I work Heather into the one single day I have? She would slit my throat if she somehow found out that I was in Minnesota and didn't make an effort to see her."

So asking and then receiving the skipper's permission, Paul took off for Rochester instead of staying in Saint Louis for the charter flight to Chicago. He decided that rather than crashing on Sam's couch, it would be better to get his own place, especially if he could not connect with Heather. The closest he could get to the bar and the Meyer Clinic (a quick meeting with the doc might do some good!) was at the Brentwood Courtyard Suites—a nice place, but not quite as nice as he was accustomed to with the Cardinals. Funny, it wasn't too long ago that he could have just as easily slept in the front seat of his automobile, especially if he had a few too many drinks the previous evening.

He pulled a rental car into the side parking lot of Sam's place, walked in, and sat at his endowed barstool at the end of the bar, overlooking the front windows of the establishment.

"Hello, Paul!" shouted Sam as he saw Paul sitting down. "Damn, you look like you are in great shape. Guess it helps to be around a pro sport to keep you goin'. And what's up with all the homers? Do you realize you are the king of swat right now?"

"Yeah, and that will get you a cup of coffee and maybe some pine blisters on the bench after you strike out four times. It's too early to get too excited, Sam, but it is a little gratifying that I know I can still get the job done. But we're talking about April stats, too, Sam."

"Tell me about your friend, Paul. You're not planning on seeing Joe Fisher, are you? You know he's been dead since 1975?"

"I'll be honest, Sam. I don't know who or what my friend is. I honestly thought I was talking to Joe, as the guy knew all the stats, the stories, the 'beaning' incident after he was traded from the Cardinals, everything. If it wasn't Joe, and I fully understand why it couldn't be, then I don't know who in the heck I was talking to. And if it wasn't Joe, who left me the tins of pine tar? Maybe a relative who knew Joe well growing up? Maybe someone just trying to mess with me? I'm willing to suspend my disbelief if this pine tar stuff works. Boy, do I look silly, though, batting without gloves on and using that gunk. I get asked in every visiting city about it, but I try to minimize the impact it has on me. I certainly don't want to mention the Fisher connection, or the team will have me committed to the psych ward at a local mental institution!"

"I don't know what to say, Paul. But I do know what to do. Here is a twenty-ounce glass of ice-cold Rheinhold Supreme and a room temperature shot of Jack Daniel's. On the house. Welcome back to Rochester. Paul eyed the combination and hesitated for a moment, remembering how good these two drinks tasted, how relaxed he felt when he drank, how everything just started to fade away—until the next day, of course. "Oh shit," he thought. "I don't need to be afraid of this stuff. I'm a major leaguer and, dammit, a damn good one at that."

One concession, though, was to keep the phone number handy of his favorite cab driver. The last thing he needed was the massive potential for disaster brought about by driving while intoxicated.

Paul placed the shot of Jack inside his draft beer glass and gulped the entire contents down in a matter of seconds. "Whew, that tasted good," he thought. It had been a long time since he'd had one of those. Maybe another one just might take the hair off the dog while he waited for his favorite spirit or whatever to show up. "I'll have another, Sam."

"Damn, Paul, where did the last one go? Did you pour it out somewhere? Okay, but slow down on this one."

The second one did not last much longer than the first, as Paul gulped down the drink again in a matter of seconds. The third one, at mild protestation by Sam, stretched further to around ten minutes. The fourth and fifth ones went down very slowly, as they were nursed by an increasingly tipsy and tired Paul Kolbe.

"Hey Sam, I'm going to rest up in the booth over there in the back of the bar area for a while. Let me know if my friend shows up, okay?" Paul almost immediately fell into an alcohol-induced sleep.

"Good for him," Sam thought. "He doesn't need to be driving in his condition, and I'll just take him to his hotel when we close tonight." As he continued to putter around the back of the bar (it was a slow night in Rochester), the phone rang, and surprise, it was Heather Alexander.

"Hey there, long time, no see! How are you, Uncle?"

"Damn, Heather. It's so good to hear your voice. What is this momentous occasion?"

"I'm trying to track down our mutual friend, Paul Kolbe. A little bird told me he was in Rochester, and I wanted to, first, give him some grief for not contacting me, and second, give him some TLC this evening if I can get out of Minneapolis in a little bit."

"Your little bird told you right, Heather. Paul is indeed here. Said he wanted to meet his friend, the guy who reminded him of Joe Fisher, and get some more pine tar. Seems as though Paul thinks the stuff is helping him grip his bat."

"Did the gentleman friend ever show up?"

"Not yet, but the night is still young; we're open for another three hours. I must tell you, however, that he is completely wasted. He had five jumbo draft beers along with shots of Jack Daniel's. I think I'll pour him into my car when we close this evening and let him sleep it off. He can pick up his car tomorrow when I come in."

"Why that shithead!" exclaimed Heather. "I fly all over the country just to spend some quality time with this guy, and he can't even pick up the phone and tell me he's within an hour's drive. Damn that Kolbe. He is a jerk!"

"Ouch," Sam thought as he heard the loud thud from Heather slamming her phone against a hard surface. "Is she pissed or what?"

The evening concluded with Sam helping Paul to Sam's SUV after the bar closed. "Hey, buddy, you better just stay on my couch and sleep this one off. I'll get you some coffee in the morning before you have to bail out of town."

"England swings like a pendulum do, bobbies on bicycles two by two, Westminster Abbey, the tower of Big Ben, the rosy red cheeks of the little children," sang Paul in his drunken stupor.

"I'm not sure what prompted that rendition of an old Roger Miller song, but my advice is to stick with your day job as a ballplayer!"

"Roger Miller. Roger the Dodger. The Los Angeles Dodgers. Baseball. The Saint Louis Cardinals. The Rochester Honkers. It's all connected, don't you see, Sam?"

With that pithy insight, Sam escorted Paul to his couch, found a pillow and a blanket, took Paul's shoes off, and turned off the lights. Morning came too early for Paul, as he had gone on his first bender since he got back to the big leagues.

"Morning, buddy. Looks like you got two called strikes on you last evening."

Paul warily got up from the couch, still in a bit of a fog. "Two strikes? What do you mean Sam?"

"Well, your pine tar friend never showed up. Plus, Heather called and was rather upset that you didn't tell her you were in town. And you passed out in one of the booths at the bar."

"Shit!" Paul responded, which seemed to be the appropriate response for his predicament. "My head is killing me. You wouldn't happen to have a barrel of aspirin, would you? Oh for two. Things can't get any worse, can they, Sam?" But things were about to get worse. Much worse. "Sam, what time is it?"

"It's 10:00 a.m. I didn't want to wake you. You seemed to be in need of sleep."

"Shit!" Once again, the exclamation seemed appropriate. "I needed to be in Chicago first thing this morning, since we have a one fifteen day game against the Cubs."

"Sorry about that. I should have known that the Cubs would play a day game, but they are usually at three fifteen, not one fifteen!"

"How quickly can you get me to the airport, Sam?"

"Is that before you take a shower and freshen up, Paul? You look like death warmed over!"

"No time for that, Sam. I am in big trouble, one damn month after I started playing with the Cardinals."

"What about your car rental?"

"I don't have time to screw with it. Can you drop it off later today?"

"Sure. Let's go."

Rochester was not a large town, but there were traffic conventions like stops signs and stop lights that most drivers paid attention to. Sam did his level best to not get either Paul or himself maimed or killed, but he pushed speed limits to the max and ran a few stop signs and one stop light when he didn't see any cars coming from the opposite direction.

"Do you always drive like this, Sam? If so, I think you have a future as a getaway car driver!"

Meanwhile, Paul was tapping his phone, looking for flights to Chicago, either from Rochester or Minneapolis. The best Paul could do was to get into O'Hare by 12:45 p.m. By the time he got to Wrigley Field, it would be 1:30 p.m. He had to call the skipper and give him the not-so-good news.

"Tony? This is Paul Kolbe. I'm stuck in Minneapolis and won't be able to get to the ballpark until around one thirty."

"You're what? What in the name of Jesus is wrong with you? You can't be late for a game. This is why we put our folks up at a hotel…in Chicago!"

"Yes, I'm aware that I'll be late and that it's totally inexcusable. Yes, I understand that I'm letting the team down and that there will be consequences. Yes, I understand that this puts you in an embarrassing situation with the local media. I'm extremely sorry, and this will not happen again."

"Just get your butt to Wrigley, and we'll talk after the game."

After thanking Sam for his breakneck effort, Paul hustled through the Rochester airport, proceeded to the correct gate, and grabbed a seat on the first available aisle. He tried to relax on the plane but couldn't and then, once in O'Hare, sprinted through the airport, jumped the line of passengers waiting for cabs, overtipped the driver to get to Wrigley Field as fast as Chicago traffic would allow, and sprinted again though the players' entrance.

"How embarrassing," thought Paul. Showing up for the game late like a little leaguer. You just don't do that at the major-league level. He showered and dressed in his Cardinals road uniform in record time and then headed out to the dugout. Tony caught him out of the corner of his eye, walked over, and said softly that Paul would be fined $5,000 and wouldn't play today, maybe not tomorrow.

He suggested that Paul sit at the far end of the bench away from the skipper so he could concentrate on the players that would be playing today. Lastly, he suggested that he work on his "speech" to the players, as he wanted Paul to personally apologize to the team before tomorrow's game.

The guy that seemed most happy about the situation was Colby Rakers, who suggested to Paul that he should go to Walmart and get an alarm clock. "Funny guy," thought Paul.

Meanwhile, the Cardinals won the Tuesday, May 10, game 6–4, thanks to two run-scoring doubles by Colby Rakers and a home run by Al Robles, giving Al nine for the season and tying him for the league lead with the guy in the doghouse.

ONE LAST HURRAH

It was time for another letter, this one to Paul at the Majestic Hotel, where the team was staying for the road trip. The letter was postmarked once again from Augusta, Georgia, and included the following message:

Greetings, asshole:

Any possibility that you might get a part-time job at a watch shop so you know what fucking time it is? Good thing you're not an air traffic controller or even a waste disposal engineer, both professions requiring some degree of on-time performance, something most of us learn in the second or third grade. Here's a tip, ass-wipe. Go to Walmart, buy an alarm clock with big numbers, and ask someone to set it for you. You might even ask your idiot manager to help you. After all, he does such a fine job managing the club, especially young players.

A concerned fan

"Wonderful," thought Paul. "This guy needs to get a life and quit picking on mine. I'm in too deep of a hole with the skipper to bring this up right now, so I'll just have to deal with the situation myself. In the meantime, I need to track down a certain lady from Minneapolis who I'm sure is just as mad at me as Tony is, maybe worse. Yes, definitely worse."

Before the second game, Tony asked all the players to come to the center of the clubhouse for an announcement.

"Thanks, guys," said Tony. "Paul here would like to say a few words."

"Hey. I had some personal business in Rochester, Minnesota to clean up, and I screwed up getting to Chicago yesterday. I'm too old to be making rookie mistakes like not being ready to play on game days, and I feel I let you down. I'm sorry, guys, for screwing up, and I can assure you I have too much respect for you, Tony, and the game to let this happen again."

"Thanks, Paul," said Tony. "He's getting more pine time today, but this is a clubhouse matter. We stick together outside these doors, so I don't want anyone talking to the media, or tweeting, or whatever the hell you do with friends on the Internet about this. We are a united team and the only way we can stay that way is to keep the clubhouse chatter to ourselves. Now let's see if can sweep these guys by winning today and Sunday." The second game of the Cubs series was a disaster, as the Cardinals starting pitcher, lefty Jay Gomez, couldn't find the plate, walking five batters in the first two innings. Before the smoke had settled, the game was out of hand, with the visiting Cardinals taking a shellacking, 11–4.

The rubber game of the series was a reverse pounding, with the Cardinals on the giving end, 9–1. Tony, in his frustration from losing the day before, decided Paul had sat long enough and inserted him into the lineup. Good thing, too, as he slammed a two-run homer in his first at bat and another two-run double off the hallowed ivy wall in left field at Wrigley.

Tony gave Paul a little smile, patted him on the shoulder, and said, "It's funny how superior performance sometimes works great for resolving differences." Paul was well aware that he was on a short leash. No more missed times and dates for games, or he might find a one-way bus ticket back to Rochester in his locker.

Meanwhile, he had called, texted, and even sent flowers to Heather with no luck. No returned calls or texts. He even contacted his buddy Sam in Rochester, who hadn't heard from her either. "Well," thought Paul, "I've screwed this relationship up, as brief and strange and wonderful as it was between us. Maybe it was for the best," Paul allowed himself to contemplate. "Then again," he thought, "when I see her smile, with her bright, intense eyes, the attentive way she makes me feel special, do I really want to give that up?"

"This will have to be resolved another day," he spoke aloud.

CHAPTER SEVENTEEN

The club left Chicago for Cincinnati early in the evening for a three-game series with the Reds, starting Friday, May 13. The Reds were the previous year's Central Division winners. There was no love lost between these two clubs, and fans could envision the possibility of at least one bench-clearing battle or more before the series concluded on Sunday, May 15.

Unfortunately, the weekend did not go well for the Cardinals. The Friday night game was theoretically sewn up early for the Redbirds, having built a 5–0 lead in the first three innings. Then they stopped scoring while the Reds pecked away. And in the eighth inning, the Reds took the lead for good, coming up with their sixth and final run. The Cardinals made an effort in the ninth, having put two men on base with one out, but they were derailed by a bugaboo that would follow them throughout the season: a 6-4-3 double play to end the inning and the game. No beanballs were tossed on either side, as the umpires knew there was always the potential for fisticuffs to break out between these two foes and took the extra measure of warning both managers that they would be on a tight leash if trouble started.

Paul was instrumental in helping build the lead by stroking a rare triple with two men on in the third. After that, his bat fell silent, like those of his fellow teammates. All in all, it was a game that got away, and when a team was in a pennant race, it could ill afford to gift wrap too many of these encounters with its chief competitors.

Saturday, May 14, was no better for the Cardinals as they lost 7–3. On Sunday, the Reds jumped out to a 7–0 lead, and all the Cardinals could do was chase them down with three runs in the ninth inning.

Too little, too late. And now the club faced the prospect of a sweep by Cincinnati, something the players would hear about from the Reds for quite some time. And true to form, on Sunday, May 15, it was a slugfest, with both teams trading off hits and runs until the last inning, when the Reds pulled away to stay, 9–7.

The series was a tough one because it set the tone for bragging rights between the two teams. And, to make matters worse, Milwaukee appeared to be a contender as well.

Paul didn't have a great series, although he hit a homer in the last game after several near misses on Friday and Saturday. It was extremely tempting to swing for the fences at Great American Park, as it was a bandbox for hitters. "Next time," thought Paul, "I'm going to revert to just having good at bats and trying to put good swings on the ball. No shooting for the fences. It just doesn't work for me."

And to cap off the weekend, Colby Rakers continued to struggle at the plate and in the field. In the Friday game, he went hitless and caused a routine fly ball to drop in for a double after he inexplicably stopped chasing it. In a radio interview after the game, he was quick to point out that he backed off, even though it was obvious to everyone in the park that the ball was hit to center field. "It's going to be a long season in the field. I've got two older players on either side of me, neither who will win a Gold Glove this season. As a result, I feel that I have to cover an awful lot of ground."

When Tony found out about the remarks, he called in Colby to his office and reminded him of a cardinal rule: no throwing your teammates under the bus.

"But Skipper, these guys run like they have concrete shoes on. I don't mind playing with them, but I can't get to every ball hit to the gaps."

Tony looked at Colby and with a deep penetrating stare, "I said, no bad-mouthing teammates to the public. I'm the manager on this team, and if I see a need to replace one of these so-called older guys for defense, I'll do it. But the fact of the matter is you flat-out quit on that ball today. It looked bad to the team, the fans, and the media, and your excuses only make it worse. You've got to start getting your head into the game for a full nine innings, not just when you feel like it. I don't want to have this conversation again with you, or you may be spending a lot of time on the bench in Memphis. Got it?"

"I got it. I don't like it, but I got it," said Colby. As he walked back into the players' clubhouse and to his locker, you could hear him muttering "that sonofabitch."

Meanwhile, Paul was facing his ongoing internal battle with Jack, as in Jack Daniel's. Other than his unfortunate stop at Sam's on his off day and his wonderful weekend in Buckhead, Paul had refrained from drinking alcohol. He knew, deep down, that it was his Achilles' heel. "How to cope…how to cope," he wondered. He needed Heather to get through the rough patches ahead.

One thing that helped was hitting the workout room, both at Paul's summer residence and at the stadium. As an older player, Paul felt the games starting to accumulate and take their toll. Baseball was a six-month marathon, not counting spring training games, and not a day or a week-long sprint. Baseball also had ups and downs, just like real life. A sweep of a three-game series could easily be followed by a six-game losing skid. The key was not to panic and to play through the inevitable tough times.

Paul started to experience more symptoms that his liver was not functioning at peak condition. He was getting fatigued faster; he was seeing blood in his bathroom visits; and he was experiencing aches and pains with routine activity, including swinging a bat or throwing a ball.

CHAPTER EIGHTEEN

The Phillies came to town Monday, May 16, and Tuesday, May 17, for a short series. They were the odds-on favorites to win the National League pennant, but that didn't stop the Cards from sweeping them in two well-pitched games, 3–1 and 2–1. Paul's homer in the second game with a man on board was the difference maker.

The "old" Paul would have celebrated with alcohol well into the wee hours. The "not-so-new" Paul knew better and headed back to his home after a postgame sandwich and quick shower. The message light on his phone was flashing—a surprise, since almost all communication nowadays came via texting. The message, repeated several times, was from Nikki. "I'm in trouble and need your help. Please call me at this number as soon as you get in."

Paul immediately dialed the number.

"Nikki, it's your 'sailor' friend," Paul said after he called the unfamiliar number. "What gives with the cloak and dagger stuff? Where are you? This area code sounds like Dallas."

"Hi, Paul."

"Wow," thought, Paul. "It's unusual for her to use my actual name."

"Sorry for the gamesmanship, but I am in the Dallas area. I didn't want to call you on my cell because I was afraid the call might be more easily hacked versus the line I'm on. All I can tell you is that I'm pretty sure we're safe on this connection."

"What the hell is going on, Nikki? This is starting to sound like an episode from *Law & Order*."

"You're right about that. Do you care about me? Can I trust you to ask you for help and not have you run away from me?"

"Those are loaded questions, Nikki. Of course I care about you. I'm not sure what our relationship is all about, but you should know I'll try to help you. Do you need money?"

"My problem is deeper than money. More like control and influence, leading to money and perhaps bragging rights among competing bad guys."

"You've lost me."

"Are you going to be visiting the Astros in the near future?"

"Let me check," as Paul looked at a minischedule he kept in his wallet. "It says here on the schedule that it won't be until June 7."

"It can wait till then. Can we plan to meet on the evening of the sixth?"

"Probably. Looks like we're playing the Cubs at home on the fifth, and we have a day off on the sixth. Damn. You say you're in trouble, you call me multiple times, you are hiding somewhere, and you say it can wait for a couple weeks?"

"Yes."

"Just yes? Okay, I'm through prying. I'll touch base with you as we get closer to the sixth."

"Thanks for kinda sorta understanding. I have to go now. Take care." And then the line was dead.

"Wow, what the hell was that all about?" thought Paul. "If she thinks it can wait, then so be it. But it sure is a curious twist to what so far has been a little innocent fun."

Speaking of the Astros, they, like the Phillies, came into Saint Louis for a short two-game series on Wednesday, May 18, and Thursday, May 19. The games between the two teams used to be pressure packed and were destined to be a big part of the annual pennant race. The Astros, though, were going through a rebuilding phase and did not have the seasoned talent to compete at a high level. In sum, the time was ripe for a few Cardinals wins. And that's just what the Cardinals did, winning 5–1 behind strong starting pitching by Kyle Flynn in the first game, followed by an equally good performance by reliever-turned-starter Kyle

McCormick, winning 4–2. Paul had two good days at the plate, including a home run in the second game.

The skipper was beside himself regarding what to do with Colby. His hitting wasn't coming around. His fielding was barely adequate. And worst of all, his attitude was downright crappy. Sending him down to Memphis was not an option, as senior management advised Tony that Colby would have to fine-tune his game at the major-league club level. "Fine-tune, my butt," thought Tony. "The boys upstairs have a long wait if they think all Colby needs is some 'fine-tuning'!"

His father started to become more of a fixture in the clubhouse and almost got kicked out when he tried to access tape in the video room. "This is offensive as hell to us, Tony," said Mark O'Bannon. Jose Nieves and Dave McFarlin, Cardinals coaches, both nodded as they sat in the skipper's office. "We can't have Tony Rakers hanging around and undermining our authority regarding coaching. He's got to go, even if that means trading Colby in the process."

"I hear you. I need a list of concrete examples where Tony Rakers has been disruptive to your coaching activities," Tony said. "I've talked in general terms with John, but specifics are going to be needed if we are to ban this guy from our facilities. Colby is the crown jewel of our farm system. And if you ask John, we have to find a way to make this work."

"Then can you tell Tony Rakers to butt out?" asked Jose Nieves.

"And can you remind Colby that he is not above constructive criticism by us?" asked Dave McFarlin.

"Yes, they'll both get the messages. No guarantee that they will sink in, but we will address the matters if you give me something to work with.

"And," thought Tony LoDuca, "Mr. Rakers is no doubt behind the letter campaign. Sooner or later, he'll slip up, and that will be the end of this problem with his son."

It was times like this that made Tony think seriously about hanging his spikes up. On one hand, his years as manager of three teams had been thoroughly enjoyable. Sure there were ups and downs but the over-all experience had been a positive one. Baseball was his life for a good portion of each calendar year. Sure there were things to get involved in at home, but after a few weeks he was itching to put his uniform back on. And his family was certainly glad to see him, and the feeling was mutual. But still, as winter gradually made way towards spring, Tony knew deep down that it would be very difficult to call it quits after the 2011 season.

CHAPTER NINETEEN

It was back on the road for the Cardinals, with three games in Kansas City from Friday, May 20, through Sunday, May 22; three more in San Diego from Monday, May 23, through Wednesday, May 25; a day off on Thursday, May 26; another three games in Denver from Friday, May 27, through Sunday, May 29; and then a chance to return home.

The Kansas City series was always compelling, even though the Royals had not been a very good team in many years. They treated the series with the Cardinals like postseason baseball and filled the ballpark each game. The Cardinals were shut out the first game 3–0, but they came back to win the second one 9–8, as well as the finale 3–1. Paul, once again, had a good series, including home runs in each of the wins. And his defense was just as outstanding, having pulled back home run–bound balls in each victory with leaping catches at the left-field wall.

Paul became extremely concerned about his supply of pine tar, as well as his continued bouts with fatigue. He even looked at the possibility of getting some commercial pine tar if necessary, but he was somehow convinced that the North Woods pine tar had some special features that worked with his grip. He was most concerned that any changes midstream would put his fluid swing in jeopardy.

In addition, things were not going so well chasing Heather down. Despite his best efforts, he still had not made contact with her. Was this the end of what could have been a great relationship? Did he even deserve to have one with her, based on his recent dalliance with the mysterious Nikki Cole?

And still no word from the Meyer Clinic. He knew that the liver issue needed resolution. Could he last the rest of the season during his one last hurrah, or was he destined to pull up stakes and end what had so far been a most gratifying experience with the Cardinals?

Paul's old response to these issues would be to find a barstool and solve his problems with a cold beer or two, or six or eight. Paul's current approach was to take one day at a time—no revolutionary concept, but it was working for the most part. Still, the absence of Heather in his life left a hole, something he hadn't felt in a considerable amount of time.

The team headed to San Diego following the Kansas City series and continued its trend of winning two games out of three. The San Diego ballpark was not known for being kind to right-handed batters and was considered one of the better pitcher's ballparks in the major leagues. Paul had a double in each game, but was not able to launch one out. When asked about it by a newspaper reporter, he said, "I always was a gap hitter and am content with any kind of hit that helps the team score runs."

Trite, but also true in the case of Paul Kolbe. Of course, the pine tar/no batting gloves issue surfaced again in San Diego. As was the case in the other cities Saint Louis had visited during the season, local media personnel used the "throwback" term again, though they couldn't argue with the success Paul was having.

"Paul, do you think that you are going to spark a trend back to the Cardinals' Gashouse Gang days when batting gloves didn't exist and batters routinely used substances like pine tar to maintain a good grip on their bats?" asked one particularly attractive female beat reporter for Fox Sports Southern California.

"I highly doubt it. I'm not trying set a trend. I'm trying to deploy a strategy that is working for me. If that means I have to stand on my head to bat, I'll try that too. I think the so-called throwback approach is fun for the fans and media, but it really is just a technique that is working for one batter in the league: me. I would encourage any hitter, especially those in their early years of playing baseball, to take the advice of their coaches, and that generally means the use of batting gloves.

"On the other hand, I think the stuff might help you and the other on-field reporters grip your microphones better. Let me know if you'd like to give it a try," laughed Paul. By trivializing the issue he had hoped that it would finally go away. It finally did, once Paul cycled through each town on the Cards road schedule.

With that matter addressed for the umpteenth time, Paul and the rest of the team headed for their hotel via a chartered coach.

The club had another day off on May 26 as the team worked its way to Denver to visit the Colorado Rockies for three games. This was a sobering time for Paul, as he experienced a birthday, thirty nine big ones, which is ancient by baseball standards. The team gave him a cake in the clubhouse and had fun over-the-hill gifts for him, plus the Colorado Rockies acknowledged his birthday through their electronic scoreboard.

When asked to confirm his age at thirty nine by the local Denver newspaper, he was quoted as saying this one "was north of thirty." After a chuckle or two, the subject of age was dropped, except for a note that appeared in his locker. Paul knew who had put it there and what vile crap it would say, but he was curious anyway:

Happy Birthday, Paul

What does this make you, fifty? Isn't it time for you to hang those spikes of yours up now? Have you seen the kids on the bench? They deserve to play. You deserve to be put out to pasture. Sure you had a few hits and snagged a few balls. Bravo for you. Do you really think you can continue doing this for a full season? Maybe you ought to have a drink or two or three and think about asking for your release. It's time, birthday boy, for you to go.

A very concerned fan.
PS: Take Tony LoGoofball with you, too!

"Damn," thought Paul. "I have to show this one to Tony, too, because 'concerned fan' mentioned him again."

With the birthday safely tucked away on Friday, Paul went to Coors Field a little earlier than usual; he knew that Tony would be in his office sorting out which batters had had the most success against the scheduled Rockies starter. He would also look at rest and injury issues, plus who was hot and who was not. Another issue unique to consider was the thinner air in Denver. Even though the Rockies have developed an innovative procedure to store game balls in climate control humidors, their ballpark is still known for producing a high number of home runs. And finally, he would take into consideration his intuition based on over thirty years of managing in the major leagues. He was a big believer in the numbers associated with the game, but sometimes he just went with his gut instinct about a player and his position in the batting order.

Paul checked in through the players' entrance, proceeded directly to Tony's office, and waited by the door.

"What's up, Paul?" asked Tony as he looked up from studying lineup options.

Paul simply smiled and handed the "birthday" note to the skipper.

"Sonofabitch!" exclaimed Tony as Paul showed him yet another note from "concerned fan."

"This has got to stop. This goes beyond fan criticism. This is an ongoing campaign of harassment, and if our senior management won't do something about Tony Rakers, then I will." Paul hadn't seen Tony this angry before in his brief time with the club. And unless he was an unfortunate umpire on the other side of the argument with him, it was doubtful that anyone else in the club had seen this side of Tony either.

He was so angry that he left the clubhouse and marched up to John Nowicki's suite. John was in the middle of a conversation with several scouts when Tony interrupted him, literally throwing the letter at John as he spoke. "I've had enough of this crap from Colby's dad. You said you would take care of this matter. It's going to come down real soon to

Colby or me. You will have to make a choice. It's a month to the trade deadline. You need to think real hard about changing your mind about keeping our problem child. Don't be surprised if you hear that Tony Rakers has been banned from the clubhouse, and don't be surprised if you hear about him getting punched out by one or more of my coaches, or maybe even me."

"Whoa, Tony," John said, backing up from LoDuca. "This isn't like you at all. Let's go inside the anteroom here and have a closed-door session about this matter." With that gesture, John was able to take the discussion away from anyone else inside or outside the organization's purview. John also finally realized that Colby and his father were more than just prima donnas. They were disruptive to the coaching staff, the manager, and one of the best players on the team: Paul Kolbe.

"You've got every right to be upset. I didn't realize how deep this situation was, and as much grief as a trade would cause me with ownership, I'm willing to start research into getting whatever we reasonably can for Colby, if that is what you think needs to be done at this point in time. But we can't just give him away."

"That's only fair, John. I could play games and sit him down for every game until you and ownership forced me to play him, but you can imagine how disruptive something like that would be. No, the best approach is to remove this cancer in the clubhouse, even if his offense and defense was good, which of course it's not! Lastly, you pulled sending him back to Memphis off the table and I agree; it would only prolong the issue and, frankly, disrupt the development of others in our system." With that, Tony turned and left the GM's office.

Next up were the Colorado Rockies in Denver. Coors Field was a challenge for outfielders due to the field dimensions, particularly in right. In fact, some teams actually moved their center fielder to right at Coors. Tony, however, did not do this, as he did not want to play Paul and Lance next to each other for fear of potential balls getting past both of them.

Al Robles, Matt Bradley, Lance Champlin, and David Page all homered at least once, including Paul, who chipped in two of his own. And the Cards won the first game of the series 10–3, lost the second game by a whopping 15–4, but came back to win the finale 4–3. All in all, it was a tiring but successful trip.

CHAPTER TWENTY

Home sweet home. Road trips like the completed one can take a lot out of a player and the team as a whole. In Paul's case, it was especially tiring because he was not used to the daily grind, and his general health, thanks to his deteriorating liver, was below par. He tried to hide his lack of energy by drinking cup after cup of coffee before and even during games, but then he would experience a caffeine crash when each game ended. On the lighter side, he wasn't used to holding such volumes of liquid, and there were a few times in left field that he almost asked for a time-out so he could visit the bathroom in the bullpen.

Extra-inning games were especially tiresome, and, of course, the past road trip had one ten-inning game in Kansas City (a 9–8 Cardinals win) and an eleven-inning game in San Diego (another Cardinals win at 3–2). Sensing the fatigue factor was taking hold of Paul, Tony LoDuca started to sub one of the so-called kids (either right-handed-hitting Alan Cooper or left-handed-hitting John Keyes) after Paul's final at bats in the eighth or ninth innings. The upside of this action was to rest Paul a little, but the downside was a loss of his bat if the game went into extra innings. So far, the strategy had not backfired, as there was only one twelve-inning game played in early April before Paul started to be pulled from games.

And on cue, another letter arrived to address this issue. This time, it was written directly to Tony LoDuca.

Dear Tony:
Interesting new strategy deployed to get Paul
Kolbe out of games in the late innings. What
are you going to do when geezer Lance needs a

break too? Is the club too cheap to acquire legitimate talent? Does the club realize it has a farm system and might want to let some of the kids play every day to develop? And the way you've buried Colby Rakers is a crying shame. He is the best prospect you've had since Al Robles came up and you treat him like a clubhouse attendant. He is a legitimate five-tool talent; I thought a "future hall of fame" (ain't that a crock) manager like you could assess talent when you saw it. Any possibility that John Nowicki could trade you for a decent manager who knows talent and how to use it?

An extremely concerned fan

Once again, Tony sought John out. This time, he found him in his office, where he was alone on his phone.

"I've got to talk to you, John, right now!" said Tony as he marched into the office and slammed the door shut.

"Tony, calm down," said John. "Look, Hank, I've got a situation here I have to take care of. Let me get back to you in our suite tonight. Thanks!

"That, for your information, was our boss and owner, Hank Rheinhold. I suppose I'll have to explain what you were upset with tonight. Which, by the way, is what?"

"Tell Hank. Tell Hank's son. Tell Hank's daughter. Tell everyone at Rheinhold. Maybe something will get done. You and I had an agreement that you would take care of Tony Rakers. I'm telling you straight out, John, that if you don't, I'm walking out of the clubhouse, and my coaches will follow too. Are you prepared to put on a uniform?"

"Look, this isn't like you, Tony. I said I would address this matter, and I'm doing so. I did not think that Mr. Rakers would choose to harass you and Paul again so soon. You and I both know you wouldn't bail out on your players in the middle of a season, so can we sit down and map out a plan of action on how we're going to resolve this matter? We also need to discuss to what degree Mr. Rheinhold should be involved."

"That's fine, John," Tony said, as he started to calm down. "But several things. I have a team to run. We have a game tonight. You need to address this matter now, not later, directly with Tony Rakers. You also need to think about what you need to say to Hank. I don't want to talk with ownership when I need to be focusing on tonight's game. And as for bailing out on my players, you're absolutely correct, although I might consider sitting Colby for a while, quite a while, if he is not traded."

"Please don't do anything that you wouldn't normally do, Tony. I know you want to win as badly as anyone in the game, and this whole situation has angered you more than anything I can think of. I will make it my top priority to discuss the matter with Tony Rakers, and I will talk to Hank about the possibility of trading Colby.

"I'll tell you what I'd like you to focus on," said Tony. "We need a couple of relief pitchers, one righty and one lefty, and I don't care if they are rental players or not. We are losing games because of our bullpen, and I can rearrange things, but I still need a dependable seventh-inning guy and a lefty specialist. Whether that is fair market value or not, it's what we need. We can replace Colby with John Keyes, Alan Cooper, or even Adron Channing for the remainder of the season. So you don't need to add any prospects from the minors to any deals you make for an outfielder in return."

"Let me work on this, Tony. And for God's sake, calm down. I've never seen you like this."

"I'm sorry, but this guy gets my goat. And his son is wasting his talent. I can't get to him, and it doesn't seem that anyone outside of his father can either. In hindsight, he should have spent another year in the minors, but I agree with you. It's too late to send him down now. He would just brood and be the worse for it. I think this is one time we have to take a deal that will help us right now and move on. Maybe a trade will be a wake up call for him. Some folks might think of Colby as the next J. D. Dylan, but at least he netted us an outstanding pitcher in Adam Cartwright in return. I'm not so sure other teams will see as much potential in Colby as we have over the years."

"You're probably right, Tony," said John. "But I'll do my best to convince ownership a trade is necessary, and I promise you I'll get some help for the bullpen."

"Thanks, John. And sorry for barging in on you several times about this subject. I'm ninety-nine percent done with ranting and raving about it. Good luck and good hunting!"

With that matter settled, at least strategically, Tony walked briskly down the stairs to his office in the clubhouse and was ready to finish his prep work for the evening's game.

The Cardinals started off the home stand with an unusual four-game set with the San Francisco Giants, beginning Monday, May 30, and running through Thursday, June 2. This allowed the Giants to make only one trip to Saint Louis during the regular season instead of two. One visit per season was especially tricky when it came time to make a decision about calling games due to weather issues.

Fortunately, there was no inclement weather during this series, but perhaps it would have been helpful: the Cardinals dropped three of four to the Giants, squeaking by in the second game with a 4–3 win. Paul had an okay series, continuing to hit a few singles, a ringing double, and one homer in twenty plate appearances. He also stole a base when the pitcher completely ignored him. He was replaced in the third game, an eleven-inning affair, in the eighth inning. His replacement, Adron Channing, walked in his only plate appearance and stole second base, but he was stranded without scoring in the tenth. Although his team lost the game, Paul took some good-natured ribbing from his teammates about his stolen base.

"Hey, Kolbe," said Jake Hudson, one of the more vocal players (especially when he wasn't on his starting pitching day). "Just because you're playing left field doesn't mean you have to think you're Lou Stock. I know that Al loves those easy RBI opportunities, but don't you think you'd be better off hugging that first base bag until you could see a hit, walk, or an error? We don't want to be hauling your butt to the hospital now, do we?"

"No worries on that front, Jake. You might just have seen the first and the last stolen base of the season for me. Hopefully Skipper wasn't paying too close attention on that play or he might recruit me on his track team. I'm sneaky fast, with the emphasis on sneaky. I think I just caught the pitcher napping a little."

The Cardinals fared much better over the weekend of Friday, June 3, through Sunday, June 5, winning all three games against the Cubs—including a twelve-inning game Saturday and a ten-inning affair on Sunday evening. And it was a great series for Paul: 7 hits, 2 homers, 6 RBIs, several great running catches, and one assist at home plate in the second game of the series in extra innings. Who knew how that game would have ended without that great defensive play? Meanwhile, just about everyone else was hitting, too, including Colby Rakers. But Colby was still struggling in center field. He let several catchable balls drop in front of him. Plus, he didn't even try to catch one hard-hit ball to left center, preferring instead to take it off the wall on several bounces and make a rather weak attempt to get the runner at second base. The whole play looked so lackadaisical that the fans in the left- and right-field bleachers loudly booed Colby when he returned to his position. To acknowledge that he heard them, Colby ever so slightly tipped his cap, an act that brought on even more boos. At this point, Tony LoDuca decided he had had enough.

"Channing, out to center field. Tell Colby he's done for the day." This delighted bleacher fans to no end, as they all stood in unison and cheered as Channing came out, and Colby, with a look of surprise and then anger on his face, jogged into the dugout.

As he walked by the skipper on his way to the clubhouse, he glared at LoDuca and said, "I don't appreciate being shown up in front of forty thousand fans, especially since some of them were booing me."

"Then play better. Get your head in the game. You're done for the day. And it wasn't 'some' fans, more like both bleacher sections. Take a shower and leave."

Smelling a story, Bernie Madlock sat in the press booth high above home plate and observed the action through his binoculars. He could even make out the words exchanged between Colby and Tony, as they were short and sweet. He promised himself that he would talk to both Tony and Colby about this matter, but not tonight. He would give it a day or two to get past the first angry reaction from either party. After all, he reasoned, he did not work for the *National Intelligencer*. But he couldn't wait too long, or the story would become a nonstory; old news is just that—old news. Bernie took only a few road trips a season with the club, but given the relative urgency of following up with the key characters, he decided to take in the first series of the road trip in Houston.

CHAPTER TWENTY-ONE

Monday, June 6, the day finally came for Paul to see Nikki Cole and perhaps unravel the mystery surrounding her last several phone calls to him. She asked to meet at a small hotel in Sugar Land, southwest of the downtown area and away from where the team traditionally stayed near Minute Maid Park. The evening air was typically muggy for June in Houston: over ninety degrees, with humidity above 90 percent. Nikki walked into the lobby bar and looked quite cool in a pale yellow sleeveless dress, flip-flops, a large straw hat, and oversized sunglasses. Then again, Nikki always looked the essence of cool. But this evening, she had a worried look on her face even before she sat down next to Paul.

"So we can finally have a discussion about your issue," Paul said in greeting as he hugged her ever so slightly.

"Can we have a drink and then go to my room?" She said. "I'm staying here, at least through your three-game schedule."

"Sure. Grey Goose and tonic for the lady?"

"Yes, but light on the tonic."

In what seemed like record-setting time, Nikki downed her drink, and Paul decided to leave his on the bar. "Are you ready?" she asked Paul as he looked at his just-filled drink.

"Sure," said Paul. As he walked briskly to catch up with Nikki, he said to himself, "I wasn't planning on drinking anything anyway."

They proceeded to the lobby elevator and headed up. Paul then had to walk quickly again to stay up with Nikki. As soon as she walked into her suite, she made a beeline to the bar and duplicated her drink from downstairs. "Damn, Nikki, slow down," said Paul. "You're making me a nervous wreck, and I don't know why!"

"That's because I'm a nervous wreck. Here's the deal. I acquired a new client in Las Vegas awhile back, and everything was great. I got big tips, nice presents, and access to some of the nicest places in Vegas and my own town of Atlanta. In short, I got just what a girl in my profession likes—a nice guy with a big pocketbook. At some point, though, the client wanted to make the business relationship more than it was, even started discussing how he could divorce his wife. I told him that was where the invisible line was being crossed, and that I would have to end the appointments we had scheduled on an ongoing basis.

"Meanwhile, his wife found out about his philandering—and not just with me. There were others. And so she decided a preemptive strike was in order. She filed for divorce in California, and was planning on taking half of all his assets.

"In order to keep his business intact, he went to what could only be considered a nontraditional source for capital funding—loan sharks.

"These so-called investors have given my client until the end of the year to repay the loan, plus a hefty interest charge. He is desperate and started to think about legal and, if necessary, illegal ways to salvage the situation. He thought about me and, indirectly, about you. One evening we were, of all things, talking about baseball and he mentioned that you were the story of the year. I shouldn't have, but I told him you were a friend of mine. Besides being a bit jealous, he mentioned that you might be a perfect fit to help him get out of his jam, since it was highly unlikely that you would play again after this season.

"He also was aware of your talent and that you have a great chance to win the Triple Crown as long as your body holds up. In short, he thinks you're a perfect candidate to manipulate games—to the degree that you, as one individual, can. A missed hit here, a botched catch there could allow someone like my client to make and win bets and get the monkey off his back."

"So how is this pressure being applied to you?" asked Paul.

ONE LAST HURRAH

"As I said, my former client is a desperate man. He says he has friends who could cause me great physical harm. And if that doesn't work, they could come after you."

"Why did you wait so long to tell me this, Nikki?"

"I wanted to see if I could work things out on my own. Obviously, I was unsuccessful."

"I don't know what to say, Nikki. Have you ever heard of Pete Flowers? He amassed more hits in the majors than anyone, but he admitted to gambling on baseball as a manager, and as a result, he was banned from the game for life. It even meant he couldn't be voted into baseball's Hall of Fame because of his misdeeds. Every major-league clubhouse has a large sign upon exiting the door to go on the field that reminds all personnel that gambling is illegal. It's the most basic rule in the game—don't fucking gamble!"

"And that is precisely why my client sees this as a way to get back on his feet. All he needs is an outstanding player who is on a potential pennant-winning team, a player with little time horizon beyond the season. In a word, you."

"It's not gonna happen, Nikki. Sorry, no can do. My advice to you is to go to the authorities, something I'm very tempted to do myself."

"You can't, Paul. Please, think about me for a minute. You couldn't prove anything anyway. I didn't get to the part where this benefits you and me. My client is willing to share in his good success. Both you and I would ultimately get a nice package in cash or a wire transfer if we prefer. If you're game, you and I could take an extended vacation after your liver transplant, maybe to Europe, maybe to the Far East, maybe to Tahiti, wherever, but we both would be set for a long time. I could retire from my 'profession' along with you retiring from yours. And what harm would have been done?

"You have twenty-four other teammates that could bail you out if you supposedly failed every once in a while. Even you aren't good enough to affect the outcome of more than a run or two. Where my client is going to benefit from this idea is in the run total: less of your production equals more for the other team. It's not unusual for a star to get into a funk. Look at your teammates' totals over the season so far. Almost every player has undergone a hitting drought. It usually comes with the long season."

"You didn't hear anything I said, Nikki. I can't and I won't gamble or tank or whatever you so casually call it. We're done here. I'm leaving, and I don't think we'll see each other again. I hope you get some protection, preferably from legitimate resources. How 'bout the Houston Police Department for starters?"

"That's it? You're going to just walk away from me when I need your help? When I'm in danger?"

"I'm very sorry, Nikki. But don't include me in your mess. I can't be a party to your scam. After a lot of years, I'm finally doing something that is meaningful and worthwhile. I'm going to see it through."

"And what about us, Paul?"

"Nikki. Us as in you and me never existed. I like you, and you like me. Maybe we even like each other a little more than that. I certainly do. But there is another woman in my life. And there is something bigger than me with this baseball season. I'm seein' it through."

As Paul headed to the door to leave, Nikki grabbed her purse and pulled out a small handgun. "I can't let you walk away from me like this, Paul. I thought we were going to be a team after this discussion. My life is going to be in danger. I need your cooperation."

"What the…? Nikki, put the fucking gun down. Are you out of your mind? Are you really ready to shoot me? What the hell would that accomplish?"

"I can't let you just walk out of my life. I need you, and I need your help."

One of the advantages Paul had in such a unique situation was the element of surprise and his athletic agility, or what was left of it. He instinctively picked up a glass vase near the door and threw it, not at Nikki, but toward the other side of the room.

Nikki's initial reaction was to turn toward the vase crashing on the floor, giving Paul enough time to lunge at Nikki and knock the gun out of her hand. After a bit of tugging and wrestling on the floor, Paul subdued Nikki with a hammerlock hold, collected the gun, and then released her from his grip.

"I don't believe what just happened. Would you really have shot me?"

"No, the gun doesn't even have bullets in it. It was a last resort. I'm scared, and I don't know what to do. I also don't want you to walk out of my life."

After examining the gun, Paul said, "You're right: no bullets. I'm surprised I didn't crap in my pants when you pulled that thing out of your purse!"

"I'm sorry. I'm desperate."

"I know you are. Go to the police or hire a private bodyguard. If you need some money, I'll scare some up for you. As for me, I'll take my chances. I'm a dead man soon anyway, unless I get that liver. I have to go now. Unlike what I said, I will be in touch, but don't try to solve this guy's problem on your own."

"I don't want you to go. Stay with me tonight. Leave in the morning if you have to."

"I can't. This whole discussion has freaked me out. I'll check back with you later. You can do the same, but I have to leave," as he headed for the elevator door down the hallway.

CHAPTER TWENTY-TWO

The Houston series went about as predicted, with the Cardinals winning the first and third games and dropping the second one. Winning two of three at home and splitting on the road over the course of a season usually meant flying a division pennant at the end of the year. Things were going well for the club. The Cardinals were in first place by two and a half games over Milwaukee, and the future couldn't be any rosier. Which meant things were about to go wrong.

After the first game of the series, Bernie Madlock showed up in the clubhouse and stuck his head in Tony's office. "Hey, Tony. Congrats on a good win tonight. Do you have a minute?"

"Road trippin', Bernie? I thought you just sat behind a desk nowadays and popped into the Busch Stadium press box once in a while," replied Tony.

"You act like I'm retired or something. No, I'm still around. And please read my column sometime. I have one in the Monday, Wednesday, and Friday editions of the *P-G* and on-line, plus a wrap-up on Sundays. And I still get out once in a while, like on this first leg of your long road trip."

"Well, I'm flattered that you followed us to Texas. And believe it or not, I do read your column. Now what did you want to ask?"

"Are the Cardinals going to move Colby by the trade deadline? Based on the ongoing rift between him and just about everyone on the club, but especially because he looks lost at the plate and in the field."

Not wanting to start rumors that might be disruptive to the team (even if they were true), Tony tried to sidestep the question. "Bernie, you know I wouldn't speculate on something like a trade. And you know that every clubhouse has some degree of tension among the players. Guys are competing for playing time or for their next big contract, plus the vast majority on any team are interested in winning, in competing, and that brings tension when things aren't going as well as they could be."

"So Colby is a fixture in center field? My guess is that it won't be long before someone takes a swing or two at him because of a screw-up, and I suspect it might be Paul Kolbe or even you!'"

"Bernie, you've been on this same story since spring training. This is starting to sound like something out of a soap opera. Is that why you came to Houston, to check out this rumor?"

"No, Tony. But I thought I would ask while I'm here."

"Do me a favor, and maybe one for yourself, too. I ask that you drop this line of questioning, especially if you are in contact with Colby or Paul. I'm starting to feel like this subject is borderline soap opera stuff, I don't appreciate it, and I'm sure it irks the players as well."

"I can't promise that, Tony. You know I've hardly touched on this in the *P-G*, maybe more so on the web, but I look like a shill for the club if I ignore a potential big story like this one."

"Bernie, that's my point. It's a nonstory. If you and the others persist, we'll tighten up our clubhouse rules. Right now, you know you pretty much have access to anywhere except the training room and the showers. I'd like to keep it that way."

"I understand, but don't ask me to put a lid on this matter either if other media folks persist on following rumors about Colby."

"That's fair, but I'll say it again: I'll lock down the clubhouse if this issue becomes distracting to the team."

"I hear you. I'm not sure we're on the same page, Tony, but I hear you loud and clear."

CHAPTER TWENTY-THREE

The Cardinals continued their road trip with a three-game series in Milwaukee, starting Friday, June 10, and running through Sunday, June 12. It couldn't get much worse for the Cards, as they dropped all three games to the Brewers.

The first game of the series started the momentum rolling downhill. After loading the bases with no outs in the first inning and not getting a run out of it, the team could feel the momentum shift to Milwaukee. The Brewers scored one run in their half of the first inning, another in the second, third, fourth, and each inning through the eighth. Meanwhile, the Cardinals were totally stymied by the Brewers' pitching. Final score: 8–0. The Cardinals' lead shrank to one and a half games over Milwaukee.

The second and third games of the series didn't bring a win either, as Saint Louis lost 5–3 and 4–3, dropping out of first place by a half game.

After a rough weekend that netted only a few singles, Paul had virtually no pine tar left. He decided to take a clandestine trip to Rochester and be back in time to make the charter flight to Washington, DC, the following day. Staying overnight in Milwaukee was a departure from the norm, as the team routinely moved on to the next city as soon as possible, even if it meant arriving in the wee hours of the morning. In this case, several players, Tony LoDuca, and John Nowicki were invited to the MLB offices in Milwaukee on Monday, June 13, to provide their insight into incorporating meaningful instant replay into games at the major-league level. Of course, ownership, the players' union, and the umpires' association all would officially have to weigh in on the subject. The commissioner was conducting what could only be described as "what if" discussions to see where the hot buttons were. It was certainly enough of a reason to keep the team in Milwaukee for a little while longer, so Paul was off to the races Monday morning.

He rented a car at the hotel and started the four-and-a-half-hour trip to Rochester. On the way, he gave Sam a call and said he was coming to town again to look for Joe Fisher. He also asked whether he thought it might be a good idea to call Heather, even though he would be in town for just a few hours.

"You're welcome to hang around my place, Paul," advised Sam. "I hope your guy shows up. I'd hate to see that fast start of yours go down the tube just because of some pine tar. With regard to Heather, I would suggest you leave sleeping dogs lie. She'll come around. But give it a little more time."

Most of the trip was on interstate highway, and with only one pit stop for coffee and a bathroom break, Paul beat the projected time to Rochester by a good half hour.

"Hello, Sam. Am I too early for lunch?" he asked. It was 10:00 a.m.

"Hello, Paul. You're too early for a lot of things. We don't even open until 11:00 a.m., but come on in, and you can help me empty this coffeepot."

"Great idea. I'm at a loss as to what to do, Sam, about *both* subjects I mentioned to you over the phone. I don't know what else to do about Joe Fisher. Wait and hope he shows up? I don't have any other plans otherwise. And as for Heather, I'll take your advice and lay low for a while. In both cases, waiting with no end in sight is very frustrating."

"Call me a crazed optimist, but I think you're going to bat five hundred today."

"I would prefer Heather be the half that gets resolved today, but I really, really am in need of seeing Joe Fisher."

The lunchtime crowd started filing into the All Pro Sports Pub & Grill, and Paul noticed a distinctly different type of clientele during the daytime workweek. These folks were interested in a quick lunch and perhaps a beer, but for the most part, they were in a hurry to get back to work. Sam, recognizing this activity, created a separate menu for week-day lunches, consisting of cold and warm sandwiches, soups, and salads that could be ordered in ten minutes or less and allow for a thirty-to-forty-minute window for lunch. As a result, All Pro was as packed for lunch as it was for the early evening happy hour/dinner crowd.

"Sam, I'll take a Rueben with a side salad. Low-cal light ranch dressing on the side and an unsweetened ice tea when you get the chance. I'll be hanging out on your patio to get a little sun and some reading done."

"Got it. I'll have one of our servers bring it out shortly."

Paul became absorbed in a book and did not immediately notice the server was standing over him. "Mr. Kolbe, I have your lunch here. Seems as though there is an additional item on the tray that I don't see on your order ticket."

"Great, thanks. Would you mind just putting the food on the table? I appreciate your quick turnaround on my order."

"I'm afraid, sir, that we still have this item on the tray to discuss. Do you have a moment, sir?"

"Sure, but I'm confused. Just what is this item?"

"It seems to be an old-fashioned tobacco tin with some kind of substance inside it."

Just then, Paul looked up, and his "server" was actually Joe Fisher.

"Joe, is that you? What the…? Am I going crazy?"

"Yes, it's me. Put your book down, and let's talk for a minute before your sandwich gets cold."

"I don't know what to say, other than I'm very, extremely glad to see you!"

"I'm glad to see you, too, Paul. You're doing well. You're taking care of business, using the pine tar religiously. I'm very gratified that you took my advice on this matter and that it's working for you. The fact that you came up here on your own, risking potential severe penalties by your manager, is a testimony to your conviction on this matter. I thought you were the right person for the job early on, and I think you've proved this so far this season."

"I appreciate your confidence in me, Joe. But I've gotta ask you: Just what are you? A ghost? A spirit? A figment of my imagination? I know the pine tar is real—I use it, and it works. But I don't know about you. You're supposed to be dead, Joe. And you've been dead for decades. I don't understand who and what I'm dealing with."

"I'm afraid I can't answer your questions. Someday it will all come together for you, Paul. In the meantime, go with it. Let's face it. It's not every day that you can talk to someone whose body is six feet underground!"

"Okay, Joe. I'll accept you on faith. Faith that someday it will all be sorted out. In the meantime, thank you so much for the pine tar. I was worried that I might have to don the batting gloves if I ran out of tar."

"Not to worry, Paul. And you won't have to come up to Rochester before the end of the season. I'll find you! I hear you have a new hang-out—D.D.'s, near my 'hangout,' if you get my drift!"

After the exchange and Joe's departure, Paul quickly consumed his sandwich and headed back into the pub to look for Sam.

"Hey Sam, what's up with your serving staff?"

"I'm sorry, Paul. We are a little short-staffed today, and the patio is where we don't have good coverage. We'll get your sandwich out very soon to you."

"Sam! I'm done. The meal was served by none other than Joe Fisher. He left me this big tin of pine tar. I'm not kidding. He must have picked up my sandwich when no one was at the window. He's something else. I left enough money on the table to cover the meal and a nice tip. I've got to run. I'll call you when I get a chance to get back to Rochester. Take care, my friend!"

"You and this Joe apparition are some pair. Take care of yourself, Paul. I'm counting on being able to display your Triple Crown trophy for a while this winter. Don't let me down!"

Paul headed to the parking lot, but had a weird feeling all day that he was being followed. Nothing materialized out of this, except that he was constantly looking over his shoulder and his surroundings. He tried to talk himself out of doing this, but to no avail. For a while the drive back to Milwaukee was uneventful. Then a black Ram pickup truck with a hemi engine and blacked-out windows appeared seemingly out of nowhere and followed Paul all the way back to Milwaukee before peeling off the interstate to Saint Louis. It passed Paul doing what had to be at least eighty-five miles per hour, but he couldn't make out who was driving the truck. All he remembered was that it was big and noisy, and the driver was very aggressive about lane changes as it passed him. It would not be the last time he saw this vehicle.

Feeling quite satisfied after his long day, Paul made it back to the hotel in Milwaukee in time to join his fellow team members, and they were soon on their way to Washington, DC, for a three-game series with the Nationals.

He was one of the last players off the coach bus to the ballpark and walked swiftly to the players' entrance of the Nationals' sparkling new stadium and sat at his assigned locker. He started unbuttoning his shirt, and something startling struck him: the remainder of his original supply of North Woods pine tar was missing.

"Shit, I wonder who's playing games," said Paul to himself. "That stuff was supposed to be set in my locker like it always is by the bat boy." He immediately looked around the clubhouse and spotted Colby Rakers, who appeared preoccupied with tightening the laces on his fielder's glove.

"Hey, Colby."

"What's up, geezer?"

"You keep that line of crap going, and you and I will have a discussion outside of the clubhouse. I warned you in the past about being a smartass to me. You haven't seen my pine tar tin, have you?

"First off, anytime you wanna go, old man, we'll go. Secondly, jerk-off, I don't know a damn thing about your pine shit."

At that point, Paul gave Colby a shove, and Colby's whole body was slammed against his locker as he fell over his chair. The force of fall cut the side of Colby's head enough to bleed, enraging Colby in the process.

"You son of a bitch." He came up swinging with a left hook, which missed Paul wildly. Paul followed up with a right cross, which landed square on Colby's jaw, followed by a left uppercut to the same place. Colby slammed against the locker again, then slumped semiconscious to the bottom of it.

A pair of Cardinals came over and restrained Paul from inflicting further damage, and the trainer and Tony, as well as several coaches, converged on the scene.

"I don't know what the hell happened, but both of you are sitting out today's game. Paul, go back to the hotel now. And we'll send Colby back after the trainer takes a look at him. We are in a fucking pennant race, and you guys are acting like you're on the school playground!"

Knowing it would be futile to get into an explanation at that point, Paul did a one-eighty, returned to his locker, retrieved his personal items, and left the clubhouse, slamming the door in the process.

Of course, timing is everything, and who did he bump into on the way out? None other than Bernie Madlock, on yet another leg of the team's road trip.

"Hey Paul. Where're you goin'? There's a game to be played tonight."

"Ask Tony about that. I'll see you later, Bernie."

Curiosity now getting the best of him, Bernie entered the clubhouse and immediately saw a commotion around Colby's locker. Looking up, Tony advised the clubhouse attendant, "Get him out of here now."

Bernie, nonplussed, left and headed up to the press box, thinking he would wait till after the game to find out what the heck happened with the players. Meanwhile, the lineup was announced, and both Colby and Paul were missing.

The road trip continued to go badly for the Cards.

The first game of the series on Tuesday, June 14, saw the Cards jump out to a 3–1 lead, only to give up a total of eight runs in the middle innings. A ninth-inning charge netted three runs, but it was not enough to catch the Nationals. Final score: 8–6.

ONE LAST HURRAH

The second game of the series, on Wednesday, June 15, was a blow-out, 10–0, for Washington and continued the Cards' consecutive losing streak at five games and counting.

And the trip continued to be a miserable one for the Cards as they dropped the getaway day game on Thursday, June 16, 7–4. The losing streak was now six and counting.

The replacement kids, John Keyes and Alan Cooper, drove in a run each for the series, but they did not possess the power potential needed to push across more runs—at least not this early in their rookie seasons.

Following the first game, Bernie made his way down to the visiting team's clubhouse in search of Tony LoDuca.

"I thought you were only going to make the Houston leg, Bernie. What brings you to Washington?" asked Tony when he spotted Bernie.

"Hello, Tony. You keep telling me that the Colby story is a nonstory, then I see a ruckus going on at his locker before the game, and then I see both Colby and Paul out of the lineup. I'm trying my darndest to work with you, Skipper, but you're stonewalling me now, and I don't appreciate being manipulated on this subject.

"Someone is gonna run with this, and both the *P-G* and the Cardinals are going to have to justify why some third-rate media outlet got the jump on both of us. What do you say, Tony? How 'bout giving me something I can work with, something I can satisfy my bosses with when this thing hits the fan."

"Come into my office, and let's talk." Tony ushered Bernie into his office and closed the door. "I admit, I have been a bit evasive about what has been going on, but I don't want to handcuff Nowicki regarding what he can get for Colby if we do trade him. Yes, we are seriously exploring talks, but they have to be hush-hush at this stage, or we lose leverage with any potential trading partners. And frankly, it will be virtually impossible to get fair market value for Colby if the other teams think we have to move him.

"And my point of view, especially after what happened today, is that we have to move him. As for Paul, he is doing a hell of a job keeping us in this pennant race, something Colby isn't. Colby has all the talent in the world, and I just can't get through to him. Then again, it doesn't seem that any other professional baseball person can either."

"Any thoughts about hiring Colby's dad on a temporary basis to help Colby sort things out?"

"Bernie, you're insulting your own intelligence when you ask that kind of question. Maybe we should hire his mother to change his diapers, too?"

"Sorry, Tony. I thought a little levity might diffuse this conversation a bit. Look, I'm all for the Cardinals doing well, and I don't want to sabotage the team's efforts to make personnel moves. I can park this for a while, but you'll have to come up with a really good reason why you sat down two starters for the series at tonight's press conference. Otherwise, I'm going to have to spread some ink on this matter sooner than later."

"That's fair, and I appreciate your cooperation. I'm going to tell the media exactly what occurred—both players are sitting out the series for violating team rules. And those team rules violated—which, by the way, are related to fighting in the clubhouse—are confidential. Both players will be back in the lineup when we return home for the Kansas City Royals series.

CHAPTER TWENTY-FOUR

Maybe some home cooking was all the club needed as it returned to take on Kansas City again for a weekend series from Friday, June 17, to Sunday, June 19. But adding insult to injury, the Royals won a squeaker, 5–4, taking the Cardinals' losing streak to seven.

Knowing that seasons ebb and flow, Tony wasn't ready to panic. After all, the team was only a game out of first place now. But the team wasn't hitting much. Only Al and Lance seemed to be holding up the offense, with two homers apiece for the series. Colby was hitless in twelve at bats, and as a result, his season batting average shrank to the .225 range. He hadn't said a word to Paul, and other than him glaring at Paul from time to time, it appeared that an uneasy truce had settled between the players.

Paul was in a terrible hitting slump, and he was convinced it was because he had lost his original pine tar and had sent his replacement tin back to Saint Louis for safekeeping.

With the end of June fast approaching, it didn't appear that a deal was imminent for Colby. Then out of the blue, John Nowicki stopped by the clubhouse after the loss to Kansas City and asked Tony if he could meet with him.

"Sure, John. Let's go in my office," Tony said as he ushered John in and closed the door.

"Tony, I'm pretty excited about a potential deal for Colby, but I wanted to run it by you first. Toronto is interested. They need a center fielder, and his potential and relatively low salary for the next few years appeals to them. They are offering two relievers and a very good double-A shortstop prospect. The relievers, I think, fill the immediate need you have for this season—and maybe beyond if we can negotiate something, plus the double-A prospect has a legit chance of getting to the big club in the next year or two."

"I wouldn't know the prospect, so I'll respect your judgment on that. Who are the two relievers?"

"Octavio Doty and Mark Recipko."

"I like that. Octavio has been a closer in the past, but he is more suited as a seventh-inning guy nowadays. That's just what we need. Mark is even potentially more valuable because he can get lefties out, eat up innings if necessary, and even start if we get in a pinch. Those two guys would help us a lot, John. Nice work!"

"Great, I'll advise Hank what we're considering, and unless he has an objection—especially since we will be adding a chunk of payroll with this move—then we'll proceed. We might even be able to close this out by the weekend so you have your new guys at the start of the Philadelphia series."

"Works for me. By the way, Toronto comes to town after the Phillies series, so we might be able to get an early read on the trade if it works out. Can you imagine the kind of response Colby would get when he steps into the batter's box for the first time in a visitor's uniform?"

"By comparison, it would probably make Barry Blake look good if he came back to play for the Giants," chipped in John.

"That's not all that's been on my mind lately, John. I'm sure you're thinking that getting rid of Colby is my number one priority, but winning games is my main objective. You may as well know now so this trade idea doesn't get caught up in what I'm going to tell you. I've been giving a lot of thought to retiring after the end of this season, regardless how things work out. I want to solve the Colby Rakers issue because I think it's important to the organization that he moves on. But the most important thing to me is winning. I'd love to bring home an eleventh World Championship in 2011. Then maybe someone else can talk about number twelve in 2012!"

"I knew this day would come sometime, but not this season, when we're doing so well."

"You and I both know there is never a good time to call it quits. Frankly, the thought of it scares the hell out of me! I don't have any hobbies. I live alone six months out of the year. What am I supposed to do, especially when baseball starts up again?"

"I have the feeling that you'll be in high demand within the baseball industry immediately after the World Series, if you do decide to retire. Don't do anything hasty, Tony. Give this some more thought. I appreciate the heads-up this early, but damn, I can't envision anyone in that dugout but you!" said John.

"I appreciate that, John. Let's hope it's perfect timing because we won, but we can cross that bridge a little later. I also don't want to mention this to anyone just yet either. I'm not sure when, but definitely not now. I think the focus for everyone should continue to be on the team."

"I agree, Tony. I'll keep a lid on this conversation. Now can we win a ball game? This Kansas City bunch needs to be taught a lesson!"

John Nowicki left Tony's office and promptly went to his suite. He called Hank Rheinhold's private cell phone number and waited through a half dozen rings.

"Hank here; how're you doin' John? It's not too often we hear from you pregame. Anything wrong?"

"I need to talk to you about a trade for Colby. But that can wait for a few hours. I thought, more importantly, that you should know about a conversation I just had with Tony. He told me that he has given a lot of thought about retiring after this season. It's not about trying to get more money or staff support, or frankly anything other than an acknowledgment on his part that he has had enough."

"Dammit, John! We can't afford to lose Tony. He's been a big part of the team's success since he came here in 1996. I can't imagine anyone else in that dugout."

"Me neither. But let's let the process play out. In the meantime, I'll start thinking about options."

The second game of the series on Saturday, June 18, saw the Cardinals break through and win a one-run game 5–4. And they did it in style with a walk-off homer in the ninth inning by Paul. After the game, longtime Cardinals announcer Mike Shaughnessy asked Paul if he'd ever had a walk-off homer before.

"Yes, Mike, I have. Numerous times, only it was playing sponge ball at a boyhood friend's house. A homer was a ball hit from the gate at the back of the friend's yard to the roof. Other than that, the answer is no, never, and I would have wagered it was never gonna happen. The good news is that we got the monkey off our backs, at least for one game. Now we can put that nasty little losing streak behind us and play some winning Cardinals baseball!"

In the rubber game of the series, both teams traded runs early and then just stopped hitting in the middle innings of the game. Fernando Sanchez, in his second inning of relief, shut the Royals down one, two, three in the ninth. The top of the Cardinals lineup would be up in the bottom of the ninth: Rafael Martinez, Paul Kolbe, and Al Robles. With the score tied 4–4, Martinez, swinging at the first pitch, ripped a line drive down the left-field line, but it was caught by the third baseman, who was hugging the chalk to prevent any extra-base hits. Paul, usually not one to play hunches, decided as he kicked dirt in the batter's box that the pitcher would be thinking of laying one in for a strike to get ahead on the count.

And Paul guessed right, as a moderately moving fastball, perhaps eighty-eight miles or so per hour, came belt-high near the center of the plate. Paul's eyes widened considerably for a second, and he said to himself, "Damn, I was right. Good night, Irene!" as he swung through the zone almost until the bat came around behind him, just barely missing the Royals catcher's helmet. But there was no doubt about where the ball was going to land. So for the last two games, the Cardinals won by identical scores: 5–4.

Both games featured a walk-off homer, proving that indeed lightning can strike twice. For the rest of the season, it was not unusual for a teammate to address Paul as "First Pitch" rather than by his name.

ONE LAST HURRAH

Bernie Madlock even acknowledged the new nickname in a burb on his *Bernie's Bytes* on line column:

"First Pitch' Kolbe sends the fans home happy, again

Paul Kolbe has shown remarkable patience in his plate appearances this season, averaging over five pitches per trip to the plate. Every pitcher in the league knows his approach and reminds himself of Paul's tendencies when going over 'the book' on the Cards left fielder. So what does Paul do about this 'book' on him? He changes some pages, even a chapter or two, by going after the first pitch and homering in a walk off win for the Cardinals. Not once, but twice in a row. Nice work, Paul Kolbe. Thanks for reading.

CHAPTER TWENTY-FIVE

It was at this inopportune time that Paul received news from Rochester that a liver was finally available for him. His response?

"No thanks."

"*No thanks?* But Paul, you realize that you've waited two years for this moment," his doctor reminded him. "And there are no guarantees that another one will become available in time for you."

"I understand, and I have to believe another one will become available. Trust me, Doctor, I have as great a will to get this done as ever. However, something really special is going on here with this pennant race. It's going to go down to the wire. And I can honestly say that I think without my help, this team was going nowhere. They need me. And I need this team, this opportunity to do something I've only dreamed about. The whole Triple Crown thing is nice, but this pennant race has been the crowning achievement of my checkered career. And, I'm doing it without the help, or rather hindrance, of booze."

"Well, Paul, I can honestly say I admire your passion, but I am also astounded that you would pass up this chance for a better life, or perhaps even for life itself. I'll see what I can do with the national transplant bank, but you are putting yourself way out on a limb by refusing this precious gift in front of you."

"Thank you, Doctor, for not giving up on me. I don't know how this story is going to play itself out, but I hope you're telling me that the operation went well sometime after the World Series."

Monday, June 20, was a day off at home for the club. Paul debated whether or not to fly up to Rochester to try to hunt down the elusive

Heather Alexander. He decided to take Sam's previous advice and let the situation play itself out.

Paul was getting desperate for hitting help, as other than the two spectacular home runs, he was hitting a modest (for him) .280 for the month. He decided the next best thing to do was to visit his new hangout in Sunset Place—D.D.'s Corner Pub, about a twenty-minute drive from his residence. It was late morning, and the place wasn't officially open, but D.D. let Paul in and poured him a cup of fresh coffee. Paul then went out on the patio and took in the relative quiet of the morning, watching cars go by on Gravois Road on the way to an early lunch or a business meeting, or whatever "normal" people did during their workweek.

He couldn't help but lament that he was in trouble without his original pine tar, and even said out loud, "Joe, Joe, I need your help. My hitting has gone into the tank. I can't even buy a base hit, let alone knock a pitched ball out of the park. I just gave up my liver transplant to help this team get into October. Was this all for nothing? Have I just been kidding myself this whole season about 'one last hurrah'?"

"You underestimate yourself, Paul," said a voice behind him. "Yes, it's me. I told you I'd look you up here sometime! I can see you're not ready to accept just who you are. I'm giving you one more chance, a chance to maximize your potential. Toss whatever pine tar you have left and keep this version under lock and key if you have to, but for goodness sake, don't lose this stuff again."

Paul turned around to respond to Joe, but the disembodied voice was gone. However, there was a quart-size canister on a patio table, enough pine tar to last through the season, including playoff rounds and the ultimate games: the World Series.

"Joe? Joe? Where are you? Where did you go? No answer, of course," Paul said out loud. "I would think I'm going crazy except for these cans of pine tar that keep showing up. This whole Joe Fisher thing doesn't make sense, but it's been working for me and I'm all in. Joe, I'll do you proud with this stuff, but I sure as hell would like to know what is going on!"

ONE LAST HURRAH

After the day off, the Cardinals had six more home games on the schedule, starting with Philadelphia from Tuesday, June 21, through Thursday, June 23, and then closing out the home stand with Toronto from Friday, June 24, through Sunday, June 26.

The official deadline for trading players without going through waivers was still more than a month away, but the rumor mill was working overtime in the American League. Toronto had started out of the gate very fast and was cruising along in first place when the sky fell in on them. They lost several position players for extended periods of the remaining season, including their center fielder for the rest of the season and maybe beyond after he crashed into the outfield wall and suffered a torn rotator cuff.

The one thing they had was an excess in relief pitching, so after looking around both leagues, the Blue Jays organization didn't take long before it realized that there might be a match in Saint Louis. Management knew from its scouts that there was some kind of turmoil between the manager and the player, and Colby was a true five-tool player, at least on paper. Maybe a change in scenery would allow the player to realize the high ceiling that baseball had predicted for him ever since he had started playing high school baseball in Georgia.

And a deal came together quickly, perhaps in some small way because the Blue Jays were coming to town for the first time in franchise history, thanks to interleague play. The deal was as John Nowicki previously outlined to Tony LoDuca: Colby Rakers straight up for Octavio Doty, Mark Recipko, and a high-ceiling prospect from the Blue Jays' AA farm club.

After the deal was announced, Tony advised the media that John Keyes and Alan Cooper would split time in center field for the present, and Doty and Recipko would be put to work immediately on the back end of games. Octavio would become a so-called seventh-inning specialist, and Recipko would become a situational lefty, with both pitchers used in a variety of other roles as dictated by circumstances. Also, Ryan Jefferson, key closer for the Cardinals for the past few years, was released, and Fernando Sanchez was shipped back to Memphis. To fill the closer's role, Jason Blevins was moved from his setup role, fulfilling a long-term vision that the team had for Jason when he was converted from being a catcher in the low minors.

A near-capacity crowd showed up for the Friday, June 24, meeting between these two teams. Jake Hudson kept the Blue Jays scoreless in the first inning, including a swinging strikeout on the number two hitter, Colby Rakers. The crowd roundly booed Colby when he was announced, and he nonchalantly tipped his cap, which brought about an even larger crescendo of boos. The boos reverted to cheers when he struck out swinging. And to cap off his frustration, he flung his bat and helmet toward the bat boy, forcing the kid to skip over the equipment as it skidded to the backstop. This, of course, brought on another round of boos, something that would be repeated with each additional at bat for Rakers, which included a groundout, a fly out, and finally another strikeout. Unfortunately, the rest of the Blue Jays were not as well contained, resulting in a 5–4 loss for the Cardinals. Paul had a hit, a double to the left-field wall, but was otherwise quiet at the plate.

Things did not improve for the Cardinals the next day as Jay Gomez, the only lefty in the starting rotation, stymied the Blue Jays for a few innings but ultimately surrendered a few long balls. The final score for game two of the series was 6–3 in favor of the Blue Jays. Colby had a similar day at the plate as he had the previous game against his old club—two strikeouts, a groundout, and a fly out. Thus far, he was 0-8 with his new club. Paul had a better day, even parking one in the left-field bleachers—a solo blast—but it wasn't enough to overtake the Blue Jays.

The final game of the series, before the Cardinals hit the road again, was played on a beautiful sunny Sunday. Kyle McCormick, a converted reliever, started for the Cardinals and accounted for himself quite well, trading zeros inning after inning until the sixth, when he appeared to run out of gas. By the time he was removed from the game, the Blue Jays had plated five runs, and a sweep appeared imminent. The Cardinals continued to get men on base the last few innings of the game, but couldn't punch them in. A sweep of the series did indeed occur, as the Blue Jays won the third and final game, 5–0. The three losses over the weekend, coupled with Milwaukee wins, dropped the Cardinals three games behind the Brewers. Colby did not play in the third game, as the Blue Jays' manager felt his new player had heard enough from the Cardinals fans and was pressing too much. Paul hit three balls to the warning track, but ultimately they were just long fly outs.

In separate interviews after the game, Cardinals announcer Mike Shaughnessy asked Tony LoDuca how he liked the trade with the Blue Jays. "You never like to trade away a potential five-tool player, especially one as young as Colby is, but we have legitimate needs in our bullpen if we are to compete for the pennant for the rest of the year. We also had a surplus of outfield personnel on the club even without Colby, so this gives some of the younger guys an opportunity to display their talents for the rest of the season. And as was mentioned, our bullpen got a big boost, and I got a whole lot smarter with a full house of relievers down there. I'm excited about their, and our, prospects for success."

Mike Shaughnessy's interview with Colby Rakers did not go as well as his interview with Tony. "Colby, thanks for coming on the airwaves with us. This can't be easy for you, so I appreciate you doing so. Was the trade a shock to you?"

"I'm kinda still in shock, Mike. I've only been in one organization, coming up through the Cardinals' minor-league system and arriving here to play every day."

"Were you disappointed at the fan reaction to your presence in another uniform?"

"Sure, who wouldn't be? It wasn't too long ago when they were cheering me. I don't think I deserve to be looked at here as the bad guy."

"Do you think this has anything to do with your relationship with the manager?"

"Absolutely. Tony and I just didn't get along, and I don't think the rest of the staff was very supportive either."

"There was a general feeling that your father had too much say in coaching you."

"He taught me how to play the game at six years old. He was the one person I could go to with questions when my swing was out of whack. I was just more comfortable working with my dad."

"Well I hope things work out for you in Toronto. Looks like they have the makings of a contender this season. Maybe we'll see you again in the World Series!"

"Thanks, Mike, and for you fickle fans that booed me, just remember the Jays swept your Cardinals. And yeah, it would be fun to play them again in October!"

CHAPTER TWENTY-SIX

With that parting shot, the Colby Rakers era came officially to a close in Saint Louis. Maybe so, but the case of the missing pine tar had not. Maybe Colby Rakers had his faults, but swiping pine tar may not have been one of them.

And in the Friday edition of "Bernie's Hits & Misses," Bernie Madlock had this to say about the trade:

Cardinals Error

The Cardinals pulled the trigger on a long-rumored trade to send Colby Rakers to the hinterlands of Toronto in exchange for relief-pitching help. The trade, on the surface, makes a lot of sense. The Cardinals are driving for a pennant, but the bullpen needed shoring up with dependable help. So the short-term goal of playing in October will probably be met. How far in October, who knows? I've said it before and I'll say it again: the best team doesn't always win in the playoffs, but rather the hottest team. Below the surface is where this trade is troublesome to me. Colby is a legitimate five-tool player who hasn't been able to turn his potential into reality. A little more maturation and who knows? Maybe this trade will help jolt him into realizing that playing hard every second of the day is more important than cheating yourself out of maximum performance. My guess is that he'll learn, but in Toronto and not Saint Louis. And what about the relievers the Cardinals acquired in the trade? They are free agents at the end of the season and will test the market. More than likely they'll get more years and more dollars than the Cardinals are interested in shelling out. Final score? Toronto: One potential star. Saint Louis: shut out after this season; no hits, no runs, one big error. Thanks for reading.

CHAPTER TWENTY-SEVEN

The Cardinals weren't scheduled to visit Atlanta again for the rest of the season, but Paul was worried about Nikki, as he had not heard from her since their meeting in early June in Houston. He was sufficiently concerned that he asked the skipper if he could take a different flight after the current series from Baltimore to Tampa through Atlanta to make sure a very close friend was okay.

"This isn't going to be another Rochester disaster, is it, Paul?"

"Skipper, I learned my lesson from that trip to Rochester earlier in the season. I'll be at the team hotel and in bed before most guys on the team are back from dinner!"

"This is highly unusual, especially with what previously happened, but you could use a day off anyway. Whether you make it on time or not, you can ride the pine the first game of the series, unless I need a late-inning pinch hitter or someone gets hurt. You've earned some time off, and I need you for the second half of the season."

"I appreciate it, Tony. I realize that this is that the last request you would expect from me, but I am literally dealing with a life-and-death issue here. I'll be the first player at the park in Tampa."

The series with Baltimore started on Tuesday, June 28, and ended on Thursday, June 30. It went much better, as the Cardinals swept the Orioles 6–2, 5–1, and 9–6. Paul had one homer and three RBIs for the series. He also hit .589 for the three games, raising his overall batting average to .335. The second game of the series was notable for the fact that it marked the statistical half of the season.

Following the third game in the Orioles series, Paul peeled off his jersey and took perhaps the fastest shower of his life. He had all his personal belongings and bags with him, so before anyone else could even get out of the showers, Paul was headed for BWI airport in a cab.

At this point in the season, it looked like four candidates had a legitimate shot at a Triple Crown in the National League:

	Home Runs	RBIs	Average
Paul Kolbe, Cardinals	22	58	.335
Al Robles, Cardinals	24	52	.327
Joey Costa, Reds	23	49	.328
Carlos Vasquez, Rockies	22	55	.335

Also at this point, the Cardinals were 44-38, one game behind Milwaukee for the Central Division title, and trailing Atlanta by two and one-half games for the wild card spot. The Braves' record was 46-35.

Fortunately, there was a steady stream of flights between Baltimore and Atlanta on Delta, so he was able to hop on a flight almost as soon as he could get rid of his bags outside the terminal at the check-in station.

He had only been to Nikki's place once before, but he had the address, a condo in the northwest suburbs, away from the airport, which was on the southwest side of town. He knew he would be there, out of necessity, for just an hour or two, so he had his bags sent directly to Tampa for his pickup upon arrival in Tampa.

He quick-stepped off the plane all the way to the rental car counter, picked up a rental car, drove to Nikki's complex, and, not sure of the exact location, parked his vehicle near the main office. He then went inside and asked the on-premise manager to verify which building was Nikki's.

"I'm sorry to be the bearer of bad news, but that residence is currently empty. Relatives of Nikki's are going through the contents of the place and then are going to put it on the market once disposition of her possessions is complete."

"I'm confused. What happened to Nikki? Where did she go?"

"She accidently drowned in an offshore accident off an excursion boat several weeks ago. She slipped with a drink in her hand and fell over a railing off the coast at Hilton Head. Her body was never recovered, but the ship was a quarter mile offshore. Gee, I'm sorry to have to be the one to tell you. Are you a friend or a relative?"

"I'm a friend. I haven't heard from her in about a month, so I stopped by to check up on her."

"Well, darndest thing. Nikki was an excellent swimmer, but apparently she just had a freak accident. There was no suspicion of foul play, so the coroner ruled it as an accidental death due to drowning."

"Do you have a family contact who might live in town? I'm only here for an hour or two, but I'd like to talk to someone about Nikki before I leave."

"Sure. She had a sister who lives about five miles from us. Here is her number. Her name is Reagan Cole. I don't know if she is married or not, but she at least has kept her family's last name."

Paul drove his rental car through the busy freeways in Atlanta to the address provided to him by the condo manager and waited a minute to see if anyone appeared to be home. A light was on, and one car was in the driveway. Taking a deep breath, Paul walked up to the front door and rang the bell. A somewhat older version of Nikki walked up to the foyer and peered outside.

Not recognizing Paul from any part of her life, Reagan, without opening the door, asked, "Hello, what can I do for you? If you're selling something, there are laws in our town prohibiting solicitations directly to residences."

"No, Reagan is it? I got your name from the manager of the residences where your sister Nikki lived. I'm a friend of Nikki's, but I hadn't heard from her for a while, and then I received the bad news from the gentleman I talked to there. I'm not sure if Nikki ever mentioned my name to you, but we became fast friends and had a bit of a falling-out recently."

"She never mentioned your name to me, but she talked about *you* all the time. You're the baseball player, aren't you? Why don't you come inside? I'd like to know what your thoughts are on what happened to my sister."

"Damn," thought Paul. "How do I explain the relationship without getting into what Nikki did for a living? And what about the gambling issue?"

"Paul, I'm Reagan, but you already know that. Can I get you some coffee? I'm afraid I'm having something a little stronger than that right now."

"I'd join you, but I've got a long day today. We play the Rays tomorrow, and I've got to hightail it down to Tampa or risk the wrath of the entire team."

"I appreciate you making a special effort to come see me about Nikki. She was just too good of a swimmer to drown, regardless of what the coroner says happened."

"How much of Nikki's career and personal life did she share with you, Reagan?"

"If you're wondering if I knew that Nikki was a professional escort, the answer is yes. I didn't approve of her lifestyle, but it was hard for her to give it up once she got used to making large sums of money while, most of the time, having fun, too."

"Were you aware of her recent run-in with a client who she become involved with and who wanted her to participate in an illicit gambling scheme?"

"You're referring to her attempt to get you to shave hits and runs during certain games? Like I said, we both shared a lot."

"I'm surprised, since you're somewhat detached from the immediate situation, that you would not have gone to the police."

"You're talking about my sister. I was concerned that the gentleman in question would cause her bodily harm if she went to the authorities."

"Good point, Reagan. If you come up with anything, please call me anytime."

Paul assured Reagan he would do likewise and headed back to the airport for his trip to Tampa. He arrived just in time to get on his flight; no more missed time before games for him, or he knew Tony LoDuca would cook his goose. It was still perplexing to him that Nikki could have drowned and that she was gone. Could there have been a case of mistaken identity? What other scenarios were potential explanations? Was it a chance for her to get out from under the scrutiny of the gambler? Paul decided he needed to let this one play out on its own timetable.

The Cardinals' next stop of the road trip was for three games with the Tampa Bay Rays starting Friday, July 1, and running through Sunday, July 3. The Rays were a terrible team when they first entered the American League. But several successful drafts netted them some outstanding offensive threats and pitching talent that had blossomed into excellent major-league players. The ballpark where they played, a domed stadium located in Saint Petersburg, was dark and rather dreary, despite the team's efforts to brighten and lighten up the interior. It was home for the Rays, though, and they took advantage of their environment and won two out of three of the games from the Cardinals, losing 5–3, winning 5–1, and finally winning the rubber game 8–3. The two losses put the Cardinals into a tie with Milwaukee, as they were having their own problems, having won only one of their last six games.

Paul had another decent series, going 4-12 with 2 doubles and 3 RBIs. He, like the other Cardinals outfielders, had a very difficult time tracking fly balls inside the dome, but no balls were lost as a result of tentative outfield play. This was not the favorite place for visiting teams to play, so most of the players were glad this opponent was not part of their regular season schedule.

Bernie Madlock also chimed in on the state of baseball in Florida as compared to St. Louis in his *Bernie's Bytes quickies:*

PATRICK G MCLEAN

Thank your lucky stars, Cardinal Nation

I applaud the metro Tampa and Miami markets for building new playpens for their baseball teams, but neither one of them managed to get it right. Tampa can be excused to some degree, as the rigid dome concept was state of the art technology when they were trying to get the White Sox, the Giants, anybody to come down to Florida. As we all know, they were awarded an expansion team and were just awful in their formative years. Plus, without delving into Florida politics, the dome was located on the wrong side of the metro market; it should have been in Tampa. Now the team is very good, extremely good, and they can't draw a crowd. Go figure. The Miami story is more complex, but suffice it to say the team finally got their brand new stadium, complete with a retractable dome for when it inevitably rains in South Florida. The Florida or Miami Marlins have had their ups and downs over the years, but are starting to field a young and scrappy team that just might play winning baseball in the not too distant future. So where are the fans? Maybe they've been desensitized over the years. It just might take a pennant race to get them back. And Cardinal Nation? I'm convinced that you fans would show up game after game even if the Cardinals trailed the Cubs in the standings. Thanks for reading.

CHAPTER TWENTY-EIGHT

A charter plane was scheduled to take off from Tampa an hour and a half after the Sunday game ended, allowing just twenty minutes for team members to peel off their uniforms, take showers, unpack their lockers, and get dressed for the trip back home for six games before the All-Star break. As luck would have it, by the time they got to the airport and were ready to board, the air flight operations manager advised them of a slight delay due to a gauge malfunction. While everyone was waiting in the charter lounge, Paul took the opportunity to track down Tony LoDuca.

"Tony, do you have a minute? I'd like to speak with you in private about a matter."

"Sure, we can use the room over there," as Tony pointed to a conference center. "What's on your mind, Paul?" asked Tony as they settled down and he closed the door.

"How well do you know the San Francisco Giants manager, Tony?"

"Bud Brown? He's a friend of mine. As you know, I live in the Bay Area, and he and I participate in several off-season charity events, plus our families go out to dinner once in a while."

"I'd like to bail out of any consideration by him for an extra spot on the National League All-Star team. Having the days off might just ensure that I can make it through another half of a season, or at least until Matt comes back."

"You know, Paul, playing in an All-Star game is a privilege that doesn't happen to too many players. With the season you're having, I'm sure you would be a natural to be selected by Bud. Besides, I've already put in a good word for you!"

"I really appreciate your support, and maybe you and I should have had this conversation earlier, but I have a story to tell you about me, and why this season is my one last hurrah. My goal is to get through the grind of a season, do well by the team, and frankly, show the baseball world how good I am when I'm on my game. I can't do it without some rest due to my condition." At this point, Paul proceeded to tell Tony everything that had transpired over the last several years.

"Paul, if I'd had known what you just told me, I probably would have nixed your being signed. I'm glad I listened to Dave McFarlin. So was I the only person in management that didn't know?"

"I don't know how Dave handled the communication, but I think John Nowicki knew and I'm not sure what he would have done with the information."

"I'm sure John, knowing me, thought this was the best way to handle your signing. I've never been so out of the loop before, but I can appreciate his and Dave's desire to bring you on board. They hit the mark! On the other subject, I'll talk to Bud and indicate that you have a 'nagging' injury and need the time off to get through the rest of the season. And if your lucky stars align again for a liver, I expect you to take the transplant. I doubt that you would get a second opportunity if you turn down the first one."

"Actually, I have news about that, too. I did turn one down awhile back. Call me crazy, but I want to see this season through, or at least as far into September or October as I can. The Triple Crown talk is fun and a motivator for me and would be nice to reflect back on, but I'm more interested in seeing how far this team can go."

"You are crazy, and loyal to a fault. I hope you get your opportunity to see this season through."

"Thanks, Skipper. And I'm sorry we didn't have this conversation sooner."

"As I said, I would have nixed the signing. Now I don't know how we'd survive without you! Worse case, I hope you can hang on till Matt comes back. Best case, we have you both for the rest of our run this season. But when that call comes again for your transplant, we'll do whatever we can to get you out of here on a plane to Rochester."

The rest of the trip home was uneventful after a "short" delay of two hours.

The next series was at home against one of the team's chief competitors, the Cincinnati Reds. Game one was held on the 4th of July holiday and the series ran through Wednesday, July 6. The Cardinals won the first game 1–0 on a classic performance by Chris Mitchell. When healthy, he was the go-to guy for the Cardinals, and he did not disappoint. The only run came on an Al Robles home run, thus allowing him the opportunity to inch closer to his teammate Paul Kolbe for the National League lead for homers.

Paul had a single, but was otherwise quiet at the plate. His work in left field was almost nonexistent, as he handled only two easy fly balls and one single requiring a throw to second base.

The second game of the series on Tuesday, July 5, was not as suspenseful, as the Cardinals racked up four runs in the first inning and proceeded to win 8–1. Paul, Al, Lance, and virtually the whole starting lineup chipped in with hits early in the game to take the fight out of the Reds early in the contest. Both Al and Paul homered as well.

The third game of the series on Wednesday, July 6, was another nip and tuck affair, but ultimately the Cardinals fell short, 9–8. Neither Al nor Paul hit a home run, but both doubled in the same inning and each player had two hits. At this juncture, the Cardinals were up one game on Milwaukee, with Cincinnati still well in the hunt.

The last series before the All-Star break was with the Arizona Diamondbacks from Thursday, July 7, through Sunday, July 10. The four-game series approach was a relatively new idea, designed to cut down travel for teams outside their division. Since this was the only trip for Arizona to Saint Louis for the season, it was important to get all four games in. Any one of the first three games of the series could have been scrubbed in case of inclement weather and then combined with another date within the series for a day-night doubleheader, but game four was more than likely going to have to be gutted out with delays in order to be marked as an official game in the books. And, of course, that's how the series played out. The Cardinals lost the first two games 4–1 and 7–6, and then came back and won the third game 7–6. Paul played every inning in each game of the series, since he was not going to the All-Star game and several other Cardinals were doing also so, including outfielder Lance Champlain. And he was having an outstanding series, hitting a total of four homers and driving in eight runs in the first three games.

Game four started on Sunday afternoon under heavy clouds, and rain started coming down after the end of two innings. Jay Gomez was on the mound and had given up no runs through the first two innings, so Tony LoDuca was inclined to let him return to the mound if the delay was reasonable. That proved to be true. The rain stopped after twenty minutes, and the grounds crew took an additional ten minutes before the game could resume. Two more innings flashed by, and neither team could mount any offense. And then the rain started again, so the umpires called time once again. The second rain delay was in effect. Since this was a getaway day for both clubs for the All-Star break, the Diamondbacks and Cardinals managers both approached the umpire crew and encouraged them to let the teams play as long as the rain remained rather light, as was the current case. The umpires, more than likely anxious themselves to start their midsummer break, agreed. The fifth inning started with a light rain falling, and Jay Gomez continued to pitch a masterful game.

The D-Backs starter, Zack Prince, returned the favor, with the game still knotted at no score. The sixth inning, with rain still falling, saw the D-Backs score two runs on a pair of doubles and a single. The Cardinals scored two of their own, thanks to a double and two straight singles, the last one by Paul to drive in the tying run. The seventh and eighth innings came and went, still under a steady rain, with both starters still in the game and throwing up more zeros on the scoreboard.

Finally, the ninth inning. Jay started off by walking two batters. Tony and Yadier paid a visit to the mound to give Jay some time to regroup and ask if he felt he could get three more outs. Jay responded in the affirmative. Tony read his body language, made eye contact, promptly agreed, and walked off the mound, much to the delight of the hometown crowd. The next batter hit a ball sharply on the ground, but right at David Page, who then threw to Skip Russell covering second, who then fired a bullet to Al Robles covering first. Two men were now out, with a runner on third base. Any kind of miscue or hit would more than likely result in a run scored. At this point, Tony thought that Jay had done all he could. He came out one more time and summoned Eduardo Alonzo from the bullpen. After his warm-up tosses, he faced the D-Backs' slugging outfielder Chris Greene.

Generally, it's a good idea to take a pitch or two when a new pitcher comes into a game so everyone—batter, on-deck hitter, manager, and so on—can see what the new pitcher is throwing and how well he is hitting his targets. In this particular case, Greene expected that Alonzo would lay the first pitch in just to get ahead on the count. He was partially correct. Alonzo threw a sharp breaking slider that appeared to drop off the table as it streaked across the plate. However, Greene, looking for a lollipop fastball, swung way too early and way too high. Strike one.

Alonzo, thinking that Greene would be expecting something high and outside and then low and inside, followed by whatever the circumstances dictated, threw the same pitch. Same result. Strike two.

Now Greene was very upset with himself. He looked foolish on two straight pitches. "Dammit," he said out loud, "I should be able to hit this guy." Little chance of that, as Alonzo came right back with the same pitch and the same result. Strike three. End of the inning for the D-Backs.

Alan Cooper pinch-hit for John Keyes and promptly drew a walk from Zack Prince, who was still in the game. Paul was up next and was having a pretty good day against Prince, going two for four, with a single, a double, and an RBI. Having seen enough of Prince's pitches all evening, Paul told himself that he should swing at the first pitch unless it was way out of the strike zone. Prince did not disappoint. Like Gomez and Alonzo, Prince was bound and determined to get a first strike on Paul to establish the advantage on his side.

He was normally a patient hitter, preferring to let the game come to him versus trying to change the game itself. This time, he skipped the rules. He swung at a pitch normally too far outside to be called a strike and put as much body language as he could into his swing. Normally somewhat of a pull hitter, this time Paul hit one of his rare home runs to right-center field.

The ball carried almost to the top of the bleachers and then bounced back into the Cardinals bullpen. Walk-off home runs are rare, so the bullpen coach grabbed the ball and presented it to Paul in the clubhouse. Final score: 4–2 Cardinals. At this point in the season, the club was 49-43 and tied for first place with Milwaukee.

CHAPTER TWENTY-NINE

Non-All-Star players were free from baseball obligations through Wednesday July 13, but they were expected to be at the charter air operations on Thursday, July 14, at 8:00 a.m. for a flight to Cincinnati and a three game-series with the Reds. Meanwhile, Milwaukee would be headed to Denver to take on the Rockies in a four-game set.

With a few days off, Paul decided that he would go to Rochester. He hoped to accomplish several things: try to see Heather and his old friend Sam; try to conjure up Joe Fisher; visit his former team, the Rochester Honkers; and check in with the Meyer Clinic.

The first part proved to be the hardest, as Heather was apparently still upset with Paul from his earlier trip to Minnesota. Sam was easier to track down, as he held his normal position behind the bar at the All Pro Sports Pub & Grill in downtown Rochester.

"Well, look who the cat dragged into my place," said Sam upon seeing Paul.

"It could be worse. I could have brought a cat in; something like a mountain lion would probably do," said Paul to return the good-natured greeting. "How've you been, Sam?"

"I've been keeping up with your exploits. Plus, there doesn't seem to be a day goes by that the local TV sports folks aren't talking about the Saint Louis Cardinals. It looks like this town has adopted you as its favorite son."

"Well, I'll be darned. Thanks for the feedback. Maybe I'll have to use a disguise to fend off the paparazzi."

"I'm not so sure that will be necessary, but there is a lady in town the next few days who somehow knew you were going to be here, too. I'm guessing this time you might want to make sure you hook up with her. She left a cell phone number, in case you didn't have it."

"Could that lady have a name like Heather?"

"You guessed right, and good luck this time, Paul! By the way, do you want your usual beer and Jack?"

"Sam, I'll take a Diet Coke for now, maybe with a lime twist so I don't look too stupid drinking diet soda in a bar."

"Comin' right up, and if you have too many of those, I'll call a cab. Where are you stayin' this trip, Paul?"

"Sam, I haven't gotten that far ahead yet. There's one really good option if my phone call is successful."

"I hear you on that one. Let me know if it doesn't work out!"

Paul called Heather's number and got a voice message saying she was out of town. "Well," thought Paul, "strike one on my list of things to get accomplished, and it was my number one priority, too."

"By the way, I'm glad you're drinking a diet soda. But if you drink that stuff every time you come in here, you'll lose your chair endowment. I can't afford to have a bunch of sissies swilling soft drinks around here. That's just too bad for my reputation."

"That's why I asked for a lime to go with the soda. Looks like a real drink if you ignore the carbonation!"

"Just kidding—you do what you need to do to get well. If that means being a teetotaler, especially after you get that new liver of yours, then so be it. Come in anyway and class this joint up anytime."

"Thanks for your support, Sam. I know I can always count on you, my friend."

"Any luck getting in touch with Heather?"

"Nope. Her answering machine said she was out of town."

"That's because I'm in Rochester, Paulie," said a familiar voice behind him.

As Paul turned around, he almost gasped for breath. "Wow, you look great! Hello, Heather!"

They both stood looking at each other until Paul finally reached out and gave Heather a warm and friendly hug, followed by a tentative kiss.

"I wish I could say the same about you, Paul. You, frankly, look tired, very tired. Is the baseball stuff catching up with you, old feller?"

"Yes and no. Games almost every day. Travel from city to city; even home games are road games for me. And I miss you. I'm glad you came to Rochester, regardless of the reason."

"Well I do have a political policy consulting client in town, but I was able to arrange my schedule around you being here in Rochester. Tell me when you have free time the next few days, and let's catch up on each other's lives."

"Other than spending a little time at Meyer and with the Honkers, I'm on cruise control. I'd like to hook up with Joe Fisher, but I think my chances are better in Saint Louis nowadays than up here."

"Paul, speaking of Meyer, I assume that part of your health issue is your deteriorating liver. I'm starting to think things are going to get worse for you before they get better. Have you had *any* indication from the folks at Meyer that you're still on their radar? Isn't going on three years a little ridiculous to wait for a new liver?"

"Unfortunately, that's the major issue with me right now. I feel that I'm getting weaker by the week. It doesn't help that I have a relatively rare blood type, AB negative."

"Is it true that you rejected the offer of a liver that they finally had for you?" asked Heather.

"How do you know that?" asked Paul, incredulously.

"*What?*" asked Sam, overhearing the conversation.

"Paulie, Paulie, my job is to stay connected. Just what in god's name were you thinking? That liver transplant would have solved your health issues. And with your history and blood type, who knows if there will be another opportunity for you?"

"I know this sounds absurd, but I'm having a signature season and I don't want it to end. I'm finally realizing my potential as a professional. There's also a lot of pride in helping this team achieve its goals. Call me crazy, but I'm willing to take the chance that the transplant won't happen, or continues to be delayed."

"You are crazy, Paul!" Sam chipped in.

"You *are* crazy, Paulie!" Heather added.

"Maybe," Paul concluded. "On the plus side, I've stopped drinking altogether. I don't need to pour any more gasoline on the fire. And for another, I'm finally getting past three or four hours of sleep a night. Not much—five or six—but it's better. I'm also trying to stick to a high-protein diet. And lastly, I'm trying to hit the gym at least three, maybe up to five times a week. And hopefully, I have you back in my life."

"Well, you were a shithead, but I'll chalk it up to your excessive drinking—the 'old' Paul, not this new, sexier version standing in front of me."

And with that matter resolved, Paul and Heather left the busy pub and walked down the street to a small Italian café with an outdoor patio and spent the rest of the afternoon, evening, and well into the morning enjoying each other's company.

In the meantime, just prior to his trip to Rochester, Paul started to have the same dream every night. He was at the plate with the bases loaded in the middle of the game, definitely not the ninth inning, during the last series of the regular season at home. The score was 3–0 in favor of the other team. Most of the time he would hit a grand slam in his dream, win the game, and clinch a playoff spot for the team. But some of the time, he would strike out swinging on three pitches. And this evening, in the absolute comfort of being next to Heather, he had his dream again. He wondered if he should mention it to Heather.

Paul got up early, figured out how the coffeepot worked, found some freshly ground morning blend coffee, and got a head start on the day by reading the local newspaper.

Heather woke to the smell of fresh brewing coffee a half hour later and joined Paul on the outdoor patio. The patio received direct sun in the afternoon, but in the morning, they enjoyed the cool shade that felt so rare in July. Paul was dressed in a Cardinals practice T-shirt and shorts. Heather was dressed in an XL Minnesota Twins T-shirt, thong, and nothing else.

After she settled into her chair, she asked Paul, "You know, your career year is half over. What are you going to do after the season?"

"Come back to Rochester short term. I'm assuming that I get a liver transplant at some point, and I'll need some R and R. May as well do it here. Besides, that keeps me closer to you."

"Does that mean you see a future with 'us,' versus you and me?"

"You're putting me on the spot here, aren't you? Truth be told, I do see an 'us.'"

"Well now, Paulie, that is refreshing to hear from you. In any event, I like what I'm hearing. Let's keep it real and see where this ends up. For now let's enjoy each other's company. Okay with you?"

"Okay with me, Heather!"

"I have a meeting this morning. I'll be back in time for lunch. Will you be available then?"

"Absolutely. I'm free all day other than scheduling things for tomorrow. I hope to visit with the Meyer folks tomorrow morning and try to mend some fences, and then see the Honkers in action tomorrow afternoon. I'll treat you to lunch today if we can find a place where fans won't mob me."

"A celebrity. I can't wait. Then again, Rochester folks are pretty respectful. You'll probably only have sign to autographs and have your picture taken throughout lunch," Heather laughed.

"By the way," said Paul, eyeing Heather's T-shirt. "I don't think the Twins were ever better represented than just now. You wear that shirt very well. I suppose that is the politically correct one in these parts, but couldn't you at least consider my feelings and wear something with the Cardinals logo on it once in a while?" he said, feigning mock hurt.

"I would if I could find someone who had connections with the team. You wouldn't happen to know anyone that works for the Cardinals, would you?"

"I'll see what I can do about that. Maybe, if you're a really good fan of the team, especially their left fielder, perhaps something could be bartered off for a T-shirt."

With that comment, they moved to the bedroom for some additional negotiation. Later on, Heather was seen wearing an XL Cardinals practice T with the number forty-seven and the name Kolbe on the back.

"Too bad I didn't ask for number ten," remarked Paul. "You would make a perfect one in that shirt!"

Before they went about their day's duties, Paul brought up a subject he wasn't sure he would broach, but he finally decided Heather might make a good sounding board. "I've been having recurring dreams for some time. But the weird thing is they don't always have the same ending. For example, here is last night's version: I take a pitch over the plate for strike one. I then see a big fat lollipop of a pitch coming my way, but halfway to home plate, out pops the skipper. The pitch is declared a 'no pitch,' and I turn to meet Tony. He tells me it is time for me 'to go.' I respond, 'Now? I was just about ready to pop one over the bleachers.'"

"And then what happens?" asked Heather.

"I give the skipper a look of anguish, walk briskly to the dugout, and then literally run through the clubhouse to gather my clothes. I rush to the airport, get on a plane, and get to Rochester in record time, but it's too late. The liver has degraded to the point that it can't be used. The clinic people then tell me to stop wasting their time and resources and kick me out of their facilities. Then I woke up in a cold sweat. This new twist is not a good one, Heather."

"Paulie, it's just a dream. Sounds like stress overload to me. Didn't you tell me that you're meeting with Dr. Arthur on this trip? Let's see where you stand after this discussion. And don't minimize what you are doing on the field. You have a chance to do what no one in the National League has done in more than seventy-five years. That, plus dealing with the intensity of someone like Tony LoDuca on a daily basis, must be accelerating the effects of your weakening condition."

"Tony's intensity is overstated in the media. He wants to win, and he takes losses badly, but he is the ultimate players' manager. He has our back with the fans, the media, senior management, and even ownership. With the potential distractions minimized we can concentrate on playing the game. You're probably right about the stress overload, but right now I think I'm looking at my therapist. That's you, Heather!"

"Then maybe I ought to be worth *two* T-shirts instead of just one!"

"Don't push your luck there. You may just be in possession of something the Baseball Hall of Fame is interested in someday!"

Later, Paul and Heather met for lunch, which somehow became quality time together the rest of the afternoon and evening. Heather had more business to attend to in town the next day, and Paul met with the Meyer staff in the morning and took in a Honkers game in the afternoon.

During Paul's meeting at the clinic, the news was not so rosy, as the staff reminded Paul of his rare blood type and the lack of success they'd had for a similar transplant. Dr. Archer advised, "At your age, Paul, we only have one opportunity for a successful operation. It's critical, therefore, to have the right blood type. The staff admires your courage in rejecting the liver transplant that we had for you, but it better not happen again." To Paul's credit, 'his' liver went to a teenage girl with a rare liver disease, and Paul's decision allowed doctors to save her life.

"And remember, you must be here, at our facility, within twelve hours of our call. Your cell phone is the first contact. The Cardinals' landline is the next one."

"I understand. I'll be ready!"

After that admonishment, Paul headed over to his old hangout for the past few summers. The Honkers were playing a rare day game, starting at noon, and Paul was able to get there just in time for batting practice. The Honkers greeted him with open arms, including a big hug from Kate Williams, the team's owner. The announcer at the game advised the crowd that there was a potential National League Triple Crown winner in attendance. Paul received a standing ovation when his name was called. Baseball fans in Rochester were following his exploits on a regular basis and had endowed him with favorite son status.

The Honkers played Paul Kolbe's "walk-up" song with the Cardinals, Survivor's "Eye of the Tiger," at the bottom of the sixth inning as a salute to Paul. The announcer then reiterated that Rochester was pulling for Paul to get the Triple Crown. Paul stood up from his seat near the Honkers' dugout and acknowledged the crowd by waving his well-worn Honkers coaches hat. The time off came and went too quickly for Paul. Fortunately, he was able to spend quality moments with Heather, invest the necessary time with the Meyer folks, and cap off his stay by taking in a Honkers game.

The trip back to St. Louis was uneventful this time; no frantic phone calls to the skipper, no suicide car rides with Sam, just a leisurely plane trip from Rochester to Chicago to St. Louis, some rest, and a ready Paul Kolbe for the second half of the season.

Here's what Bernie had to say about the state of the ball club at this juncture in the season in his *Bernie's Bytes on line column*.

Halfway to the division crown?

The Cards are past the statistical half of the season but the All-Star Game has always symbolically been considered the halfway point in the baseball season. So far, the ball club is hanging around where they need to be. But then again so is Milwaukee, and so is Cincinnati. In one respect, it's easier to get into the playoffs nowadays in that there is a wild card option for one team that did not win its division (rumor has it that there will be not one but two wild card teams per league as early as next year; let's not go the way of hockey and basketball, guys). Still, if you want to get to the World Series, let alone win, you have to get past the first round of best-of- five, then another round of best- of- seven. Then you play another best- of- seven for all the marbles with your counterpart from the other league. Does the best team always win the World Series? If you assume the team with the best regular season is the 'best' team, then my short answer is 'hardly ever." Who wins? It's usually the team with the hottest hand going into the playoffs. That situation usually can be seen in the wild card team, as they more than likely had to scratch, crawl, do whatever was necessary, to get to the playoffs. Thanks for reading.

CHAPTER THIRTY

And the second half started off with a bang, as the Cardinals met the Cincinnati Reds Friday, July 15, through Sunday, July 17. The first game of the series went to the Reds 6–5, with a complete-game performance by their fifth starter.

Paul had a good day with a homer, and Al Robles also homered, showing signs that he was going to give Paul a legitimate run for the Triple Crown. The team had better luck the next day with a 4–1 win behind Chris Mitchell, but then it dropped the rubber game of the series 3–1. The Cards also lost ground to the Brewers in the division race, as they were now one-half game out of first place.

Both Paul and Al continued their power displays, with each homering one additional time during the series. The rest of the team was relatively quiet, although they managed to squeeze in a run in each game to keep them interesting.

The team then enjoyed a day off July 18 in the Big Apple before playing the Mets Tuesday, July 19, through Thursday, July 21. Unfortunately, the team stumbled, losing the first two games of the series 4–2 and 6–5, but coming back to win 6–2 behind Jake Hudson. The losses were disconcerting, but the Cardinals were still only a game out of first place. Paul and Al continued their hot hitting. Their performance, along with the Reds' Joey Costa and the Rockies' Carlos Vasquez, indicated that the prospects for a Triple Crown winner in the National League had dimmed because there were too many candidates hitting very well in some, but not all three, categories of batting average, runs batted in, and home runs.

From New York, the team continued its road trip to Pittsburgh for three games from Friday, July 22, through Sunday, July 24. The Cardinals reversed recent trends and won the first two games 6–4 and 9–1, but they missed a chance for a sweep by losing the third game 4–3. The Cardinals were now tied with the Brewers for first place.

Paul got the third game off, at least part of it, before he managed a pinch-hit two-run double in the top of the ninth; it was one of those games where the players knew they were going to look back toward the end of the season and wish they had that extra win in their pocket. The old adage that all games count applied in baseball: winning teams maintain their competitiveness whether it's April, July, or October.

CHAPTER THIRTY-ONE

Home sweet home, if only for seven games, but the brief home stand made it possible to pick up some ground on both the Reds and the Brewers, as the Cardinals were playing the lowly Astros from Monday, July 25, through Thursday, July 28, and the Cubs from Friday, July 29, through Sunday, July 31. The Houston series started off promising, as the Cardinals won the first two games 10–5 and 4–3.

Both Paul and Al feasted on Astros pitching in the first game, collecting three hits each, including a homer, but both were shut out in the second game.

Things did not go as well in the third and fourth games, as the youth-oriented Astros won the next two, 4–2 and 5–3, for a series split. Meanwhile, Milwaukee swept a three-game series with the Cubs, which pushed the Cardinals one and a half games out of first place.

Next, the Cardinals played host to Chicago and did well, winning the first two games convincingly 9–2 and 13–5, but then dropping the finale 6–3. Meanwhile, the red-hot Brewers swept the Astros, pushing the Cardinals two and a half games out of first place.

As the month of July came to a close, there was still a four-player race for the Triple Crown, or at least parts of it:

Player	Home Runs	RBIs	Average
Paul Kolbe	32	71	.330
Al Robles	29	62	.326
Joey Costa	31	58	.329
Carlos Vasquez	27	65	.337

The end of July also marked the end of the trade-without-waivers deadline. This season, the period proved to be a nonissue for the Cardinals, as the club had previously made its move for relief help in the Colby Rakers trade. Colby was not faring much better in Toronto than he had in Saint Louis. After a slow start, he went on a tear before settling in around the .230 mark, with several homers and a few RBIs, hitting mostly in the seventh spot of the lineup. There was no indication that the Blue Jays were any more tolerant of having Tony Rakers around than the Cardinals were, but at least there was not any public revolt by the coaches and managers. Perhaps a change in scenery and the sheer distance from Augusta, Georgia, to Toronto, Ontario, had a lot to do with the situation being somewhat resolved.

CHAPTER THIRTY-TWO

What a way to kick off the dog days of August! Up first, over Monday, August 1, through Wednesday August 3, the Cards had a three-game series with the Brewers in Milwaukee. The Cards started ace Chris Mitchell in the first game and the Brewers countered with ace Zack Brantley. The game went scoreless for the first three innings, but a four-run fourth swamped the Cardinals. They were able to cut the gap to 4–2 in the fifth, but the Brewers countered with two runs of their own to push their lead to 6–2. That's how the game ended, which pushed the Cardinals back three and half games.

Neither Paul nor Al were involved in the scoring, but they both helped their respective batting averages out with a hit in two official appearances and two walks apiece.

Converted reliever Kyle McCormick started game two, and with the help of the new relievers, Mark Recipko and Octavio Doty, the Cardinals' won a back-and-forth game 8–7. Al Robles was particularly effective, going 4-4 with 2 doubles and 4 RBIs. Paul was silent in the game, except for one home run in the first inning, a solo blast deep to left field.

Paul trudged back to his hotel room, thoroughly spent. As soon as he was in his room, he noticed the house phone was flashing. Picking up the receiver, he dialed the front desk and was advised that he had a voice message. He then dialed his extension and listened.

"Good evening, Mr. Kolbe. My name is Jimmy John Harris. I was a friend of Nikki Cole's, and I was hoping she would have had a discussion with you about a business arrangement I was most interested in working out with the two of you. I'm in Milwaukee for other business purposes, but I'd love to have a drink with you this evening, or perhaps coffee in the morning. I have a sense of urgency on completing our arrangement, so please free up some time to see me. Thanks, Mr. Kolbe."

"I don't believe it! First he harasses Nikki to the point that she either took her own life, or faked it, or more likely was murdered," thought Paul. "I'm not going to give this loony the time of day, let alone meet with him."

The phone call made Paul restless the remainder of the evening, and he slept on and off until four in the morning. Finally, he got out of bed and headed for coffee and a newspaper in the downstairs lobby. On the way back up to his room, he noticed someone rather out of place in the lobby at the early hour of five o'clock. He didn't break stride and walked briskly past the person seated in the chair, overlooking the elevator bank. He punched his floor number, looked straight ahead, and proceeded to walk into the elevator after another glance toward the lobby.

Nothing else out of the ordinary occurred that morning and Paul took a cab to Miller Park to get an early jump in the trainer's room before other players came into the clubhouse. Paul was the first Cardinal to show up at Miller Park for the rubber game of the series. The game pitted Edwin Johnson for the Cardinals against a rookie call-up for the Brewers, an apparent mismatch on paper. Unfortunately for the Cardinals, the games weren't played on paper. The Cardinals lost 10–5 in a slugfest, pushing them back to three and half games. Both Al and Paul had multiple hits, but the Brewers kept pounding the fences for their win.

The road trip continued on to Florida to play the Marlins in a four-game series from Thursday, August 4, through Sunday, August 7. It was important, given the struggles that the Marlins were having winning games, to do no worse than a split of the series. And if the Cards wanted to make up ground on Milwaukee in the division race or Atlanta in the wild card race they needed to win three or even four of the games.

The first game was won by the Cardinals, but was closer than the final score of 7–4. The big guns all went deep, including both Al and Paul.

Game two went to the Cardinals as well, 3–2, but it required a two-inning save out of Jason Blevins. Power in the game was nonexistent for the Cardinals, but the team bunched enough singles together to generate the three runs needed for the win.

Game three was a pitcher's duel between Redbird ace Chris Mitchell and Marlins starter Ricky Narleski. The game was scoreless until the ninth, when Lance Champlin did the honors by stroking a two-run homer with Paul Kolbe on–board as a result of a walk earlier in the inning.

Could they complete the sweep? Yes, they did. The Cardinals closed out the four-game series with a more comfortable 8-4 win in the final game. Both Al and Paul homered again, but despite their success in south Florida, they managed to stay status quo with Milwaukee and pick up only one game on Atlanta after the series.

While the Cards were winning, so were the Brewers, as they swept a three-game series of their own against Houston. Meanwhile the Braves won two out of three against the Mets. Although Tony LoDuca never publicly admitted to it, scoreboard watching for the wild card, especially with regard to what Atlanta was doing, became a daily obsession for him. Currently, the Braves were four games up, but they had recently been as many as ten games ahead of the pack. That did not mean that Tony, nor the club, had given up on chasing Milwaukee down, but it did mean that it was time to look at the potential for a wild card slot versus a division championship.

CHAPTER THIRTY-THREE

It was time to get back to business and look toward a long stretch of division games coming up in the next few weeks. A win against a Central Division opponent was like two wins: a simultaneous plus for the victor and a minus for the opponent.

It was the dog days of summer, and the players baked during day games with the field temperature in excess of ninety-five degrees. Plus, it was very difficult to pick up the rotation and keep track of fly balls for the outfielders due to the sun's glare. Fortunately, many Cardinals fans had the tradition of wearing red to home games. The color contrast for fly balls was outstanding. In most other parks, fans would wear white for home games, which would make it much more difficult to pick up the ball in flight, especially on sharply hit lines drives.

For now, Paul had a day to relax on Monday, August 8, sit around the complex pool, and maybe even have a light beer or two (skip that thought). But mostly, Paul could relax and get mentally prepared for the rest of the season.

The day started out like all other off days—normal. But normal could not define events as they unfolded over the next twenty-four hours. For starters, Paul decided to head to the city and have breakfast at one of his favorite places, South Side Diner on Grand Avenue near Tower Grove Park. The area had been undergoing a rebirth of sorts, with a number of suburbanites moving back into large but run-down, two- and three-story early twentieth-century homes and frequenting the eateries and shops that were springing up on Grand Avenue to serve this new influx of residents.

Paul usually sat at the breakfast bar, but since the early morning air was unseasonably cool for the time of the year in Saint Louis, he decided that he would sit outside in the patio area. Whether it was too early in the morning or folks just assumed that it would be too hot, Paul found himself the only customer inhabiting the area.

He immediately ordered a pot of coffee and asked the server to come back in fifteen minutes or so. He opened the day's copy of the *Post-Gazette* and turned to the sports section to see both what Bernie Madlock had on his mind and also how the other Central Division teams had played the previous night. Bernie had a very complimentary comment or two about Paul, but implored the general manager to "do more" than just dump Colby Rakers on the trade market for a short-term fix in the bullpen, even though the previous month's trade seemed to be working for the Cardinals.

Of course, Bernie knew that as of this date, any trades would have to clear waivers first, but the Cardinals had a long and successful history of picking up players in just such circumstances for the stretch run to the pennant.

While Paul was reading, he noticed some movement across the street, which he picked up out of his peripheral vision. At the same time, he absentmindedly dropped his napkin on the patio brick pavers. As be bent over to pick it up, he heard what seemed to be a buzzing sound, followed by a sharp ricochet off the brick wall just behind his seat. As he sat up, he noticed a good portion of one brick facing was shattered. The diner's server came out almost at the same time and asked what had happened.

Paul stood up, looked across the street, and responded, "No idea. If I didn't think it was a crazy idea, I would assume someone just took a shot at me."

"Holy shit. Are you sure? That brick does look like something hit it. Could it really have been a bullet?"

"I'm not sure, but I think I'll take the rest of my breakfast inside at the bar," said Paul. "If I were a drinking man, I'd ask for a very stiff bloody mary. I'll settle for some more coffee."

Coffee was all Paul could handle, and his stomach was churning after the patio incident. As he was about to get up and leave after paying the bill, the day manager came rushing over to Paul.

"Mr. Kolbe, I just heard what happened and I called the district police captain. He is coming here himself in just a minute. Can you stay and make a statement on what happened?"

"Sure, and thank you for acting on this matter."

After reiterating his account to the police captain, Paul decided he had enough excitement for the day and left the diner. He was assured by the captain that the police would conduct some follow-up detective work on the matter such as interviewing neighbors, and would increase patrols in the immediate area.

"So now what?" thought Paul. "Maybe I'll just hang out at my place and not venture out the rest of the day," he said aloud.

He pulled out in traffic on Grand and headed north to get onto I-64. He noticed a large Dodge Ram pickup pull into traffic behind him after it made a U-turn from across the street. "Where have I seen that bad boy truck before?" thought Paul. Rather than go directly onto the highway, Paul decided to continue north on Grand to see if the pickup followed him. Sure enough, as he headed past Saint Louis University, the pickup continued north too, first three cars behind Paul and then gradually edging closer until it was directly behind him.

Paul decided that, coincidence be damned, he was going to make an effort to lose the tail. He made an abrupt left turn on Delmar as a light was turning red, and sure enough, the truck ran through the light to stay with him. He now remembered. It was the same truck that he saw pass him on the interstate between Rochester and Milwaukee earlier this summer. He decided that it was time for hardball, and he snaked his way over to the interstate. At this point, he pressed the pedal to the floor, at one point getting up to eighty-five miles per hour. He was hoping to attract the attention of state or local police, but none were out on the highway at that particular time. And where was his cell phone? "Dammit," he thought out loud. "It's sitting on the bathroom counter top, where I always leave it when taking a shower. This, of all days, to forget to pick it up!"

Fortunately, there wasn't much traffic, and he worked his way around vehicles that looked like they were standing still at fifty-five miles per hour.

At one point, he was driving on the other side of the street and moving in and out of the direct flow of traffic in order to get around cars in his lane. "Where in the hell are the cops when you need them? Dammit!" thought Paul.

He looked in his inside and outside mirrors and decided he had finally lost the truck and then figured his best defense was to go home and call the Virginia Heights police. Sergeant David Kelly came by shortly after his call and, in addition to asking for his autograph for his son, advised Paul that there wasn't much his department could do at this point. "There was no overt crime committed, even though I hear you about the possibility of a shot being fired in your general direction and the car following you."

"General direction? If the shooter was any good, I'd be dead. More like specific direction, Sergeant."

"I understand, but there's nothing the county or your municipality police can do without some more tangible evidence. If the Saint Louis Police Department recovers a spent bullet, then we're talking about attempted murder. Short of that, we have nothing to go on. What we can and will do is patrol your street on a regular basis for the rest of the baseball season and follow up on any further activity that you call in. You have my number. Feel free to contact me directly."

CHAPTER THIRTY-FOUR

With that matter somewhat resolved, the Virginia Heights sergeant left Paul's residence. Meanwhile, around the corner, the driver of a parked black pickup truck observed the contact and then decided to leave shortly after the police car did. Paul was nonplussed about the whole day, but decided to go out for dinner rather than stay in.

He called first base coach Dave McFarlin, who agreed to meet him at Maguire's in Soulard, an inner-city Southside neighborhood pub and grill. Maguire's was known for its Irish heritage, and had expanded in recent years with the building of an outstanding outdoor patio area, complete with two bars, a water fountain, and TVs strategically placed so sporting events could be seen virtually anywhere on the patio.

Dave beat Paul to the restaurant and chose a table near the water fountain, but close enough to the bar so they could watch baseball on Fox Sports Midwest. Tonight's game featured the Kansas City Royals and the Chicago White Sox.

"You want a beer or something else, Paul?" Dave asked as Paul came into the patio area from a side street. "Love one, Dave. But I'm better served by ordering an ice tea. Maybe after the season. After the long season. I forgot what a grind one hundred sixty-two games are, Dave. And throw in spring training and hopefully the playoffs, now you're looking at two hundred plus games." Just then, another bullet whizzed by the table and almost hit a lady sitting immediately behind where Dave and Paul were sitting.

"Enough of this shit," shouted Paul as he took off after a shadowy figure down Twelfth Street. In retrospect, it probably wasn't the smartest thing to do. After all, the mystery figure had a gun. Still, Paul was tired of being harassed, not to mention extremely angry, and wanted to get to the bottom of the mystery.

He chased the figure down three blocks before he encountered a police patrol car headed in the opposite direction. "Officer, that man I'm chasing just took a potshot at me at Maguire's." The officer slammed on his brakes and made a U-turn to go after the shooter. The shadowy figure turned and fired a shot at the police car, shattering the windshield but missing the officer. The officer caught up with the mystery assailant, drove up the sidewalk, and bounced his front bumper against the shooter, causing the shooter to fly several feet in the air before landing headfirst into the trunk of an oak tree.

By then, Paul came running up to the scene and was quite shocked to see who the shooter was. "Nikki? How could this be? I thought you drowned! And what the hell are you doing taking shots at me?"

Nikki tried to get up, but couldn't. "I faked the drowning to get that jerk gambler off my back. Besides, I was just trying to scare you into realizing how short life was and that you and I might just be meant for each other."

"That doesn't make a lot of sense, Nikki. And your bullet almost hit a lady back at Maguire's. You are one crazy lady!"

"I thought you'd be very glad to see me. And you should know that I didn't intend to hurt anyone." Those were the last words Nikki would utter. She rolled over on her side as Paul noticed a massive cave-in on the back of her skull. Blood spurted out like an overrun bank in a spring flood. Her death was quick and hopefully painless.

"Did you know this young lady, sir?" asked the arriving Saint Louis Police officer. "Hey, aren't you the ballplayer for the Cardinals?"

"Yes on both," answered Paul.

By this time, Dave McFarlin had arrived, and he told the officer that it would be best if he could extricate Paul from the situation before any media showed up. Dave also told Paul, "Don't worry about this situation. We'll take it from here. In the meantime, you've got to get the hell out of here before the TV folks storm the scene."

The Saint Louis patrolman then said, "We'll need a statement later, but I can have someone stop by your place tonight. Since there were shots fired, including one at me, we need to get to the bottom of this matter. I also need to go back to Maguire's and get details on what happened there."

Later that evening, police detectives from Saint Louis and Virginia Heights stopped by Paul's residence and quizzed him about the day's events and what led up to Nikki's shooting spree. "You are a fortunate man, Mr. Kolbe," said the Saint Louis detective. "You sure you don't have nine lives?"

"It doesn't feel like it right now. I still can't believe this friend of mine was taking potshots at me all day."

"Well, it's over, and you can get back to the business of hitting that baseball," said the lead Saint Louis detective. "Any chance I can get an autograph for my son?"

Grabbing a ball sitting on the kitchen counter, Paul quickly signed it and handed the keepsake to the detective. "Better yet, here's something he just might have some use for!"

"Thanks, Mr. Kolbe!"

That's how the upside-down day ended. It was indeed time to get back to baseball for Paul.

CHAPTER THIRTY-FIVE

Things were getting dicey. The Brewers came to Saint Louis for a three-game series Tuesday, August 9, through Thursday, August 11. The Cardinals needed to win at least two of the three games to make up some ground on the Brewers. A three-game sweep would be even better. Unfortunately, the Brewers did not cooperate, winning the first two games 5–3 and 5–1. The last game was won by the Cardinals 5–2 behind ace Chris Mitchell. Losing two out of three left the Cardinals four games back. And things were not so rosy on the wild card front either. Atlanta swept the Marlins over three games, pushing their lead to six games over the Cardinals.

Al and Paul were both somewhat effective, driving in two runs apiece with several doubles, but no home runs.

The Rockies were next up for the Cardinals, with three games scheduled for Friday, August 12, through Sunday, August 14. The Cardinals managed to take two of three from Colorado, winning the first game 6–1, dropping the second game by the same score, and then winning the rubber game 6–2. Meanwhile, Milwaukee beat the Dodgers three straight, putting them up a full five games on the Cardinals. Meanwhile, the Braves lost two out of three games to the Cubs. This allowed the Cardinals to creep to within four and a half games of the wild card spot.

Paul was leaning on his patio fence, still having a difficult time separating his game from the recent death of Nikki, debating his lingering concerns over what to do about Jimmy John, thinking about his relationship with Heather, and finally—the elephant in the room—confronting his deteriorating state of health. On top of all this, he was trying to help his team win games and hold off three outstanding ballplayers with at least as good a chance at the Triple Crown as he had.

"I'm getting too old to be carrying all this crap around in my head," remarked Paul to himself. And another voice, one that sounded just like Joe Fisher's said, "Looks like you're feeling sorry for yourself."

"Joe, how did you get in here?"

"I knocked softly and then walked through your door, and I saw you out here."

"What brings you out tonight, Joe, from whatever spiritual, mystical, magical corner of the universe you usually hang out?"

"I detect sarcasm in your voice, Paul, and it's not very becoming of you. I'll chalk that off to pure frustration on your part, based on the number of things stacking up in your life."

"You hit it on the head, Joe. I'm sorry for jumping at you. But dammit, you come, you go, and I don't know what to think about you. Am I going crazy, is this some out-of-body experience, or am I just hallucinating when I see and talk to you?"

"None of the above, Paul. Believe me, I'm real. Maybe not the kind of real you're used to, but I'm real. I told you that it will all be sorted out someday, but that day isn't today. I'm here this evening to serve as a reminder that you can achieve your goals for this year. For tonight, let's focus on the Triple Crown. You can't control what the other players do, but you can control what you do. Don't take an at bat off, even if a game is in the bag. Even if you're dead tired. Even if Jimmy John has bet money against your team."

"You know about—"

"Yes, I'm aware of his proposal. Be vigilant, as the slimeball won't go away until he is forced to do so."

"Damn, Joe. You're good. I don't know how you know what you know, but you are on top of things. I will try to keep my chin above water and not let these issues overwhelm me." Paul dropped his gaze for just a moment, and when he looked up again, Joe was gone.

"Just like that," thought Paul. "I don't know what to think at this point, but it seems my best course of action is to deal with all this stuff on a day-to-day basis. I suppose I owe Joe Fisher, whoever and whatever he is, a big thank-you for reminding me of what is important."

It was time once again to read Bernie's take on the state of Cardinal Nation. In his *Bernie's Bytes on line column he wrote:*

Dog gone those dog days of August are here

Remember last winter when you complained about how cold it was? Guess what? Bet you would like a little of that chilled air back about right now. I recently had the occasion to sit out in the bleachers for a ball game, something I like to do once in a while to get a feel for what the average fan is experiencing. The sun was bearing down until well past seven o'clock and I had to resort to pulling the bill down on my trusty Post-Gazette ball cap just to be able to see what was going on in front of me. Then the sun receded behind the stadium facade and a welcome breeze came in from the west. It's nights like this that you can truly understand the mentality of Cardinal Nation. Through thick and thin, they push the turnstile, game after game, until another three million of so in attendance comes and goes. I've got to hand it to you fans. I couldn't do this on a regular basis. Give me the relative comforts of the press box, emphasis of the word relative, or my favorite watering hole if I'm not working. Now is the time for pennant winners to push through the fatigue, the humdrum of summer, and make some progress. Games lost in the doldrums of August are just as important as late September. Let's see what this team is made out of. Thanks for reading.

CHAPTER THIRTY-SIX

The Cardinals moved on to Pittsburgh for a three-game series from Monday, August 15, through Wednesday, August 17. They needed to make up ground against Milwaukee or Atlanta if they wanted to take the division flag or the wild card. This series was seen as a crucial one for the club. Unfortunately, the Cards took a step backward, losing 6–2 and 5–4 in the first two games.

Both Al and Paul were nonfactors in these games. Al had some nagging injuries, but he would just as soon fight Tony LoDuca than to be pulled out of the lineup. Paul, on the other hand, wasn't going to volunteer to sit down. A quick look at the Triple Crown "standings" revealed the following:

Player	Home Runs	RBIs	Average
Paul Kolbe	38	98	.330
Al Robles	36	92	.319
Joey Costa	37	89	.323
Carlos Vasquez	33	90	.335

CHAPTER THIRTY-SEVEN

Days off like Thursday, August 18, were precious and few this late in the season, so the key was to get some rest and relaxation if possible. R and R is more difficult on the road, as normal eating and sleeping habits are disrupted. Fortunately, the trip from Pittsburgh to Chicago was a short one. It was a relief to get to the hotel early in the evening and look forward to an entire day off. The first thing Paul did when he got to the room was throw himself on his king-size bed and let out a sigh. Staring at the ceiling felt wonderful. "Just me and my beat-up body for a whole twenty-four hours," he thought. But at the same time, he smelled a faint whisper of a familiar aroma. A woman's perfume? A scent that only...?

"Hi, Paulie," she said, from an oversize love seat facing the bed.

"Heather?"

"Were you expecting someone else?"

"No, of course not. But how did you get in here?"

"I had my persuasive skills in high gear with the front desk manager. Besides, I thought a nice dinner is overdue; we can't eat my Uncle Sam's food all the time, can we? And I have a conference in town so our timing worked out perfectly."

"I'm impressed. I'm very glad you surprised me. I'm also very tired from this day-to-day grind. Could we settle for room service, including a nice bottle of wine—for you? I'm afraid I'm still on the wagon while I'm waiting for my liver transplant, which may never come, but that doesn't mean you should be, too!"

"I'm glad to hear that, Paulie. I can settle for a nice glass of ice tea and room service—this time!"

"Great. Let's order, and then I have to take a hot shower and try to get some life back into my body."

"Good idea, but I have a better one. I'll join you, then we'll continue your therapy on this king-size bed, and then we can order room service—either dinner or breakfast depending on the time!"

"You're on. And thanks, Heather, for breaking and entering into my room. I'm glad you tracked me down."

Paul quickly undressed, scattering clothes on the way to the shower. He turned on the hot water to build up some steam in the enclosure, and he then cut the hot water back and added cold water to get the temperature to a more moderate setting. He got into the shower and just let the water cascade off his body. Heather, with her hair covered, entered the shower with a bottle of black raspberry vanilla shower gel and a large shower sponge and proceeded to squirt gel all over Paul's body. She then alternated between soft kisses and using the shower sponge to massage him.

"Now it's my turn," said Paul, as he used the shower gel to squirt on Heather's front and back. He decided his magic fingers would be a better approach than the shower sponge and proceeded to massage Heather all over.

They embraced, kissed passionately for several minutes, and then decided to quickly rinse and dry off. Once they settled onto the king-size bed, they took turns being the aggressor for what seemed like hours for Paul. And it was.

"Holy moly. It's midnight," said Paul. "Let's order some food and then head back to bed. I'm pooped." The rest of the evening and early morning hours came and went far too quickly.

The daylight coming through the bedroom window woke Paul up, and he wandered into the foyer looking for a coffee maker. He also found a note from Heather, indicating that she had an early day downtown and that she would like him to hit a home run for her today. "You got it!" said Paul out loud, with as much conviction as he could muster.

ONE LAST HURRAH

Paul had until 11:15 a.m. to enjoy some relative peace and quiet before the raucous weekend ahead that accompanied Cards versus Cubs action. He put on Cards sweatpants, a short sleeve Cards warm-up jersey, a pair of athletic shoes and headed for a quick walk around the hotel block to get some fresh air. Once again he sensed that he was being followed, stopping occasionally to pretend to be interested in something in a store window. As in previous cases, nothing materialized, but he swore to himself that he saw a black Dodge Ram truck with blacked out windows pull away from across the street when he reentered the hotel. Just a coincidence? Maybe, but Paul started to think his health issues were causing him to hallucinate about potential danger lurking around corners, manifested in the form of an aggressive looking black vehicle. "This is crazy. I'm not letting this get the best of me. Next time I see a Dodge Ram truck like the one on the highway, I'm going to make a point of trying to track down the driver and see just what the hell is going on," said Paul to himself.

CHAPTER THIRTY-EIGHT

The Cardinals next played the Cubs in a three-game series from Friday, August 19, through Sunday, August 21. Weekend series in Chicago always brought a bunch of Cardinals fans to Wrigley Field. It almost felt like a home game. Shouts of "Let's Go, Cardinals" were almost as common as Cubs cheers. They were always fun games and, regardless of the standings, were very competitive.

The Cardinals continued to struggle on the road, losing the first two games 5–4 and 3–0, before winning the third game 6–2 behind starting pitcher Jake Hudson. Paul was taken out of all three games in the late innings again, but he did manage two home runs, including a grand slam during the series, pushing his RBI total past the century mark. He headed to the locker room after being pulled in the first game to get some quick therapy from the assistant trainer and noticed former reliever Ryan Jefferson nosing around his locker, seemingly looking for something. Not sure about Jefferson's status with the club, Kolbe waited until he could talk to Coach Dave McFarlin about the situation.

"Hey, Dave."

"Back at you. Paul, What's up?"

"How well do you know Ryan Jefferson?"

"As long as he has been on the team, plus he is now a special assistant to John Nowicki. What's bothering you about him?" asked Dave as he read Paul's face.

"I saw him nosing around my locker. I didn't confront him, but maybe he was the guy who took my pine tar in the first place."

"You mean as opposed to Colby Rakers? Colby was just a butthead and probably took your stuff just to piss you off—even if the team lost a few games in the meantime. There's no reason for a front office guy to take anything out of your locker, Paul, or frankly even to be in the clubhouse."

"I agree. That's why I'm asking. If it happens again, I'm going to confront him, and I don't really care that he works directly for Nowicki."

"I'll have a talk with Ryan, and let's see what he was up to."

"Thanks, Dave. It's a sensitive issue with me. I don't have that much of the pine tar left, and I really need the stuff to grip my bat. And please spare me the 'batting gloves are good' mantra. I swear, sometimes I think you guys work for Rawlings, Mizuno, or Franklin!"

"We just might be if you don't start pulling your weight around here, old fella. I guaranteed ownership that you would hit at least forty homers, and you're going to have to gut it out to get those last few!"

"Dave, I've known you a long time, and the last time you had a guarantee of success was the year we finished in last place! I hope they know how to discount whatever you tell them!"

"Okay, you got me there. I will, no kidding, have a chat with Ryan and let you know what I find out. Meantime, do me proud and get a few more long ones!"

So the six-game road trip against lesser division foes netted two wins and four losses, not exactly what the Cards needed this late in the season if they were going to play into October. The Los Angeles Dodgers came to town next from Monday, August 22, through Wednesday, August 24. They, like the Cardinals, were battling for a division pennant and the wild card. The last thing the Cardinals needed was to be swept in a key home series, but that is exactly what happened.

The first game was a thriller, with the Dodgers prevailing 2–1. Chris Mitchell gave up only one run, but the bullpen couldn't hold off the opposition and took a tough loss for the Cardinals.

The second game of the series was a blowout for the Dodgers as they blasted starter Kyle Flynn and three relievers 13–2.

The final game of the series proved no better for the Cardinals as the Dodgers pounded Jay Gomez and another slew of relievers 9–4. The three losses pushed the Cardinals a full ten games behind the Brewers. Maybe it was time to seriously start thinking about the wild card.

The only bright spot was Paul Kolbe, as he continued to crank out hit after hit, along with an occasional home run. But RBIs were getting difficult to get, as the team just wasn't putting runners on base in front of him.

Pittsburgh then came into town for a four-game series from Thursday, August 25, through Sunday, August 28. This series represented an opportunity for the Cardinals to pick up some ground over a club headed nowhere. The team responded well, with 8–4 and 5–4 wins over the first two games, followed by a 7–0 loss (ace pitcher Mitchell just didn't have it that day), and concluding with a 7–4 win. The club, therefore, did its job, winning three out of four games. However, Milwaukee was even more efficient, winning all three games of a series against the Cubs. This pushed the Cardinals even farther back at ten and a half games, with a little over a month to go in the season. Meanwhile, on the wild card front, things didn't look much better, as the Braves enjoyed a nine-and-a-half-game lead on the Cardinals.

Tony LoDuca sat in the dugout of the final game against Pittsburgh longer than usual, as he was now convinced that retiring after the season was the right thing to do. It also seemed that the season was slipping away from him and his club, and he wondered if he had somehow telegraphed to his players that it was okay to slide through the rest of the season. "Damn," Tony thought. "Looks like this season is over anyway."

The question he was wrestling with in his mind was how and when to approach ownership, the players, media, and the fans about his final decision to retire. He was convinced that it was time. But if he said something right now, it would look like he had folded the tent on the season. However, if he waited till the team was officially out of the race, it would appear like he went out a "loser." If he could wait till, miracle upon miracle, the team actually won the division, league, or World Series pennants, that would be ideal, but what were the odds of that happening?

CHAPTER THIRTY-NINE

"Why does it always seem that a day off falls on a Monday? Wouldn't it be nice to have a Saturday or Sunday off?" mused Paul. "Don't kid yourself," he added. He hadn't had a weekend off in the summer since before he'd gone pro, and this year would be no different. He let his mind wander a bit. "Now," thought Paul, "just why did I turn that liver down? It was for the right reason, but dammit, it doesn't feel that way right now."

"For some reason," he said out loud to no one in particular, "I still think it will happen. But when? Will it be too soon? Will it be too late?"

A sense of urgency had fallen on the club, but especially on Paul Kolbe, as he was increasingly aware that his body was wearing down. Without a liver transplant soon, he would not be physically fit to continue playing baseball at any level. With just a month of the season left, the club would need him and everyone else pushing and pulling their weight to overcome the long odds facing them to get into the playoffs.

Plus, he was confused about what would motivate someone like Ryan Jefferson to mess with his livelihood. "Why would he care if I was successful or not?" he thought. "Wouldn't it be better if everyone on the team did well? What ax did he have to grind?"

And then there was the old bugaboo—alcohol. A day off during this stretch might just be more pleasant if he could just lay around the pool, drink a beer or two, enjoy some barbecue, and have a nice conversation on the phone with Heather. A minivacation? "Yes," thought Paul. "I earned this day off. I earned the right to have a little innocent fun, sun, beer, whatever." And then reality hit: there was no such thing as a beer or two for him. A beer or two would soon be a beer or three, followed by a shot of Jack Daniel's, followed by a quarter bottle of Jack over ice, followed by more beers and more whiskey. The end result would be a very bad hangover the next day and a real possibility that he would land in Tony's doghouse. And he still had an opportunity to go out on top with a Triple Crown. "Why waste this final chance?" thought Paul.

He wandered out to the pool around 10:00 a.m., still a bit groggy from lack of sleep, but ready to face the day. The only people brave enough to face the August heat—already at ninety degrees—were a few kids and their moms, with the exception of one attractive lady whom Paul had never seen before.

Not only was she attractive, but she also appeared to be working on a chilled pitcher of bloody marys, as evidenced by the large stalks of celery sticking out.

As Paul wandered by her chair on the way to secure several pool towels, he couldn't help make a comment. "Breakfast of champions?" he asked her.

"I'm not playing ball today, and neither are you, Mr. Kolbe," she said.

He abruptly stopped. "Do I know you? And how do you know what I did for a living?"

"Everyone here knows who you are, Paul. You're our residential hero, if not the whole town's. Certainly for us more mature folks, you are the real deal."

"Why thank you. Have we met before? And is that all you're having for breakfast?"

"Yikes no, Paul. I've been up for hours. I already did yoga, rode a bicycle, and swam a few laps, all after a high-protein breakfast. This happens to be a little 'wind me down' concoction I've developed to get to a nice lunch. Would you care to join me and have a sip?"

"You know, it's very flattering of you to ask. But I'm not a drinker, at least not now, and I really would prefer just a cold Diet Coke for now."

"You should try a little of this. I hear there are some additional side benefits to males, including increased stamina and performance."

"What the hell is she talking about? Is she coming on to me?" thought Paul.

"Perhaps I can stay a minute or two. You know I'm a ballplayer. What about you? What is your name, rank, and serial number, soldier?"

"My name is Alanna. I have a friend who lives here, a neighbor of yours, and I'm watching her place while she is on vacation."

I've never seen you here before."

"I'm relatively new in town. I'm originally from Atlanta, or 'Hotlanna,' as some of us prefer to call it."

"Yes, I've heard of 'both' towns. By the way, isn't a bit warm to be drinking something like a bloody mary? And isn't it a bit optimistic to have such a large quantity?"

"Actually, it's not too hot yet for this drink. It's kinda like a bloody mary, but not quite. And as far as the quantity, I was actually hoping you would wander by so I could entice you to sit down and join me for a spell. I'm a big baseball fan, but I'm afraid my hometown Braves are starting to make things a bit easier for your club to get into the playoffs."

"I don't know about that. We're taking it, as the cliché goes, one day at a time. It's tough enough handling your own business, let alone watching the scoreboard, too."

"I can see that. I was askin' before, but now you don't have a choice. Please sit down and join me."

"My, you are very persistent. Okay, for a minute or two. Now explain to me what is in your little pitcher."

"Take a sip and see if you can tell what it is. And, by the way, it's alcohol free."

Paul sampled Alanna's concoction and remarked how relatively mild the drink was. "I can't even taste anything specific. It sure is spicy, though. Very refreshing, too, in a citrusy way. Now I know why you like this stuff," he said as he took a bigger sip.

"Well, it works for me," said Alanna. After a few more minutes of baseball chatter, Alanna asked, "How do you feel?"

"Why would you ask a question like that?" Just then, Paul started to feel a little tipsy. "Wow. That stuff has an afterburner kick to it. I'm starting to get a little woozy."

Several minutes passed by, and he suddenly started to feel a bit disoriented. "I'm not sure if it's the sun, your drink here, or what, but I'm not feeling so good."

"I'm sorry to hear that. You do look a little under the weather. What if I helped you back to your place and tucked you in for a while? And if you don't feel better, I can take you to a doc-in-the-box or even the emergency room. Goodness knows there are enough hospitals near here."

With that suggestion, Alanna helped Paul negotiate his way back to his place. "Here, just drop me off here," Paul said as they approached his couch.

"Will you be okay? I can stay awhile to make sure you're all right."

"I'll be…" he said as he fell into a deep sleep.

"Paul? Paul?" Alanna Rakers Jefferson checked and made sure Paul was still breathing. She then dialed her husband, Ryan Jefferson, and said, "Done deal. He's out like a light. Should be for at least long enough to miss the team charter to Milwaukee. Boy will Tony be upset with this guy. Not much consolation for having my brother shipped off to Toronto, but it helps a little bit."

"I agree. Now dump the stuff you had left. Throw the pitcher away, and get the hell out of there. Don't do anything in a hurry. Just look natural. I'm glad to get a little revenge for Colby, too, but enough is enough. We're almost done with the subterfuge after this little caper. I promised Colby one more swipe of Kolbe's pine tar and then we are officially done with these shenanigans."

Alanna disposed of the evidence, including what was left on the pool patio, and was out of Paul's place, including one more check on Paul, in less than five minutes.

Meanwhile, Dave McFarlin was growing anxious. He had called Paul on the spur of the moment while near his neighborhood to suggest lunch and left several messages. He then stopped by and noticed Paul's vehicle in the carport, lights on inside, but no response when he knocked on the door and rang the bell.

He then drove to the manager's office, introduced himself and explained his concerns. "That doesn't seem at all like Paul Kolbe. He's usually very responsive whenever I've had to stop by for something. Can we go by his place and make sure he is okay? I don't think he'd mind if he knew we were concerned about him."

"Normally I would say no, but you've convinced me that this is not usual behavior by Paul. Sure. Meet over there in a few minutes, and I'll have someone from housekeeping stop by and let you in."

What seemed like an eternity passed by, and Dave was finally let into Paul's residence. What he found was Paul sprawled out on the couch in some kind of deep sleep. "Paul, wake up. Paul, can you hear me?"

"What the...?" Paul replied faintly. "Alanna? Alanna?" he asked.

"Paul, it's me, Dave McFarlin. Who's Alanna?"

"Ala..." He fell back to sleep.

"We need to get this man to the hospital quickly. Something, or someone, has done something to him," said Dave to the housekeeper. "Please have your office call 911 now!"

Fortunately, Paul chose an area of Saint Louis County that was teeming with hospitals. A Virginia Heights ambulance responded in less than ten minutes and was hauling Paul out the door in fifteen minutes flat. Once in the ER facility of Saint Edwards, the presiding doctor asked Dave what happened and what Paul had in his system.

"I have no idea. Only that he repeated the name Alanna several times before falling into a deep sleep. Sounds like he ran afoul of a lady bent on doping him up for some reason."

"Not to worry," advised the doctor. "His heart rate, pulse, and oxygen levels are all consistent with someone in the deepest part of their sleep cycle, so I don't think we need to be concerned about anything truly harmful. Why would someone want to put your friend in a deep freeze, probably for the next twelve hours or so?"

"I'm not sure," replied Dave. "But that time frame would have caused Paul to miss our team charter flight to Milwaukee, perhaps the most pivotal series we'll have this season."

"Sounds like you have a motive, and who knows what the reason might have been. Perhaps you should contact the Virginia Heights Police Department for additional insight."

"I might," replied Dave. But he also knew that inviting the police department in meant that media would soon follow. Did the team need that kind of a hit at such a critical point in the campaign?

Forty-five minutes later, the doctor came out to the waiting area and advised Dave that the tox screen came back and indicated that Paul had high, but not damaging, levels of Ambien in his system, a drug designed to assist patients with sleeping disorders.

"Because of the relatively mild amount of drugs Paul has in his system, we'll be able to release him in time to make your charter flight to Milwaukee tomorrow. You might want to advise your manager that it would be wise to take Paul out of the starting lineup. He might be able to play at full speed later in the game."

CHAPTER FORTY

Paul made it on the charter flight the next day for the critical three-game series with Milwaukee from Tuesday, August 30, through Thursday, September 1, but he was indeed a bit woozy. After Dave McFarlin conferred with Tony LoDuca, it was determined that a start on the pine was in order for Mr. Kolbe. "I want our security personnel to look into this situation, too, Dave," said Tony. "There's been too much crap going on against Paul, and it's time to put a stop to it."

The first game was a masterful pitching performance on both sides of the diamond, with the Cards' Edwin Robinson prevailing 2–1 after an assist from the bullpen. First baseman Al Robles supplied the power with a two-run homer after pinch hitter Paul Kolbe coaxed a walk from the Milwaukee closer.

Game two of the series was a lot more comfortable for the Cards, as they cruised to an 8–3 win behind the pitching of Jake Hudson and the robust hitting of nearly the entire lineup. Home runs came from Robles, Kolbe, and Champlin, and the team pounded out fourteen hits overall. At this point, the team was 72-64 and still trailing Milwaukee in the Central Division and Atlanta in the wild card by eight and a half games each.

Game three of the series was more good news for the Cardinals, as the team pulled out an 8–4 win with a major assist from the bullpen and late-inning heroics by the same three sluggers—Robles, Kolbe, and Champlin—just as they had done in game two of the series. The win moved the club to within seven and a half games of first place in the Central Division. They remained at eight and a half games out of the wild card race, as the Braves also won.

CHAPTER FORTY-ONE

The Cardinals came off the road for a three-game series with the Cincinnati Reds from Friday, September 2, through Sunday, September 4. Going into the Labor Day holiday weekend, the Triple Crown race was still alive in the National League, with all four candidates in the hunt:

Player	Home Runs	RBIs	Average
Paul Kolbe	48	129	.335
Al Robles	42	119	.329
Joey Costa	44	121	.329
Carlos Vasquez	40	116	.334

Matt Bradley would be returning to the club effective August 30 so he could be placed on the postseason roster. The timing of this move was near perfect, as it was obvious to most fans, the media, and Cards management that Paul, for whatever reason, was running down physically. Plus, a full-time effort in the outfield did not seem like a good strategy with a healthy Matt Bradley ready to play for the first time this season. Questions by fans started appearing in Cardinals blogs regarding Paul's "sudden" decline, and Bernie Madlock elected to go semipublic with a statement in his own on-line column:

Out of Steam?

It should be obvious to most fans that Paul Kolbe is running out of steam...whether it's age or some health-related issue, I'm not sure, but the timing of Matt Bradley's return could not have been more fortuitous.

With Matt's official return, Tony called a meeting in the clubhouse to make a formal welcoming back to the Cardinals.

"Gentlemen," said Tony, addressing the assembled players and staff, "I'd like to personally present to you our newest Cardinal—Matt Bradley!"

Shouts of joy and applause broke, along with some nervous glances at Paul Kolbe.

"Although Matt would rather fight me than being taken out of the lineup the rest of the way, he will need some time off to rest his shoulder. In the meantime, we are very fortunate to have Paul with us this season. He will play, as he has done all season, when we need him out there, and the same applies when Lance Champlin needs a break in right. All other times, we'll deploy Paul as our pinch-hitting weapon, something he has shown great skill at."

"Matt, would you like to say a few words?" asked Tony.

"A few words, Tony!" said Matt, as everyone chuckled. "Seriously, it's good to be back. I'll be fresh for September and hopefully beyond. I'll be honest and realistic at the same time—I'm not one hundred percent healthy, as Tony alluded to, but I had to be activated now or miss any potential playoff games altogether. I also want to acknowledge the fantastic job done by my replacement for this season—Paul Kolbe!" continued Matt, to a now standing, cheering staff, players, coaches, and even Hank Rheinhold and John Nowicki, who slipped into the room to observe the meeting.

"And," continued Matt, "I hope either Paul or Al get the hardware for that Triple Crown; we need to keep this spectacular achievement as a Cardinals one!"

Spying John and Hank, Tony asked, "Hey Boss One and Boss Two. Do you want to add anything to our discussion here?"

John looked at Hank and Hank gestured to go ahead. "Hey guys, and ladies from the front office. I just wanted to reinforce what's been said here already. This team has a chance, albeit a long shot, to go deep into October. We have Matt back, plus Paul. That's like trading for a superstar for 'future considerations.' I've never seen a group of guys like you who continue to fight day after day. Keep it up and let's enjoy this ride!" John concluded to cheers and applause.

Later, as Paul was getting dressed for the game, Matt wandered over to his locker, extended his hand, and said, "Thank you, Paul. I know this whole season has been wearing you down, but I'm amazed at just how good you've played so far. I know this is your so-called last hurrah, but I think there are an awful lot of fans pulling for you around the country to win the Triple Crown. Count me as one of those fans, too. I'm proud to say that I'm one of your teammates! Don't be too surprised if you get more at bats than advertised. Both Tony and I were conducting a little PR today to give our opponents something to think about. I won't be one hundred percent healthy until next spring training, so you'll still get plenty of hacks in!"

"Thanks, Matt. It's been a fun ride and I'm going to enjoy it wherever it takes me and whenever it lets me off!" said Paul.

Home cooking usually worked for the Cardinals, but, unfortunately, it did not translate to big success against the Cards' next division foes. The Reds took the first game 11–8 in a slugfest, and they also won the rubber game 3–2. In between, the Cards won 6–4, with Paul Kolbe supplying most of the power in the win.

In what appeared to be the new strategy for Tony's club, the lineup included Bradley and made Paul available for late-inning pinch hitter duties. Paul was also starting to feel that he could not field adequately in the outfield, but he was not about to turn down an assignment if Tony felt that Matt needed a day off due to his long rehab. In his only at bat in the Cardinals win during this series, Paul belted a bases-loaded double, scoring three runners and breaking the game open at 6-4.

Following the series, the Cardinals found themselves increasingly in trouble in the division at nine and a half games out. They were still eight and a half games out of the wild card. The calendar was relentless in September. Game after game, the season was dwindling with not much hope of a postseason appearance without some dramatic spurt by the Cardinals and/or a corresponding swoon by either the Brewers or the Braves. And speaking of the Brewers and Braves, the Cardinals had a chance to make some inroads against them as they started a three-game series against the Brewers on Monday, September 5, through Wednesday, September 7, followed by a rare late season day off and then a three-game series against the Braves on Friday, September 9, through Sunday, September, 11. It was time to make a run for the finish line.

CHAPTER FORTY-TWO

The Cardinals began using Matt Bradley as their near-everyday left fielder, and he did not disappoint, hitting a home run in game one of the crucial Brewers series. Unfortunately, that was all the scoring that the team could muster, as Milwaukee plated four runs in the top of the second inning, and the scoring ended for the game, 4–1. This pushed the Cards back into the double-digit range at ten and a half games within the division, not a good scenario given that it was game 141 of the season. Meanwhile, Atlanta left a crack in the door open, losing to the Phillies 9–0. Paul, in his new role as pinch hitter deluxe, walked his only at bat and was stranded at first with three consecutive strikeouts for Saint Louis batters to end the game.

Paul felt like he had played what Tony liked to refer to as a "hard nine," even though he spent 99 percent of the game on the bench. It was getting tougher and tougher to put on the uniform and take it off, shower, and head home. Paul felt particularly bad about the situation, because he knew that this was crunch time and the team could use a bat off the bench. Getting up and out of bed the next day wasn't a walk in the park for Paul either. He was bound and determined to see the season through, but it seemed as though his body wasn't listening. "Triple Crown?" thought Paul. "I'll be lucky to finish in the top ten of any offensive category the way I feel right now."

It's amazing what a good breakfast can do, however, for a person's disposition. Paul decided that, rather than sitting around his residence and feeling sorry for himself, he would motor into the city and start the day off with a good meal. He selected a small downtown café within walking distance of the ballpark, looking as nonchalant as any casually dressed visitor to the city. Paul couldn't help but grin when he was recognized by a group of attractive ladies who worked for a law firm in the building where the café was located.

"Are you Paul Kolbe, *the* Paul Kolbe?" one of them asked.

"I'm not sure who you are referring to, Miss, but I did notice that there is a nice article about someone of the same name here in the sports section of the *Post-Gazette*. The guy looks kinda old to me to be playing baseball, doesn't he?"

"Not at all," chimed in another lady.

"We were just remarking how handsome a man he is and that we wouldn't mind seeing his slippers next to our beds!" said another, as they all giggled like high school girls.

"My, my, ladies, surely you jest. After all, there are some very nice looking younger guys on the Cardinals baseball team, not to mention the hockey and football teams. Surely there are better opportunities out there for your speculative pleasure!"

"We beg to differ, and are you sure you're not Paul Kolbe? Other than the unshaven face and maybe slouchy clothes, there is a strong resemblance!" added one of the ladies.

"Slouchy clothes? Ladies, that is hitting below the belt!"

Just then, as luck would have it, Bernie Madlock sauntered in and ordered a coffee and bagel with cream cheese to go. That is, until he saw Paul.

"Paul Kolbe, what brings you here this morning? The game isn't till this evening, which makes you about six hours ahead of schedule."

Paul looked at the ladies, glanced at his half-eaten omelet, grabbed a piece of dry whole-wheat toast, threw some money on the table, and promptly left the premises. He managed a "Gotta go" response to Bernie and a "Pleasure to meet you, ladies" comment to them, as they were momentarily quieted by the sudden turn of events. Paul, based on Bernie's recent blogging on his "sudden decline," did not want to get into a protracted discussion with the writer on his health, which, no doubt, would have worked its way into one of Bernie's future pieces.

As he was leaving the restaurant, a man wearing sunglasses, dressed in a cream-colored summer suit, and sporting slicked-back hair was waiting at the curb next to a sleek, black, two-seat foreign sports car. His arms were folded as if he had anticipated running into Paul Kolbe.

"Mr. Kolbe? May I have a word with you for a minute?"

Paul stopped, looked at the gentleman, tried to appraise the situation, and then decided that it may be better to meet the individual head-on versus walking away from him. "Do I know you, Mr....?"

"My name is Jimmy John Harris. Remember our telephone conversation about me needing to meet with you as soon as possible? Can we sit in my vehicle for a few minutes? It's hot out here already this morning, and what I need to tell you needs to be with the utmost of confidence."

Paul was not sure what to do now, but the mention of the previous phone call piqued his interest, so he said, "Fine, but I don't have a lot of time."

"What I have for you won't take long. Hop in!"

Once both men were in the vehicle, Jimmy fired up the engine and the AC and then proceeded to lower the temperature control.

"Mr. Kolbe, as you know, I'm the guy that Nikki mentioned to you with the gambling proposal. Things haven't gotten much better for me since her untimely death. It may even be worse, as the amount I owe to my so-called bankers has gone up twenty percent. I'm a reasonable guy, and I would like to think of a reasonable solution, but I am really being squeezed."

"And I suppose your strategy is to roll some of that stress off on someone else if you can. Someone like me."

"Not so much that. It's just that you are in a unique situation to help me. You're doing really well. You have only this season to play. Your team still has a chance of going to the playoffs, where the big payoffs occur. In short, you can help me, and I can make you very comfortable in your retirement years."

"There's just one glitch in your scenario, Mr. Harris."

"Please, call me Jimmy John."

"Jimmy John, you can go fuck yourself. I told Nikki there was no way, and I'm telling you the same in no uncertain terms. It's not going to happen, at least not with me."

Paul then unlocked the passenger side door and got one foot out of the car.

"It's unfortunate that you feel that way, Mr. Kolbe," said Jimmy John. "Think about it. The next time I come back to see you, you may not have a choice, and it won't be so lucrative for you." With that comment, Jimmy John sped away and was gone from sight within a few seconds.

"What an asshole," Paul said out loud. "Come back and we'll see who has a choice. I'll use your noggin for batting practice!" Paul was livid.

With so much time on his hands, Paul decided to retrace his steps and head back to his residence. A short nap turned into a two-hour one, but he felt more refreshed than he did at the start of the day. "Slouchy clothes?" wondered Paul. "I thought I looked casually stylish!"

Paul eventually decided it was time to head to the stadium and be ready if needed off the bench. He called his favorite cabbie, Mario, who showed up in less than fifteen minutes.

The second game of the series went better for the Cardinals, as Kyle Flynn pitched a masterful game and the team won 4–2. Paul, once again, had a pinch-hitting appearance and made the most of it, driving in a run with a double, and then scoring on a groundout and a fly out, the latter in relatively short right field. Meanwhile, the Braves continued to struggle against Philadelphia, losing 6–3. Paul felt like he had played in a doubleheader. He barely had enough energy to peel his uniform off, jump in the shower, and put on a polo shirt, jeans, and sandals. He was about to call a cab when Dave McFarlin came to his locker and offered him a ride home.

"Are you up for getting a quick bite to eat on the way out to your place, Paul?" asked Dave.

"Sure, Dave. I'm really beat, but if I don't eat something, I'll feel even worse in the morning. There are several places on the way. Your call, and I'll pick up the tab."

"You ballplayers are all alike—throwing your big wallets around in front of us poor coaches!" kidded Dave. "Seriously, Paul, the reason I wanted to spend a little extra time with you was to see how you were dealing with the sudden change from everyday left fielder to pinch hitter extraordinaire. And damn, you're really good at pinch-hitting!"

"To be honest, Dave, it's a big disappointment at this stage of the season. I'm glad Matt is back, but damn, I've had a good—no, *great*—season. It's tough to sit on the bench for most of the game, and it's really tough to get used to what a pitcher is throwing with a few practice swings to deal with. On the other hand, I'm getting weaker and weaker, Dave. I need that liver transplant soon, or I think my body will start shutting down on me."

"I didn't know things were getting so critical, Paul. Does Tony know about your situation?"

"Yes and no. I don't think he knows that things are starting to get bad for me. I don't think he'd use me at all if he knew that. And I don't want everyone in the locker room to suddenly start feeling sorry for me when we have such an uphill climb."

"I'll make you a deal, Paul. I won't rat on you with Tony, and you tell me if things get so bad that you might hurt yourself either at the plate or in the field. We need you in the worst way right now, but not if you're going to be a sitting duck against a ninety-five-plus fastball or if you need to make a game-saving catch."

"That's very fair, Dave. In a perfect world, I get through the season, and the club makes the playoffs. Unfortunately, I would bet against the former happening, but not the latter. I like our chances, and every game we win and the Braves lose just reinforces how the whole team feels about our situation."

"That's good to hear. How 'bout some grub, and then we'll get you home so you can get your beauty rest."

Tony LoDuca did not want to push Matt Bradley too much upon his return to the lineup and started Paul for game three of the Milwaukee series. Paul responded with one of his better games of the season. Behind ace Chris Mitchell, the Cardinals won 2–0, pulling within eight and a half games of first place. In the wild card race, Atlanta lost once again to the Phillies by a 3–2 margin, and now were only seven and a half games in front of the Cardinals, with three games in Saint Louis looming just ahead.

In his first at bat, Paul was bound and determined to change his approach from his usual routine as a pinch hitter, that being to wait out a pitcher to see what he had to offer. Instead, Paul wanted to swing at the first pitch unless it was so far out of the strike zone that he couldn't reach it with a hockey stick. Fortunately, the pitcher wanted to get control of the count and laid one across the plate around ninety-one miles per hour. Paul almost put it out of the park, sending it to the last row of the left-field bleachers.

The second at bat was a virtual carbon copy. Surely the pitcher must have thought to himself, "This guy will revert back to his 'take a pitch or two' approach he's had all season long." The pitch came in, virtually the same place without as much zip to it. Paul's next homer did clear the left-field bleachers and landed on the concourse before caroming out the open gate and rolling across Clark Street. Not the likeliest place to stand for a baseball, but some lucky kid without a ticket was able to retrieve the ball, and he had a new hero—Paul Kolbe.

The game ended on the two solo homers by Paul, and the clubhouse attendant asked him if he would sign the ball that made it out to Clark Street for the youngster who had retrieved it. "I'll do you better than that for him," said Paul as he came out of the clubhouse to personally meet the youngster and his father. "Come back tomorrow, and I'll have box seat tickets for you and your dad."

Following a shower and a change of clothes, Paul jumped into a cab to head for his local residence. He had started using cabs to and from the stadium to avoid driving in heavy traffic. What to eat? "There's only so much pizza and Chinese delivery food you can handle," thought Paul. Maybe a quick trip over to nearby Great Western Plaza would yield something different.

Paul threw his equipment bag inside, took a quick look at the accumulating mail near the door, grabbed his car keys, and headed out the door. He eased into unusually heavy traffic and made the usual five-minute drive in a stop-and-go fifteen minutes. The plaza was bustling with people, but Paul thought it might be a good idea to park in the underground garage and emerge in the center of the restaurant plaza, where all his choices would be within a few steps of each other.

Al Robles had a sports pub place—at least in name only—at the plaza. Plus there was a Mexican restaurant, a steak house, an Italian café, and a kosher-style deli. As Paul started walking toward the stairs, he heard footsteps behind him. Turning around just in time, he avoided a fist directed at the back of his head by the larger of two men, and instinct took over. Before either of them could do anything else, Paul kicked one of the men in the groin and hit the other one in his Adam's apple with an open hand. Both men went immediately to the ground. Before either of them could move, Paul managed to kick both of them in their stomachs, whereby they both moaned and laid on the garage floor, doubled up. Just then, a security vehicle came around the corner with its routine yellow lights flashing.

Before long, both men were in custody with the Virginia Heights police.

"Any idea, Mr. Kolbe, why these two men would have tried to attack you?" asked one of the officers.

"I have a suspicion that they might have been sent by a not-so-gentleman from Las Vegas."

"Why Las Vegas?"

"That's where a guy that was involved with Nikki Cole lived. She was the young lady who took some potshots at me awhile back and then was run over by a police cruiser after she shot at that vehicle. Kind of a long story, but it would be helpful to know if these punks were imports."

"I'll let you know. But if you know more than you're telling us, you need to get us involved. It's for your own safety."

"I understand, and I'll keep that in mind."

By then, Paul was completely uninterested in eating and went back to his residence to contemplate the day's events. "Drama. What next?" thought Paul. "It's tough enough to play baseball at this level day in and day out. Drama? Don't need it!" With that, Paul settled on his couch and never officially made it to bed that evening.

Paul woke up to a beautiful sunrise and a perfectly clear day in Saint Louis. It was Friday, September 9, still officially summer, but starting to feel like fall. The weather forecast called for a crisp, early chill, but almost perfect baseball weather for the entire weekend. This was it for the Cardinals—win or go home when the playoffs began. Three games with the Braves. If they lost all three, it was likely the end of their season. If they won all three, then the Cardinals were legitimate playoff contenders. Anything in between would prolong the agony, and perhaps the futility, of trying to catch Atlanta.

Here's what Bernie Madlock had to say about the upcoming series in his "Bernie's Bytes" column:

Bring on the Clichés

It's do or die time for the Cardinals as they prepare for a critical three-game series with the reeling Atlanta Braves. Baseball is funny like that. Need one more shot at a division title? You got it! Didn't work out for you? How 'bout getting in through the back door with a wild card spot? As friend and Cardinal radio broadcaster Mike Shaughnessy frequently notes, "Old Abner has done it again!" And he has. The Cardinals can make up considerable ground if they take all three games this weekend. Win two of three and the hunt for a playoff spot is still a possibility. Lose two out of three or all three and the conversation starts to drift into a discussion about next year. So c'mon, Cardinals, give the fans something to cheer about for the rest of the season and me something fun to write about. Thanks for reading.

The Cards' starting staff was not set up well for the series, but it was just as important to get past the Brewers to at least have an outside shot at the Central Division pennant. Therefore, ace Chris Mitchell had to be used the previous evening against Milwaukee.

Game one came down to bringing Lance Lyon out of the bullpen and into the starting rotation. Lance was no stranger to starting, having been a starter earlier in the season at Memphis, the Cards' triple-A affiliate. And he didn't disappoint. He kept the Braves scoreless until the seventh inning when he ran out of gas and gave up three runs. Not to worry, as the Cards' middle lineup, plus a pinch-hitting appearance for Paul, stormed back with four runs in the home half of the seventh inning. The bullpen then took over, including a three-strikeout performance by closer Jason Blevins.

Paul's at bat was textbook Kolbe. The first pitch was virtually down the middle of the plate for a strike. The second pitch was high and wide of the strike zone, and Paul looked at it for ball one. The third pitch was low and inside, but close enough where Paul thought he could yank it out of the ballpark. He came close, but the ball ultimately pulled foul, just a few feet from the pole. The fourth and final pitch was over the plate, but it would have been a ball because it landed almost shoulder-high. Paul didn't get a good swing at it, but it was good enough to lift the ball above the shortstop and all the way to the wall between the Braves' left and center fielders. The hit was good enough for a double, scoring two runs.

Paul headed straight home after the game and decided that maybe he could indeed handle pizza delivery one more evening. He noticed several messages on his cell phone, one of them from the detective from Virginia Heights.

"Hello, I'm returning a phone call I received earlier this evening." The news from the Virginia Heights Police Department shed some light into Paul's recent assault. Seems as though both individuals were hired to "scare" Paul. They were not sure who hired them only that their payment ($2,500 each) was made through a post office box in Las Vegas.

"This has the smell of Jimmy John all over it. I do want to visit Augusta and Tony Rakers after the season is over for a little payback discussion, but I don't think he is capable of this kind of harassment," thought Paul. "I'll deal with Jimmy John if or when he surfaces again."

Game two turned out to be the identical score and result, 4–3, as lefty Jay Gomez gave up three runs early, but held on till closer Jason Blevins could again save the day. Paul continued his assault on Braves pitching with a triple and two RBIs. He worked his usual routine at the plate with the Braves pitcher, looking at what was intended to be a strike on the fat part of the plate. Instead, it drifted outside for ball one. The second pitch was formula as well, moving Paul off the inner part of the plate for ball two. The third pitch was a sinker ball, designed to drop as it neared the plate. It looked too good for Paul to not swing, and swing he did, sending a wicked foul ball into the Braves dugout for strike one. The fourth pitch was low and inside, but not inside enough. Paul pulled it down the foul line and it one-hopped to the wall in left field. By the time the outfielder caught up with the ball, Paul was motoring past second base. The throw came in as a looping arc to third base, and Paul slid in around the tag. "A big hit in a big game. Doesn't get any better than that!" thought Paul.

"Looks like pinch-hitting comes naturally to you, Paul," said Tony after the game in the locker room. "I can't think of a higher pressure situation, and you handled it well."

"Thanks, Skipper. But you know I'd rather be playing every day if I could. I'm glad, though, that Matt is back for the sake of the team. His big bat adds quite a dimension to our lineup!"

"That it does, and thanks for understanding, Paul."

Game three was decided early on, as Jake Hudson pitched into the eighth before closer Jason Blevins came in and saved his third game of the series with the final score 6–3. It was never close, as the Cardinals scored early and held on. Paul had yet another pinch-hitting opportunity, and he was handled "wisely," said Mike Shaughnessy in the broadcast booth, as he drew a walk on four outside pitches.

Most wouldn't have thought a walk would produce much fatigue for Paul, but here he was, stooping over like a much older man, laboring as he tried to stand fully erect.

After the game, Tony popped his head out of his office and called to Paul as he sat by his locker: "Hey, Paul, can you stop by my office before you leave this evening?"

Paul gave a quick nod and headed off to showers, peeling his uniform off as he walked, with everything winding up in the proper bin for washing and use another day.

Paul then headed to the skipper's office. "Hey, Skip. What's up?"

"Close the door and have a seat, Paul. You know us managers are like moms sometimes. It's hard for me to see you and not think that you're disappearing before my eyes. Even Nowicki has noticed that you have not been yourself of late. What can we as an organization do to help you?"

"I appreciate your concern, and John's as well, but I'm playing a waiting game with the Meyer Clinic in Rochester. They have to find the right match for me, and due to my rather rare blood type, it's been a difficult task."

"Has your drinking had something to do with your setback? I understand your waiting time is up to two years."

"Going on three now. It hasn't helped, but those days are hopefully gone for me. It's something I battle every day, from sunrise to sunset and beyond. I don't think alcoholism is something to be taken lightly. It requires constant vigilance, but it's worth it to see the kind of success I'm having on a day-to-day basis."

"I just wanted to let you know we're behind you. I think your new role has to help, but there will be times when I need you in the field, too."

"I can handle a hard nine once in a while, but probably not back to back. My goal is to get through the season. And while I'm at it, I may as well win the Triple Crown, too!"

"It's an amazing story, what you have been able to do in such a limited role here at the tail end of the season. And actually you're really good as a pinch hitter. I don't remember anyone who has had the kind of success you've had lately!"

"I don't know, Skip, but maybe it's because we are in a playoff race and maybe it's because this is my last chance. The stress of pinch-hitting is working for me and not against me. And hey, if I don't win the Triple Crown, then it looks like our own Al Robles could do it. And with both of us cranking, plus the other guys, plus the great starting and relief pitching, this team has a great chance to get into the playoffs. And that is energizing all of us in the clubhouse!"

"As it is for me. I also wanted to use you as a sounding board for something. I made a decision awhile back that this was going to be my last hurrah, too. I'm retiring at the end of this run, whether it's the season or postseason. Outside of my family and John, no one else knows about this decision. I'm really struggling with when the right time would be to announce this to ownership, the team, the media, and our fans. I don't want to disrupt the good thing we have going for us. And right now, the emphasis ought to be what is going on day after day on the field."

"I'm stunned, Tony, and also flattered that you would mention this to me. I suppose we're both in the same rowboat in regards to leaving the team on a permanent basis. My departure will be a little bit of a jolt, but yours will be a seismic shock!"

"I've been wrestling with this decision for some time, and I'm still not sure what to do. My inclination is to ride out the season and then make the announcement. Maybe advise John and Hank as soon as this week of my timing. But even that would be a potential distraction, and perhaps even a potential leak if someone else in the front office gets wind of any conversations or e-mails. It's been on my mind for some time, but then so has this team's success. I've never seen a late-season, come-from-behind roll like this team is on, and I don't want to screw it up with something about me."

"Now it's my turn to give some advice," said Paul. "You are a major figure here in Saint Louis. And your announcement will eventually cause a major shift in attention to you. This, of course, is going to happen anyway, but it doesn't have to happen until the season has run its course, either through the regular season or through the World Series, or anywhere in between. I think an awful lot of fans are looking at box scores, pitching matchups, injuries, rookie call-ups, and who is sitting down for the current game. If your announcement occurred while there were still games to play, I think the players would get even more stressed because they had the added pressure of making sure you went out a winner."

"So you're confirming what I've been feeling in my gut: to wait till after the season. Paul, there's something else I want to talk to you about, but not here. Can you meet me at Antonio's in West County for a late dinner? I'll treat you to a little pasta. Neither of us are drinkers nowadays, but they brew a mean ice tea and have great coffee."

"Tony, I heard that no one gets to see you after games. I'm flattered that I got invited."

"Actually, I have something very interesting to talk to you about."

Tony indeed had something to talk to Paul about, and they continued the conversation throughout several more dinners over the next few weeks.

Back on the field, as a result of the Cardinals' sweep, the club pulled within four and a half games of the Braves. Whether or not the Braves voiced it outwardly, they had to feel the pressure of playing baseball every day and having a team closing in on them with very few games left in the season.

CHAPTER FORTY-THREE

It was time for the Cards to take a seven-game road trip to Pennsylvania, starting with three games in Pittsburgh from Monday, September 12, through Wednesday, September 14, followed by four games against a surging Philadelphia squad from Friday, September 16, through Monday, September 19. The clock was ticking. Time was running out for Saint Louis.

Game one of the Pirates series was a tough 6–5 loss, as the team could not overcome a rough outing by Lyon and an equally rough performance by the bullpen. Offensively, Matt Bradley was battling a slump, as his shoulder was still not 100 percent. Tony decided Matt needed a little more time off, so he inserted Paul in left field for game two. Things went better overall, with Al Robles, who always hit well in Pittsburgh, Lance Champlin, and Paul hitting solo homers en route to a 6–4 win. Atlanta had won its second series game with Miami after dropping the first game. Two more days of status quo off the calendar. Time to make a serious charge if the playoffs were going to happen.

Game three of the series was a well-pitched game with highlight-reel defensive play from both teams. The Cards won 3–2, and once again Al Robles played a big part, swatting a home run, a double, and a single. Paul went hitless, though he did drive in a run on a sacrifice fly. Yet another game came and went off the schedule, and the Cardinals were still four and a half games off the pace for the wild card.

Thursday, September 15, a rare day off this late in the season, was good and bad for the club. Good in that the players received extra time for much-needed R and R, but bad in that they could lose momentum.

For Paul, it was a welcome break of kicking back and doing virtually nothing for a whole day.

For Tony, it was a time to consider his approach to ownership regarding his retirement. Deep down he knew that Nowicki had probably confided in Rheinhold already, but it was still Tony's desire to tell him personally of his decision. He was willing to wait till the conclusion of the season, whenever that would be, but he felt he owed it to Hank to tell him earlier. "Maybe sometime during the last home series versus the Cubs," thought Tony, half aloud.

Moving on to Philadelphia, the Cardinals became serious scoreboard watchers despite Tony LoDuca's directive to "play a hard nine" and let the baseball gods sort out the standings. "If we all focus on the games we have remaining, one at a time, then we'll maximize our results. And if we fall short, then we won't have any regrets. On the other hand, just think about what we could do in the playoffs if we get in."

Game one on Friday, September 16, went the Cardinals' way, 4–2, thanks to hot-hitting Al Robles, who was making a serious charge at Paul Kolbe and the other two contenders for the Triple Crown. Paul was increasingly at a disadvantage, as he was not starting every day and sometimes received only one or even no plate appearances. His lead was slipping steadily, with the real potential for him finishing fourth versus first in the race for batting honors. Unrattled, though, Paul was increasingly more concerned about his deteriorating health and whether or not a liver transplant would ever happen.

He also was concerned about seeing the year through. "It's literally one day at a time," thought Paul. But what a day-at-a-time season he was having.

Game two on Saturday, September 18, was a clunker, a 9–2 loss against Philadelphia's newly acquired Roy Buckwald, a former Houston Astros starter and longtime Cardinals nemesis. The only positive aspect of the game was a two-run homer by Paul off the bench, something he seemed to be specializing in with his pinch-hitting role lately.

ONE LAST HURRAH

His new routine on the road was to get back to the hotel, order room service, and then head to the hot tub if the facility had one. Usually he would be the only one in the whirlpool area, as it was late and hotel pools and spas were officially closed. But every once in a while, though, someone would still be hanging out. It was this particular night that two ladies of uncertain age, perhaps midthirties, were sharing a bottle of champagne and eyeing Paul as he asked politely if he could join them.

"You bet! Did you come here this evening to save two damsels in distress?"

"No, I came here to soak some heat up into my weary old bones for a while. But you two hardly look like you're in distress. Looks like you're having a great time."

"The distress," giggled the brunette, "is that we're both pretty horny."

"That's right," joined in the other lady, a redhead.

"Wow. Do you want me to check with the concierge for you and see what the hotel can do about that?"

"Why don't you just save us the trouble and join us in our suite after we finish this champagne. Would you like some, Mr....?"

"Kolbe. Paul Kolbe. Ladies, I'm very flattered. In fact, you made my day. But my line of work requires a good night's sleep, something I don't think I could possibly get if I hung out with you two for a while. And frankly, I'm making a concerted effort to stay away from alcohol. That would be something else very difficult to do if I went back to your suite. By the way, what do you two do that brought you to Philadelphia?"

"You surprise me, Mr. Kolbe," said the brunette. "I don't know too many red-blooded men who would turn down two cutie pie elementary school teachers."

"Especially both of us!" chimed in the redhead.

"Teachers? There weren't any grade school teachers in my school that looked as attractive as you two! And perhaps I'm incredibly stupid, but I have to get my beauty sleep for tomorrow's game. I'm a baseball player for the Cardinals and we're in town to play your Phillies."

"Now that's way too cool," said the redhead. "If I take my top off, would you mind autographing my left boob?" she giggled.

"Yeah, me, too" chimed in the brunette.

"Ladies, before I get into a lot of trouble, I think I'll bid you both good night. And thanks for the memories of what could have been a very interesting evening!" Paul then extricated himself from the situation, cursing himself lightly for passing on spending time with the two lovely ladies, yet congratulating himself as well. "Maybe Heather means more to me than I realized," said Paul out loud.

He made his way back to his room and spent the better part of an hour staring at the ceiling while lying spread-eagled on his king-size bed. Somewhere during the early morning hours he dozed off for yet another night without a lot of sleep. Morning came too quickly and he took a quick shower, tidied up his appearance, dressed casually, and met the other Cardinals in the lobby for the bus ride to the ballpark.

Game three on Sunday, September 18, saw ace Chris Mitchell paired up against the Phillies' Cole Hamilton, and Chris got the best of Philadelphia, shutting them out 5–0.

Neither Al nor Paul, who started the game, figured into the scoring, but both kept Chris Mitchell's shutout intact with sparkling defensive plays. Al dug a few would-be errant throws out of the dirt, started a first-to-second-and-back-to-first double play, and made a near belly flop catch in the stands on a foul ball near the Cardinals dugout. Paul made a similar play along the left-field foul area near the stands, and he threw a runner out at second trying to stretch a single into a double.

Game four on Monday, September 19, paired Kyle Flynn against the Phillies' ace Roy Holliman, and it proved to be the game of the series. The Cards took a 1–0 lead as Holliman uncharacteristically gave up two walks in the first inning. The Cards promptly gave that run back in the bottom of the first, and then the Phillies plated another run in the second to take a 2–1 lead. The Cardinals tied it in the fourth, and the game went scoreless until the seventh, when the Phillies pushed a go-ahead run on a ground ball error to second baseman Skip Russell. It was time for heroics, for that magical something that only happens in those rare seasons when everything comes together. That magic moment came in the top of the ninth, when Paul Kolbe batted for starting pitcher Kyle Flynn.

The first batter of the inning, Skip Russell, coaxed yet another walk from Roy Holliman, and in stepped Paul. The Phillies might have been tempted to walk him, given his pinch-hitting acumen of late. But that would have necessitated putting the winning run on base, something that the baseball gods would definitely frown upon. Holliman still had his good fastball this late in the game, plus his killer curve had been nicking corners against right-handed batters all night.

The first pitch was almost down the middle of the plate. "Strike!" bellowed the umpire. The second pitch was a nasty slider. "Where was the book on that one?" thought Paul. Holliman seemed to have been saving that pitch for this critical moment. "Ball," said the umpire, much to the consternation of the pitcher and the relief of Kolbe.

"Damn, that was close," said Paul to no one in particular. Pitch three was a purpose pitch, high and tight around Paul's chest.

"Ball," said the umpire, as the catcher turned around and glared at the umpire. This was considered a neutral pitch count but the pitcher definitely did not want to go three balls and a strike if he could help it.

The next pitch wasn't ideal from Paul's perspective, but it was good enough to take a swing. The Philadelphia ballpark is considered a hitter's park because of the relatively short fences, and Paul's ball just barely cleared the left field wall at 330 feet, not his most majestic home run, but good enough to count as much as a 500-footer. The home run gave the Cardinals a 4–3 lead, which they maintained to win the game.

Meanwhile, the Braves lost two out of three to the Mets, and the first series game with the Marlins. Their lead over the Cardinals for the wild card spot had shrunk to just three games.

CHAPTER FORTY-FOUR

Back home again, another big series was looming ahead for the Cardinals. Actually, this is an understatement, as every series is big in a pennant race. There were only three series left for a total of nine games, all against teams that would be sitting out the postseason. These teams—the New York Mets, the Chicago Cubs, and the Houston Astros—would be playing loosely, as they had absolutely no pressure on them. Plus, all three teams would be mixing and matching lineups, interspersed with veterans and rookies looking to make one final impression for their next year's contract or to stay with the big club.

Game one of the Mets series on Tuesday, September 20, turned out to be an interesting demonstration of the collective will the Cardinals had in getting to the playoffs. The Mets jumped to a 6–0 lead, only to see the Cardinals roar back with eleven runs to win 11–6. The bullpen did the job of holding the opposition, and the bats for the Cardinals were booming: Al Robles had a single, a double, and two walks; Lance Champlin had two doubles; Matt Bradley had a double and a home run, and he was hit by a pitch. Paul did not get into this game and missed an opportunity to participate in the slugfest. Meanwhile, X rays were taken of Matt Bradley's elbow as a precautionary matter. They came back negative, but Tony LoDuca decided to sit Matt down for a few days, as he had a red-hot-hitting Paul Kolbe available to play in his place.

Game two on Wednesday, September 21, saw some additional success for the Cards, as they won 6–5 with Matt Bradley on the bench and in the clubhouse nursing his sore elbow. In a trend not especially suitable to playoff baseball, all the Redbird scoring came on home runs, including one each by Al and Paul.

Game three on Thursday, September 22, was not so successful, as the Mets prevailed 8–6, one of the rare occasions where the bullpen failed to nail down a win. Given that the Braves won two out of three in their series with the Marlins, the Braves held onto a two-game wild card lead over the Cardinals.

Although everyone on the Cardinals and the Braves were reluctant to admit it, scoreboard watching, without making it too obvious, was the order of the day. The habit extended from the players who would nonchalantly peek over their shoulders at the right-field scoreboard; to the managers and coaches who were constantly looking up and out at the big scoreboards in their respective stadiums; to the members of senior management and ownership, who would watch the other team's game in their suites while their team was playing on the field; to the media, both print and electronic, who constantly brought up the subject with Cardinals staffers; and finally to the fans, who speculated on how many wins the Cards and Braves could achieve for the remainder of the year.

As far as the media was concerned, it was never too early to speculate on 'what ifs.' Bernie's latest on line column spoke to this subject as follows:

Scoreboard Watching for the Birds

Let's face it, Cardinals fans. The division flag will be flying in Milwaukee this season, but all is not lost. Atlanta is in a nosedive of historic proportions and the all the Cardinals have to do to make the playoffs is play reasonably well down the stretch to the finish line. Easier said than done, as their opponents are playing loose, with nothing to prove, nowhere to go. So buckle your seat belts, Cardinals fans, as the rest of the season should be a fun ride. Thanks for reading.

CHAPTER FORTY-FIVE

Only three home games remained on the schedule, all with the Cubs, from Friday, September 23, through Sunday, September 25. And then the season ended in Houston, with three games from Monday, September 26, to Wednesday, September 28.

Matt's elbow was feeling much better, so Tony reinserted him in the Cards lineup, bumping Paul back to the bench and his pinch-hitting role. Since Paul had more clubhouse time, he started observing Ryan Jefferson's comings and goings, the theory being that Jefferson had no good reason, as a nonplayer, to be in the clubhouse for any reason unless Tony wanted to confer with him about a player development issue.

He finally got his chance to confront Ryan during the third inning of the first Cubs game when the Cardinals were in the field. Ryan was reaching for Paul's pine tar in his locker when Paul surprised him, spun him around, and pushed him over a folding chair, knocking both the chair and Jefferson loudly to the floor.

"What the fuck did you do that for?" asked Ryan as he looked at the scrape on his elbow.

"Because I finally found the dickweed who has been harassing me since I've been here. You better start talking, or you won't have any teeth left to talk about anything, Jefferson."

"I was just looking at your pine tar. Just curious. No harm. No foul."

"Sorry, at this late date in the season, I don't believe you. Do you want to go up to John Nowicki's suite with me and explain what you were doing in my locker?"

"Hey, my wife, Alanna, and I were just trying to spook you a little bit. That's all. We were doing it for her brother, who felt threatened by your presence the moment you showed up. Don't ask me to explain why. You didn't play his position."

"Your wife? Alanna? Of course, it's starting to make sense. Your brother-in-law is our dear, departed Colby Rakers! First of all, what you did, and what your wife did, was not just a little series of pranks over the summer. I don't care if the pine tar worked or not; you had no business snooping around my locker, much less taking something out of it. Your wife drugged me; I could have been left in a coma for all she knew. You are a staff member of this organization, of all people. Didn't they give you a second chance when you had drug issues with the league? Didn't Tony stick by you as the closer, even when things were shaky? And didn't he and Nowicki take you in as a member of the GM staff when your career was shot to hell earlier this year? This pisses me off so much so that I'm going to turn you over to Tony after the game. I want you to tell him what the Rakers and Jeffersons have been up to, and if you're lucky, he'll send you out to the boonies where you can play out the season as a bat boy. If you're not lucky, he'll ask John to can your ass and leave it to the media to figure out what 'for violation of team rules' means."

Tony and John met with Ryan Jefferson after talking to Paul at length following the game. "Pardon my language, but this is about as close to a clusterfuck that I've seen in a long time," said John. "For starters, you're fired at the end of the season. I'd do it now, but I don't think the club needs any more distractions as we head into the final week here. Ask the traveling secretary for a voucher for a trip to the training facility in Jupiter and stay the hell out of Saint Louis until your termination is official."

Of course, very little got by Bernie Madlock. He noticed that Ryan Jefferson, a fixture around Busch Stadium after he retired as a player, was no longer around. "Hey, Tony, what happened to Ryan? He was always good for a quote or two, and now I can't find hide nor hair of him."

"Ryan is down at Jupiter looking at several of our future prospects. As you know, Bernie, evaluating talent is a process that never ends if you want to stay competitive."

"So there's no truth to a rumor I heard that he was shipped out of town due to some disagreement."

"Bernie, this isn't a daytime soap opera. We're a ball club trying to get into the postseason. Where do you pick up your tips?"

"Tony, humor me for a moment. I wouldn't even bring it up if I didn't think my information had some credibility."

"Bernie, humor me for a moment. I'm not wasting my time talking about bullshit with you. You want to ask me a question about the club, the batting order, the pitching rotation, whatever, fine. Anything else, you're on your own."

"Man, a pennant race makes you cranky, Tony! I'm just trying to follow up on a lead, not bust your chops."

"Then stick to writing sports. There are other departments at your newspaper that deal in gossip. And close the door on your way out."

With that, Tony hoped the subject was officially closed. But Bernie did not feel that Tony had given him a fair shake, and he would continue to keep an eye open for more news on this subject.

Starting in early September, Paul noticed a dramatic drop-off in his energy levels, and it took all the strength he could muster to get to the park, play the game (even if that meant only pinch-hitting), take a shower, and head home to bed. He also lost his appetite, and not eating made things even worse. He started dropping weight, first a pound, then two pounds, then five pounds, then ten pounds.

To make up for the weight loss, he started eating heavier meals for dinner and added at least one, if not two, large milk shakes a day. "What a problem to have," thought Paul. "If I told anyone that I had to drink at least two milk shakes a day to try to maintain my weight, they would laugh me out of town." Paul chuckled to himself.

His uniform was starting to look like he borrowed his big brother's shirt and pants. Even his hat size had changed, dropping an eighth of an inch. He went to the equipment manager, talked his way into several smaller home and road uniforms, and bribed him with an autographed bat to not tell the skipper. Hopefully, no one would notice until after the season.

Fat chance of that. Eagle eye Bernie was back in the clubhouse and approached Paul.

"Paul, how are you feeling nowadays? You look like you've lost a lot of weight. Is this typical for you at the tail end of a long professional baseball season?"

"It's a little more pronounced than normal for me, Bernie. But I haven't had the benefit of a full season of work for several years," said Paul, hoping to deflect the conversation.

"Well, take care of yourself, Paul. I think the club is gonna need you down the stretch."

"Thanks for stopping by, Bernie."

With that exchange, Bernie wandered off to Tony's office.

"Got a minute?" asked Bernie as he poked his head inside.

"Depends, Bernie. Are we talking soap opera today or baseball?"

"Kinda both, Skipper. Have you noticed the rather dramatic weight loss that Kolbe has been experiencing? I couldn't tell you what kind of poundage I'm referring to, but it seems like he is a whole size smaller since the start of the season."

"Bernie, that smacks more of soap opera than baseball, as far as I'm concerned. I see him out there every day, ready to play. If he's in the field, he handles his position very well. If he is being used as a pinch hitter, then he provides dangerous power off the bench. If he has lost weight, I think it's normal for a guy like that who has been out of the game for several years."

Not satisfied with the answer, but unwilling to start a protracted conversation just before the game, Bernie gave Tony a wave and headed out the door. "This is not done," said Bernie out loud in the hallway as he waited for the elevator to the press box.

ONE LAST HURRAH

That testy exchange between Tony and Bernie led to another on line column by Bernie as follows:

One or Two Sizes Too Small

I'll be the first to acknowledge that I'm out of my league when it comes to fashion, but if you've observed Paul Kolbe all season like I have it would be obvious to the naked eye that he has dropped a significant amount of weight in recent weeks. So much so that I would bet a C note or two that he is wearing smaller sized uniforms than when he started with the club. What is the significance of this sartorial dialogue? The Cardinals need Paul's big bat down the stretch, whether it's subbing for Matt Bradley or coming off the bench in a tight game and pinch hitting for someone else. The Cardinals aren't outwardly concerned about the situation. I hope they're right. Hang in there, Mr. Kolbe. Thanks for reading.

CHAPTER FORTY-SIX

The good news for Cardinal Nation kept coming. The Cardinals still had a statistical chance of winning the division outright. But they had a better opportunity to catch the faltering Atlanta Braves, who were just two games ahead of the Cardinals in the wild card hunt.

The other race—whether or not Paul Kolbe had a shot at winning the Triple Crown—was coming down to the wire, too. With Matt Bradley activated for the stretch drive and playoffs but nursing a bad elbow, how many hits did Paul—particularly in his weakened state—have left in his bat?

The main challenge seemed to be home runs, as fellow teammate Al Robles was just three behind Paul at forty-six. Joey Costa, the Cincinnati first baseman, had forty-five, and Carlos Vasquez, the Colorado outfielder, had forty-three. Paul had a comfortable lead in batting average and RBIs, but with his strength sapping and the need to give Matt some work for the playoffs, the opportunity for Paul to hit many more homers was not very great.

Before game one of the Cubs series, Tony waited until after batting practice and then made eye contact with Paul.

"Hey, Paul, can I see you a minute?" Tony caught him coming into the clubhouse as Paul was headed to the trainer's room.

"Sure, Skipper. What's up?"

"Come into my office, and please close the door."

"Damn," Paul thought. "Is this where I get the lecture about how the club needs Matt to play the rest of the season? I can't play a full nine innings anyway."

"Paul, you know that I'm aware of your medical condition based on our discussion. Moreover, I know that you've already refused a liver transplant because you wanted to see this season through. We both know that once you have that operation, you're done. I also know that you need to get that transplant, or you could die. I've done a little checking around the country with some folks I know, and it seems as though there could be some movement in regards to your spot on the wait list because of your medical condition and the fact that the liver transplant you passed on saved the life of a fifteen-year-old girl with a rare liver disease. You earned a lot of goodwill points as a result."

"Wow, Skipper. I'm starting to think you have better resources than Bernie Madlock does!"

"Not quite. But I do want you to agree that if a compatible liver does become available again, you will not hesitate to take advantage of what undoubtedly is your last opportunity."

"I can do that. I think left field is in pretty capable hands right now, don't you? And center field, with the kids platooning and Colby Rakers long gone, looks good. And the other older fella in right—and thank goodness for someone else near my age—has had a tremendous year. I would, however, like to stick around as long as I can. Believe it or not, I like the idea of winning the division. And I've gotta be honest here: my personal achievements at my age mean a lot to me, plus I'm sure every other player on the downside of his career is kinda sorta pulling for me, too."

"I'll make you a deal, Paul. I want you to continue to be my late-inning pinch hitter for the few games left of the season. You have the skills and the mental fortitude to perform in this pressure-cooker hitting situation. We may need just one of those big hits from you to catch Atlanta for the wild card. I'm not giving up on the division title yet, but we're staring at some very long odds that Milwaukee doesn't come through at this point."

"That works for me, Skipper. I don't think I could do you much good anyway in the field, given where I'm at physically."

ONE LAST HURRAH

As soon as Bernie arrived in the press box he noticed the lineup posted for the day's game. Paul was on the bench, and Matt was back in left field. "I'm not letting go of this story," said Bernie to himself. Back to the elevator, back to the clubhouse, back to Tony's office. He once again poked his head through the doorway. "Hey, Tony, can I talk to you for another minute?" asked Bernie.

"Now what, Bernie?"

"I noticed you made a hasty lineup change before the game earlier this week by dropping Kolbe and adding Bradley. And you then followed up with that lineup change a second day in a row and inserted Bradley again in left field. You have a guy who could win the Triple Crown sitting on the bench. And you've dropped two games in the standings to Milwaukee. What gives?"

"You're very astute today, Bernie, and on top of your game. I never ask you for favors, and you never do likewise. But I'm going to now."

"No promises, Tony, but I'll give your request serious consideration."

Tony followed by updating Bernie on everything he knew about Paul's condition.

"Wow," said Bernie. "That's a real can of worms. I'll sit on this as long as someone else doesn't run with it. Otherwise, my boss would run me out of town!"

"Not to worry," advised the skipper.

It was time for the last three home games of the season, which were against the Cardinals' traditional rival, the Chicago Cubs.

Before the action started on the field, Tony felt it was time to formally advise ownership of his decision to retire at the conclusion of the season. Tony asked John to set up the meeting as a luncheon with just Hank Rheinhold representing ownership, the purpose being to minimize curious eyes and ears around the stadium. The three of them met at Charlie Giovanni's Restaurant in the heart of downtown Saint Louis. Tony had called and made the reservation personally, so Charlie was in the small lobby area when the three parties arrived.

"Gentlemen, what a pleasure to see you. I've brewed up some fresh coffee for you and have a private seating area for your luncheon."

"Thanks, Charlie," said Tony. "I know that whatever you have for us will be perfect!"

Tony went back and forth with John and Hank for the next two and a half hours, first advising them of his decision to retire and then recounting some of the highlights—and a relative few of the lowlights—that occurred during his career with the Cardinals.

When they were almost talked out, Hank asked Tony, "So who should we look very seriously at regarding your replacement?"

"I think there is one outstanding candidate, and I'm confident that when I mention his name, John will probably agree that you and he should take a hard look. The qualifications and connections are deep. There is one glaring problem, but it's not something that can't be overcome."

After Tony mentioned the name, John chipped in that he agreed and that said individual would be extended an invite to interview for the position.

Tony lastly mentioned his desire to keep his retirement under wraps until the end of the season so that the focus would remain on the field and not the dugout. With that bombshell out of the way, it was back to baseball.

The first game on Friday evening was similar to a recent recurring theme: let the other team get a big lead and play catch-up the rest of the game. It was a recipe for disaster.

Al did hit a solo homer, but it wasn't enough. Paul got into the game and sent a high fly ball that was caught at the base of the wall in left field just a little shy of the visitor's bullpen. The other Cardinals ballplayers were shut out, so it was getting late for the Cardinals to stay in the race. Final score: 5–1, and hardly a great time to lay an egg. And Atlanta? They lost their game, too, so the Braves stayed three ahead, now with five games to play.

Friday's game ended around 10:30 p.m., and by the time Paul left the park, he was at least as tired as he was hungry. He decided to stop by D.D.'s on the way home, grab a quick sandwich, and check out

ONE LAST HURRAH

SportsCenter on the tube to get a recap on the rest of the MLB scores and highlights. He became so absorbed in a BLT on whole-wheat toast (crispy bacon, fresh tomato, crisp lettuce, no mayo) that he didn't notice the gentleman standing behind him.

"Hello, Paulie. How are you doing? Mind if I join you for a minute"?

Paul turned around, and there was his "friend" from Rochester, Joe Fisher, in the flesh. "Whoa, is that you, Joe?"

"Hey, Paulie, did you think you'd only see me when you were in a drunken stupor? You quit that stuff after the AWOL incident earlier in the season, didn't you?"

"Wait a minute. The only person I've ever known as an adult who called me Paulie is a lady I'm in love with."

"And who might that be, Paulie?"

"Her name was, or I should say, is Heather. Heather Alexander."

"Actually, I believe her name, or rather her middle name, is Alexandria."

"You know her? And what would her last name be?"

"Her full name is Heather Alexandria Fisher."

"This is too much information for me to process. You, here in the flesh, and Heather...is she your daughter?"

"You flatter me, Paulie. No, great-granddaughter. My job here is almost through. You have a shot at winning the Triple Crown and helping your team get to the playoffs, even as a pinch hitter who gets only one at bat a game. All you have to do is hit a couple more homers to hold off your teammate. He's coming on strong, like he does at the end of every season."

"Your job? Who hired you? And what are you? You've been dead since 1975! And how does your great-granddaughter fit into this puzzle? Is she for real?"

"I can assure you that she is indeed very real. As for your other questions, I can't answer them. Only you can do that for yourself."

"Now you're messing with me, but maybe we can have this philosophical discussion some other time. I've been low on pine tar for a

245

while. Plus, I can hardly grip the bat being as weak as I am. And it feels like I'm getting weaker every day. Can you scare up a little of your black magic for the few remaining hitting opportunities I'm going to have in my season?"

"Paulie, first of all, it was never about the pine tar. It's great stuff, but you don't need it anymore. You have you. You're the only one you're competing against for the remaining few games you have. My advice to you is to grab a bat, grip that son of a bitch as hard as you can until it starts to leak sawdust, and smack the crap out of the first good pitch you see—probably the first pitch, if there are men on base. Be fearless. What the heck do you have to lose at this point? And batting gloves? Don't mess with 'em."

"It's not about the pine tar? Are you shitting me? I've prayed about it, obsessed over it, and hoarded that gunk. And now you tell me it's not about the pine tar?"

"It's about you, Paulie. Do you have the fortitude to get the job done? I think you do. I know you do. Just go out there and do it."

"What about Heather? Are we just going to keep bumping into each other, or is there something real between us? Are you going to tell me about who and what you are?"

"Heather and you are the real deal. Trust me on that one. And my work, as I stated earlier, is about done here. You just have to trust the system. The system works if you let it. So for starters, trust yourself. Good-bye, Paulie. Enjoy that Triple Crown trophy. It'll look great on your mantel. And think about 'Joe' as a boy's name someday. That would make me very happy. Take care."

"Wow," thought Paul. I need a drink. He turned around and looked at the bar for D.D. for just a moment, and in that instant, Joe Fisher was gone. He was by himself, and he had never felt lonelier in his life.

Paul walked over to the bar and ordered a shot of Jack Daniel's and a large Rheinhold draught beer. The bartender, someone who Paul didn't recognize, served them and asked if Paul would be running a tab. "No.

I just finished a meal and would like to take this out on the patio before I go."

"No problem," said the bartender. "Just let your server know when you're ready for your bill."

Paul took his drinks outdoors. It was getting a bit cooler, starting to feel fall-like. No one else was outside on the patio.

"Just one sip, maybe just this little, okay, not so little, glass and no more," thought Paul. He started to flash back through his journey to where he was today, back to the start of the season. Back to sitting on his endowed chair at the pub in downtown Rochester. Back to before he met Heather. Back to before he met Joe Fisher. Back to just Paul and his alcohol. Night after night. Back to waiting for a liver transplant that seemingly would never come.

He walked over to the railing and said, again, to himself, "Just who are you trying to kid, Paulie?" And then he promptly dumped the contents of the shot glass and the draught glass over the side.

He went back inside, settled his bill, and left the premises, satisfied that he was one the right track but wondering if he would ever see Joe Fisher again.

CHAPTER FORTY-SEVEN

Saturday, September 24, was a true chamber of commerce day, with just a slight breeze blowing west to east.

The game was a pitcher's duel—Cubs' ace against Cards' ace Chris Mitchell. For some reason, Chris did very well against the Cubs, and this day was no exception. The game was tied 1–1 going into the bottom of the ninth, with the Cardinals' run coming on a sacrifice fly to right field. The Cubs closer had dispatched the first two batters, but then he proceeded to walk the next one. The pitcher's spot was up, and it was time to try to win the ball game. Tony looked at his roster, and it was a no-brainer to summon Paul to pinch hit.

Once again Paul didn't disappoint. With one man on base, the last thing the pitcher wanted to do was nibble around the corners of the plate. He wanted to throw strikes and get the batter out. So that was what the Cubs' pitcher tried—emphasis on *tried*.

The first pitch was a ninety-seven-miles-per-hour fastball thrown slightly inside but still near the plate, a purpose pitch designed to intimidate the batter. Paul anticipated this strategy, shifted his feet slightly back and out from the plate, and put as much torque in his swing as he could, lifting the bat head slightly as he swung through the pitch. The ball seemed to have a rocket-like trajectory, hitting the upper section of Big Mac Land, well over 440 feet from the plate. The homer was a walk-off one and, at fifty, kept him three ahead of Al, five ahead of Joey Costa, and six ahead of Carlos Vasquez. Fortunately, the win kept the Cardinals hope for postseason alive, as Atlanta won, too. This kept the Braves four up with four to play.

Sunday, September 26, was another glorious day weather-wise. The sun came out to greet everyone without a cloud in the sky, yet could only muster candlepower up to around seventy-four degrees at its zenith later in the afternoon. It was the last regular home game of the season, and the Cardinals needed a win to stay in the hunt for a postseason berth.

As per the new norm, Paul sat on the bench, but something felt very different about this game. He had a feeling that he wasn't going to make the trip to Houston, that it was all going to end today, this afternoon, this ball game. He wasn't sure if it was going to turn out okay, but then he remembered Joe's mantra: trust the system, and trust yourself. He was at peace, and he felt that whatever happened today would be embraced and handled with the utmost confidence in his abilities.

Just before the team went out on the field for batting practice, the equipment manager handed Paul two urgent telephone messages, one from Dr. George Archer, the other from Heather.

"First the doctor," thought Paul. Could this be good news? It was.

"Yes," he heard through the phone. "We have a match for you. But you must get here no later than this evening. Otherwise, we can't guarantee the viability of the organ. Can you do it?"

There was no hesitation this time. "Yes, I'll be there. I'll leave right after today's game. I might be in my baseball uniform, but I'll be there."

"That's fine. You can scrub in, as we say here, when you get here. We're counting on you to make it this time."

"I'll be there. It feels like my work is done after today."

And then the second call. "Heather? How are you? I miss you. I want to see you. I'll be in Rochester this evening, although it'll be at the Meyer Clinic this time. Do we have a date?"

"You bet we do. And I suppose you'll need some TLC afterward. I think I can take a little time off and spend it in Rochester. I'll see you there this evening. Good luck today. I know you will do well, Paulie!"

She knows I'll do well? *Trust the system; trust yourself.*

After firming up a flight to Rochester, Paul went to Tony's office.

"Hey, Skipper, can I see you in your office for a minute?"

ONE LAST HURRAH

"Paul, I'm still working on our game strategy. Can it wait?"

"No, it can't." And then it dawned on the skipper what was about to happen.

"Paul, when do you have to leave?"

"Is every one psychic in my world?"

"Actually, we talked about this awhile back, and I knew the day would come and that it would be the end of your playing time here. I just wish it would have come a few weeks down the road."

"It's today. I have to leave no later than 3:00 p.m. to catch a flight to Rochester through Chicago. I have to make those connections."

"I understand. I'll keep that in mind if we need a pinch hitter earlier than usual, and I'll cover your tracks with the players, ownership, and media, but under one condition."

"What's that, Skipper?"

"You come back and be in our victory parade after we win the World Series."

"I can do that. I will do that!"

"Funny," thought Paul. "Life can be very fickle sometimes." He hated the thought of running out on the team in the heat of the pennant race, yet he had no choice. And he knew his time was up anyway with Matt back in action. But a good-bye wave to the fans, a few handshakes, and some bear hugs from his teammates would have been nice. "Well, win the World Series, guys, and then there will be time for that," thought Paul.

Just as promised, Tony kept eyeing his watch, the score, the number of pitches thrown by starter Jake Hudson, and even seemingly the number of pumpkin seeds that accumulated under the team's bench. Anything to keep his mind busy on this last home game of the regular season. It was a big day for Tony, too, as his own 'last hurrah.' Just like Paul, but for very different reasons, he couldn't reveal his intentions to retire at the end of the season, whenever that occurred. He wanted the focus to remain on the team and its drive to make the playoffs, and not on people saying good-byes to Tony. There would be an opportunity for that at a more appropriate time, hopefully after a World Series win.

Unfortunately, it didn't look like it was going to turn out the way Tony, Paul, and over 47,000 fans, players, and front office personnel wanted it to be. The Cubs jumped on Jake Hudson early, but he settled down before running into trouble again in the fifth inning. After allowing two runs in the fifth, the Cardinals trailed 2–0. Tony did not want to get any further behind, so he planned to take his starter out at the bottom of the inning. The Cardinals bats came alive and started to make the game interesting. A fly out. A walk. A groundout. Another hit, moving the runner over to third. Jake Hudson was due to bat, but his day was over. Tony looked at his watch, looked at Paul, and said, "Don't take too many pitches. You don't have time."

And with that comment, Paul grabbed his favorite white ash Louisville Slugger and marched to the batter's box, hardly taking a practice swing. The Cubs pitcher was a bit confused. "Why is Paul coming into the game so early? Does he think he can hit my curve ball?" the pitcher thought.

Paul wondered if the pitcher would follow the book on Paul—curve outside, fastball down central, fastball high and tight, fastball low and outside, changeup catching the outside of the plate.

He gripped the bat as instructed by Joe Fisher, without pine tar or batting gloves.

Pitch one. Just as advertised. Curve outside, just missing the black edge of home plate. Ball one.

Pitch two. Ninety-seven-miles-per-hour fastball right down the center of the plate. Strike one. "Dammit," thought Paul, "that was *my* pitch to hit."

Pitch three. Fastball low and away. "Leave this one alone," thought Paul. Ball two.

Pitch four. Fastball high and tight. "Leave this one alone, too," thought Paul. Ball three.

Pitch five. Trusting that a changeup was coming, Paul backed up and moved sideways just a little, as he had done in the previous game. The pitch was a little farther into the plate than the pitcher would have liked, and his grip on the ball had been a little bit too loose, allowing the ball to be a little too tempting for Paul not to put a swing on it. Batters will tell you that sometimes, when things are going well, the ball seems like a beach ball to hit. Other times, it seems like a pea. This time, it was at least the size of a beach ball, as Paul gave it a ride that almost cleared the bleachers and the ballpark in left center. The ball was hit with such force that it zoomed out of sight.

The three-run homer, number fifty-one of the season, accomplished several things: It gave the club a 3–2 lead, which eventually converted into a 3–2 win, thanks to the bullpen holding the Cubs scoreless for the rest of the game. More importantly, it kept the team alive for the postseason.

Paul quietly slipped away, still wearing his uniform. "Showers can wait," he thought. There would be time for good-byes later.

CHAPTER FORTY-EIGHT

The Cardinals concluded their regular season with a three-game road trip to Houston starting Monday, September 26, through Sunday, September 28, winning two out of three games to finish 90-72, a full six games behind Milwaukee for the Central Division pennant.

Meanwhile, Atlanta continued on its incredible dive and lost its final three games to Philadelphia to finish 89-73, one game behind the Cardinals for the wild card spot in the National League. The Braves had lost nine and a half games in the standings to the Cardinals in the last month of the season, even longer if one factored in late August. As cold as the Braves were, the Cardinals came charging into the playoffs as the hottest team in baseball. With Matt Bradley back, the team was at full preseason strength, poised to make a deep run in the National League playoffs and, hopefully, the World Series.

News about Paul Kolbe's departure spread like wildfire. Two local TV stations, the flagship Cardinal radio station, and the *Post-Gazette*'s own Bernie Madlock went to Rochester to follow up on the health of their one-season wonder. It was obvious to all at that point that Paul was done as an athlete. He just barely made it through his liver transplant and would face a long recovery just to function as a nonathlete.

"Paul, this is Bernie Madlock, your old friend from the *Post-Gazette*. I'm glad you're feeling chipper enough to answer this phone call. I'm in Rochester today trying to chase you down. Any chance I can come by the clinic and get some additional information for our readers? You know Cardinals fans. They want to know what's up with one of this season's heroes. Oh, and if you didn't know it, you won the Triple Crown.

Your final numbers of 51 homers, 139 RBIs, and a .332 batting average held up over the other guys chasing you, including Al.

"That's great, Bernie. For you, come on by. The others can wait till I get back to town. No pictures. Okay?"

With that, Paul and Bernie chatted a bit about the transplant, the tremendous season Paul had, and the ball club's potential success in the playoffs. Paul acknowledged that he would love to be there and would be, at least in spirit for now and hopefully in time for a World Series parade. "And stay close to Tony. He'll have several tidy bits of information for you around then, too."

"Tidy bits of information? What the...? Very interesting, Paul. Okay, get well. We'll see you back in Saint Louis, hopefully after a World Series win.

And in another "Bernie's Hits & Misses column," here is what was said about Paul in the *Post-Gazette* column:

I'll Admit to Being Wrong Once in a While

Okay, folks, I'm not ashamed to admit that occasionally I'm way off base, but I was wrong when the Cardinals signed Paul Kolbe for the 2011 season. He was just what the team needed at the time: a big bat, surprisingly good defense, amazing speed (okay, but he did steal one base), good overall instincts—did I mention he won the Triple Crown?

Moreover, he was a steady, mature voice in the clubhouse, something—along with Lance Champlin—that was most needed with a team featuring so many first- and second-year players.

I'm in Rochester, Minnesota, checking up on the recently retired Paul Kolbe. He just had an organ transplant that will save his life. None of us know, and Paul isn't saying, how difficult it was for him to come to the ballpark every day as he grew weaker and weaker toward the end of the season. And what was his reaction to his condition? One clutch hit after another and the Triple Crown, something that hasn't been accomplished in the National League in more than 75 years. Would the Cardinals have won the pennant without Paul Kolbe? My take on that answer is "no way." Good luck to you Paul. You gave us a season to remember and I personally hope you make it back to Saint Louis once in a while so we can revisit the great season that 2011 was in the annals of Cardinals baseball. Thanks for reading.

EPILOGUE

Paul made it to the clinic with thirty minutes to spare. Waiting for him there was none other than Heather. The transplant team was in place, too, consisting of two surgeons, two assistants, three nurses, an anesthesiologist, and several other personnel. While the source of the liver was confidential, it was mentioned to Paul that it came from an individual who was thirtyish, in good health before a fatal auto accident (wrong-way driver), a nondrinker, and therefore someone who gave Paul an outstanding opportunity for a second chance at life. The operation was not very long as operations go, but the preparations seemed an eternity for Paul. He admitted to himself that this would be an even tougher challenge than chasing down the Triple Crown, but he had a good summer of abstaining from alcohol and was determined to get through this operation and then seek professional help for his long-term addiction to alcohol.

First things first. He noticed, as he was lying on the operating table, that the room temperature was somewhere south of sixty-five and the lights above him were very, very bright. "Do you want a warm blanket, Paul?" asked one of the nurses.

"Yes, and I'm usually not cold. But it's freaking freezing in here. How do you work in this environment?"

"You get used to it, and it's necessary." After surrounding his body with warm blankets, the nurse asked how he felt now.

"Pretty good, but I'm starting to feel a little drowsy. You don't mind if I take a little nap during this procedure, do you?

The whole staff started laughing. "I think," said the lead surgeon, "that the drip in his arm is working quite well."

The next thing Paul knew, he was waking up in a large room with other patients lined up on the opposite wall. No one seemed to be paying attention to him, although it was obvious that someone was doing so remotely, as he was hooked up to several machines and was strapped into his bed. He lifted his head and immediately felt a little tug in his abdomen area, not really pain—he was too medicated for that—but an uncomfortable enough feeling that he dropped his head back to his pillow.

"Hello, Paul. How do you feel?" came a question from a female voice somewhere off to his left.

"I'm a little groggy. When are we going to start with the operation?"

The nurse nearest him started chuckling and said, "You just had your operation. You're in the recovery room. I'll let the doctor confirm your prognosis, but I can tell you that your procedure went exceedingly well."

"Yes, I am a little bit groggy. I suppose that's good based on what I just went through."

"That's correct. We wouldn't want you to feel any other way at the moment. This feeling won't last much longer, but for now just relax, and you'll be coming out of the fog in a few more minutes."

"Hello, Paul," said Dr. George Archer. "How are you doing?"

"I feel pretty groggy, doctor. How'd I do?"

"Well, the good news is that you sailed through the operation. The bad news is that you won't be able to play baseball for a while, unless you plan on playing a video game."

"No thanks. But you're saying I'll be fully recovered at some point?"

"Fully recovered. But I would take it easy for the first six to eight weeks. You will be in a lot of pain when the medication wears off. So let us know when you need some relief with that. We're going to wheel you into a private room for the rest of the day, and in a couple of days, if all is well, we can release you. I understand someone is already waiting for you in your room."

"It better not be Joe Fisher," said Paul.

"Who is Joe Fisher?" asked Dr. Archer.

"Just an old friend, but one that seems to show up whenever it strikes his mood."

"I believe there is a lady instead of your Mr. Fisher. Good luck, Paul. I'll be checking in on you periodically over the next day or so, and the nursing staff here will be around twenty-four seven."

Paul was wheeled out of the recovery room by two transporters, moved down the hall to a bank of patient and staff elevators, and transferred up two flights. After several turns in a hallway, he arrived in his private room, just down the hallway from the nurses' central station for the wing.

Inside the room were two side chairs, a nicely appointed couch, and a very attractive Heather wearing a smart-looking business suit. She sat at a desk with her laptop computer, appointment book, calendar, cell phone, and various folders and papers covering the entire desktop.

In an attempt to infuse some humor in the situation, Paul said, "Is this a bad time? Am I interrupting your work?"

"Paulie!" she almost shouted, getting up from the desk. "I understand that you passed with flying colors. You're good for at least another hundred thousand miles!"

"I'm really glad to see you, darling," said Paul.

"Darling? We may have to load you up with the good stuff more often!"

"Maybe it's really truth serum, as it sounds like the right thing to say right now."

"That's very sweet of you, Paulie. But let's get back to you. The doctor says you're probably going to want to rest for a while, maybe even take a nap. I'll leave my stuff here and run a few errands while I'm in Rochester, and then I'll come back later this afternoon. I'm glad the operation went well and that you should have a full recovery in just a short time."

Heather was out the door, and Paul took a nice, long nap, interrupted every hour by a nurse taking vitals or otherwise checking on him.

Day two in the hospital turned out to be routine for Paul. He was awakened around 6:00 a.m. for routine checks: blood pressure, pulse, temperature, and dressings. Nothing was out of the ordinary.

Breakfast consisted of some kind of smoothie featuring fruit and yogurt, but no solids requiring a lot of effort to digest.

Later that morning, Heather returned to Paul's room and found a decidedly perkier patient than the day before. She leaned over and kissed Paul lightly, and he smiled as he looked into her open blouse.

"Victoria's Secret, I presume?" smiled Paul.

"Well, I see you are feeling chipper," said Heather.

"Yes I am!" exclaimed Paul. "I haven't been too mobile yet. I understand that I should be using that walker in the corner over there as soon as possible," said Paul, motioning to the corner nearest the door, "but I don't think I'll need it."

"Really? Let's see you go to the bathroom on your own."

"I can't do that yet, for several reasons."

"And what would they be, Paulie?"

"I'm hooked up several ways to Sunday, and I have a catheter."

"Okay, but when you do get up from your bed, I'm going to have the walker handy, just in case."

"I won't need it, but that's fine. You'll see. I think I can dance on my way out of here!"

Day three turned out to be getaway day. And yes, Heather had to smile when Paul decided that the walker really was a good idea.

Back on the field, the Cardinals caught and then passed the Braves for the wild card. They marched through the National League playoffs, beating both the heavily favored Philadelphia Phillies and then their Central Division rival Milwaukee Brewers for the National League title. The Cardinals then met the equally heavily favored Texas Rangers, who were making their second straight World Series appearance. No matter, though—the Cardinals were underdogs all season and were not about to lose at this juncture of their journey.

ONE LAST HURRAH

It was after the successful conclusion to the World Series that Tony finally announced to the various stakeholders that he was retiring as field manager of the Saint Louis Cardinals. He would be the manager with the third most wins of all time. He was truly going out on top.

Once the shock of his announcement wore off, there was immediate speculation as to who would succeed him.

After fully recovering and after all the hoopla of celebrating a World Series victory had died down, Paul had the occasion to visit Atlanta to see Nikki's sister one last time to pay his respects. He also wanted to make a side trip to Augusta, east of Atlanta. Prior intelligence from a former teammate of Paul's indicated that Tony Rakers liked to hang out at bar near his house called the Nineteenth Hole, which catered to the golf-crazy crowd in Augusta.

Paul entered the bar alone and approached the server nearest the door, handing over a twenty-dollar bill in exchange for discreetly pointing out Tony Rakers, who was seated at the far end of the bar.

Paul wasn't sure what would happen at such a "meeting," especially on Mr. Rakers's home turf. All he knew was that it was time for payback for the season-long harassment that had Tony Rakers's fingerprints all over it.

There was a barstool next to Tony Rakers's, and Paul deftly slid onto it, looking straight ahead at the barmaid. "What can I get you stranger?" she asked. "I haven't seen you in here before."

"No, this is my first time here. I'll have whatever the gentleman to my right is having, and give him another one as well."

"Thanks, stranger," Tony Rakers said. "I appreciate the freebie, but it's kind of unusual for someone to just walk into this place and buy drinks for guys he doesn't know."

"Actually, we do know each other, although it seems as though I know you a whole lot better than you know me. I played baseball up until the end of this season."

"Really? Did you ever meet my son, Colby? Colby Rakers? And I'm Tony Rakers.

"Yes, I did know Colby. Even played with him for a while. The guy has a lot of talent. Some baseball people even say he is a five-tool ballplayer. But all I remember was a guy that just couldn't put it all together and liked to complain about his teammates."

"Who are the fuck are you to come in here and get in my face about my son?"

"My name is Paul. Paul Kolbe. I won the Triple Crown this past season in the National League. This was the first time in over seventy-five years that someone accomplished this feat. And Colby? Wasn't he traded away because he was a cancer in the clubhouse? And didn't he finish around the .230 mark after he was shipped off to Canada?"

At that instant, Tony Rakers recognized Paul and, although he was slightly inebriated, remembered with anxiety his letter-writing campaign against the man now sitting next to him. He started to get off his barstool, but Paul put one hand on his left shoulder and forced him back onto his seat.

"Look, asshole, you can't talk about my son like that, and you can't push me around. Who in the hell do you think you are?"

"Look, you're the asshole and not me. I told you my name is Paul. Paul Kolbe. I had to put up with your bullshit all season, and I just wanted to pay you a personal visit. I had every intention of reconfiguring your face with my fist. But after looking at what a pitiful human being you are, I think I'll just leave you with this thought. If I ever hear from you again, I won't just stop with altering your face. I'll reconfigure your whole body so you wind up in a wheelchair for a long, long time. And it will be self-defense, according to the witnesses I will have assembled for your beat-down."

With that, Paul took his drink—a cheap whiskey—and poured it in Tony Rakers's lap. "What the fuck are you doing?" asked Tony. He started to get up. Paul pushed him down again—this time very forcefully—and said, "Looks like you just saw a ghost and pissed in your pants! I hope for your sake that I don't hear from you again and that I don't ever see your daughter and her recently fired husband. All this happened because of you, you incredibly sad piece of crap."

Paul then left the bar and didn't look back. He never heard from Tony Rakers again.

As for Jimmy John, he was apparently more talk than action. He did indeed run into trouble with his so-called bankers and had to take an extended vacation to Argentina, where he was supposedly tending bar in a remote village catering to expatriates. The long arm of his "bankers" was ever present in his mind, and not a day went by that he didn't wonder if it might be his last day at the cantina. So much for his tough talk.

Heather and Paul got along so well that she decided to accept Paul's offer of matrimony. A wedding date was set for January to avoid the upcoming 2012 baseball season.

And then there was Paul's postplaying career. It seems that Tony LoDuca took a liking to Paul and started to have dinner with him after a few home games before Paul had to leave for Rochester. These dinners included extensive discussions on baseball strategy and player evaluations. Tony then met with John Nowicki and Hank Rheinhold and convinced them that his recommendation would pay off for the Cardinals.

In late November, the Cardinals sent out a notice to the press that a conference would be held on Monday, December 5. The letter was a tease of sorts to encourage all the local media to show up:

Attention Metro Saint Louis Media Personnel
Subject: Announcement of new Saint Louis Cardinals Manager
When: Monday, December 5, 2011, at 10:00 a.m.
Where: Saint Louis Cardinals offices, Clark Street entrance

The news conference was attended by virtually everyone in sports media in the metro Saint Louis area, plus regional and national media outlets. There had been speculation for several weeks after Tony's announcement about who would be replacing him as the field manager for next season. A number of well-known names had surfaced, but it was unlikely that the team would go in any of those directions. The majority of the media had speculated that the new manager would be a former player for the team.

"Ladies and gentlemen," said John Nowicki, general manager of the Cardinals. "We're here to introduce the new manager and a new member of the coaching staff today. And for that honor, I'd like to turn the microphone over to our president and chief operating officer, Hank Rheinhold."

"Good morning," started Hank. "We're glad such a large group showed up today. We feel very strongly that we continue to maintain the continuity of the long tradition of excellence we've had here in the managerial and coaching ranks, and we're very pleased to have filled two critical positions on our field staff.

"For starters, I'd like to reiterate our best wishes for two departing staff members. First, Tony LoDuca. Tony, as we've discussed over the past few weeks, provided us with outstanding field leadership as manager of the Cardinals from 1996 to this past season. As we've previously stated, his tenure has been one of sustained success, including three World Series appearances and two World Series Championships. It's difficult to replace a living legend like Tony, but we think we have the man who is up to the task. Let me introduce the new manager of the Saint Louis Cardinals, former catcher Mike McSweeney."

"Thanks, Hank, John, and the rest of the Cardinals staff who were involved in my hiring," began McSweeney. "First off, I've never managed before, as you members of the media will no doubt report. Second, as a catcher, no one has been more involved in the day-to-day on-field events than someone like me. That's why I think you see so many former catchers as managers in the major leagues. I've been involved with the Cardinals as a member of John's staff since I retired as a player, and I've had the opportunity to study the entire organization, from the short season single-A ball club to the triple-A club, as well as the intricacies of scouting, coaching, and managing a big league club. I'm confident that I will earn the respect of the players and that Cardinal Nation can be assured that the managerial reins of this club are in good hands. I'll have more to say on this subject as the off-season progresses.

"But now I'd like to talk about our coaching staff. There will be only one change, that being the hitting coach position. Mark O'Bannon will be leaving us and joining the Dodgers so he can be closer to home. As a family man myself, I certainly can't fault his decision. He has done an outstanding job with our players, including most of the younger players on our current roster. To replace Mark, we've brought on board recently retired Paul Kolbe. Paul, as you well know, just completed an outstanding season, having won the National League's Triple Crown, the first time in over seventy-five years that this feat has been accomplished. And he did it very efficiently, as he mainly was deployed as a pinch hitter extraordinaire during the final month of the season. He didn't even make the final road trip to Houston due to an illness.

"Tony first suggested that we consider Paul for this position because of his technical knowledge of hitting, from reading pitchers to foot placement, from swing mechanics to situational hitting. And it doesn't hurt that he has the hardware to back up what he is preaching to hitters about the art and science of hitting a round ball with a round bat. In short, Paul knows his stuff, and the proof is in last year's pudding. Here's our new hitting coach, Paul Kolbe."

"Thanks, Mike," said Paul. "I think everyone in the organization is sorry to see Mark leave, as he was highly successful as hitting coach of the Cardinals. I think that I bring some of those same qualities to the job, albeit with my own personality. And I want to categorically deny the rumor that both Rawlings and Mizuno sports equipment manufacturers have offered lucrative endorsement deals to me for the design of a line of batting gloves for aspiring Triple Crown hitters!"

With the press conference behind them, the future never looked brighter for Paul and Heather. Rumor had it that beyond the wedding planned for January, the happy couple might expect a son (to be named Joseph "Joe" Alexander Kolbe) to come along in their lives and take up baseball as he grows up under the tutelage of the last Triple Crown winner in the National League. And the Triple Crown trophy looked great on their fireplace mantel.

As for the recurring dreams? Now there were only good hits and runs for Paul, Heather, and soon-to-be little Joe Kolbe.

THE STORY CONTINUES

It's a bit of a stretch to call the next book a sequel, as the principal characters change with a focus on the front office and the team's new ownership—H. Rheinhold & Sons Brewery, Saint Louis, Missouri, which had the good fortune of acquiring the ball club just in time to win a World Championship.

The story picks up after the successful 2011 baseball season and follows the trials and tribulations of new management taking over for the soon-to-be-retiring Hank Rheinhold as both head of the brewery and the ball club.

Should Cardinal Nation be concerned about the brewery's commitment to the sustained excellence that the team has achieved season after season? You bet!

There is intrigue galore in the Cardinals front office and at the brewery. One way or the other, the business and sport of baseball clash to the consternation of Cardinal Nation.

And things get interesting when Paul Kolbe is asked to seek assistance from a supernatural resource—not Joe Fisher, but one of the greatest showman in professional sports. "Do I look like a magician?" Paul asks himself. "I can't just conjure up these characters." We'll see, Paul, we'll see.

And it all plays out under the watchful eye and pen of the ever-present Bernie Madlock, sports columnist for the *Saint Louis Post-Gazette.*

Meanwhile, there is baseball to be played, and the 2012 team does not disappoint as far as thrills are concerned. It's the off-field drama, though, that makes this story what hopefully will be a compelling read for you.

Made in the USA
Lexington, KY
10 June 2014